MARTIN DIMERY

# RULING CLASSES

Public and state school rivals engage in espionage, corruption and guerrilla warfare - with comic consequences

MARTIN DIMERY

# RULING CLASSES

Public and state school rivals engage in espionage, corruption and guerrilla warfare - with comic consequences

MEREO
Cirencester

**Mereo Books**
1A The Wool Market Dyer Street Cirencester Gloucestershire GL7 2PR
An imprint of Memoirs Publishing www.mereobooks.com

Ruling Classes: 978-1-86151-896-5

First published in Great Britain in 2018
by Mereo Books, an imprint of Memoirs Publishing



A CIP catalogue record for this book is available from the British Library.



The address for Memoirs Publishing Group Limited can be found at www.memoirspublishing.com

The Memoirs Publishing Group Ltd Reg. No. 7834348

The Memoirs Publishing Group supports both The Forest Stewardship Council® (FSC®) and the PEFC® leading international forest-certification organisations. Our books carrying both the FSC label and the PEFC® and are printed on FSC®-certified paper. FSC® is the only forest-certification scheme supported by the leading environmental organisations including Greenpeace. Our paper procurement policy can be found at www.memoirspublishing.com/environment

Typeset in 11/15pt Times New Roman
by Wiltshire Associates Publisher Services Ltd.
Printed and bound in Great Britain by Biddles Books.

# ABOUT THE AUTHOR

Martin Dimery spent many years as a drama teacher in comprehensive schools before (in his words) “shamelessly defecting” to an eminent public school. Later he became a music venue manager and is currently Director of the Frome Festival in Somerset. He has written a number of stage plays including “Terms of Engagement”; “Bombshells” and “An Audience with Ben Jonson which were commercially published. He has also contributed articles to national newspapers and periodicals.

In the mid-1990’s, after co-devising a juke box musical featuring the songs of the Beatles, Martin Dimery embarked on a secondary occupation as “a poor man’s John Lennon” touring the UK and abroad, in a tongue-in-cheek tribute -Sgt. Pepper’s Only Dart Board Band. This led to the publication of his autobiographical tour diary “Being John Lennon (SAF 2002), extracts of which were serialised in the Guardian and The Stage. There followed an e book sequel- “Without the Beatles”.

More recently, Martin Dimery has toured nationally in his self-written revue “Shakespeare Rattle and Roll”, setting Shakespeare’s songs and verse to familiar modern musical styles. He also performs with the Unravelling Wilburys.

He is married to Anne and they have three grown-up children and a grand- daughter.

# AUTHOR'S NOTE

When I began writing "Ruling Classes" I was concerned that, if published, it might cause enough controversy to put an end to my teaching career. I needn't have worried. My career ended (in no little controversy) when this story was still in its early chapters.

"Ruling Classes" compares the pretentions of a privileged public school with the struggles of its state school neighbours, as each plan to build a prestigious theatre. This scenario was directly inspired by my own experience. In reality, the schools were more distant and not in direct competition, but the way each of the schools approached their ambitious theatre projects, served to vividly illustrate the cultural divide that dominates the British educational system.

The temptation to base the characters in "Ruling Classes" on some of my former colleagues has been fully resisted. Should anyone of my acquaintance think otherwise- that is entirely a matter for them.

Martin Dimery 2018.

CHAPTER 1

# SCHOOL TIES

Adrian Pelforth studied his extensive collection of neckties. The revolving tie-rack always brought a moment of pleasure and tranquillity every morning as it rotated, electronically, to the tune of "Jesu, Joy of Man's Desiring." The rack had been a farewell present from the wealthy father of an ex-pupil, who manufactured such delights in his Hong Kong factory. The neckwear upon this sartorial carousel was observed by Adrian with great fondness, for it revealed, to his satisfaction, the story of a successful, and well connected life. He stopped the rack in its tracks and considered first the tie of Cobham Chase Preparatory School for Boys – the very first tie he ever adorned… "No, too sentimental," he thought. "And too short – without a jumper." He then studied the Convocation tie of Frobisher College Cambridge. "No – not this time." His guest was a man of self-made stock – not much of an academic. The tie of the Life Guards would perhaps more impress Jack Wildblood, his go-getting industrialist visitor. Or possibly his MCC members tie. But then Jack Wildblood was a soccer man wasn't he? Director on the Board of Brighton and Hove Albion. "Unlikely to have much time for cricket," he uttered under his breath. "Spends most of the summer in Mustique rather than Lord's." Adrian's wife Marjorie heard the last involuntary remark and stirred from her sleep.

"Ah ha!" he exclaimed, bringing Marjorie fully into the twilight world of the pale, insipid, institutionalised bedroom. "The staff tie of Headland College, Grand Cayman," he muttered with just a trace of sentimentality towards his first ever teaching post. "That should arouse the interest of a serial tax-evader like Jack Wildblood," he thought aloud, with a smirk.

Pelforth was lunching with Wildblood and the school Chairman of Governors, Simon Petherton-Pugh. According to Simon, Wildblood had ingratiated himself amongst many familiar and highly regarded social institutions, but had yet to receive a longed-for, and cherished, knighthood.

To succeed in his ultimate ambition, Wildblood needed a good cause, and Pelforth hoped that the beneficiary of that worthy quest might be Stortfield Academy. Adrian had presided proudly over Stortfield as Headmaster for the last seven years.

Pelforth meticulously fastened his tie in a broad knot before noticing a stain. "Brandy," he deduced, sniffing at the evidence. The stain proved entirely resistant to rubbing with spittle. "Bloody brandy," he said, aloud.

"What are you muttering about?" murmured Marjorie, lifting her eye mask and squinting at him beneath a rococo cluster of heated hair rollers.

"Bloody brandy. On this tie. I'll have to change it."

"I don't see the problem. You've plenty of others," Marjorie replied with characteristic early morning disdain.

Adrian was not a man of spontaneity, but his presence was imminently required in the Sixth Form Assembly. He plucked at the rotating carousel in the semi-gloom and gathered the nearest passing tie: "Ah! The Carlton Club. Just the job. Why didn't I think of that before?"

Adrian's attire was fully assembled with the addition of a matching purple handkerchief for his top pocket. With that, he marched purposefully to breakfast in the school dining room.

Gareth Chivers wondered why the modern garage was never quite large enough to house a car, at least, not large enough to get the car in, and its occupants out. Hence, abandoned to the winter night air, the frosted windscreen of his Vauxhall Carlton required a great deal of scraping and spraying before visibility could be guaranteed. The tie he wore today had been presented to him by the Carlton dealer as a free gift upon purchase. His other ties were in the wash. He wore the Carlton tie hoping no one would notice.

The car struggled to start in the cold. This was just as well, as it gave Chivers' wife Linda the time to notice that, once again, he'd forgotten his lunch box. She tapped the driver's window, overhearing his frenetic and impatient cursing.

"I hope you don't swear like that at school," she said, as she stood shivering in her dressing gown.

"Of course not!" replied Gareth turning the key to the car a little too hastily. "It's bloody flooding the engine now!"

"Your lunch – silly" replied Linda, leaning through the window.

"Oh God. Not again."

"You're getting Alzheimer's."

"Too many things to think about, that's the trouble."

With that, the car, with reverse gear already engaged, started with a jerk, causing Linda to step back smartly into a nearby hedge. "Watch out!" she yelled, but Gareth was too preoccupied to notice.

Gareth always carried a packed lunch. The official reason was his high cholesterol level which required a strictly monitored diet. Unofficially, as Headmaster of Stortvale High School, he was only too aware that:

a) The school's dinner service provided food so high in saturated fat and sugar, that his regular dining would certainly result in a triple heart bypass.

b) The County Health and Safety Officer had described Stortvale's kitchen as "a likely source of the school's recent salmonella epidemic."

And

c) A packed lunch enabled him to continue working at his office desk, undistracted by the petty demands of disciplinary duties, and the perpetual whinging of his staff.

Adrian Pelforth took breakfast in the school refectory. He was especially keen to remind the Head Chef of his important lunch guests, and the need to put on a good spread in the Sir Ian Botham Suite. He sat, as was his policy, amongst the pupils, more specifically, between Melinda Farnsworth-Rogers and Belinda Bellingham-Steele, his Head Girl and her Deputy respectively. Melinda had already received her offer from

Cambridge, but was thinking of deferring to take a gap year, teaching in a school in Nepal. Melissa would, quite possibly, be Prime Minister one day – or so Adrian thought. Of course, he desperately hoped she'd see fit to change her political allegiance along the way. He loved her, nonetheless, for her assertive intelligence, but wondered why all the bright pupils had liberal tendencies. Belinda, Adrian also loved, less for her assertive intelligence and more for her assertive breasts. He knew she was something of a wild child, but was very popular amongst her peers, and damned good at charming his parade of special guests. Squeezing between the two of them (that is to say Melinda and Belinda), Adrian was able to partake of a generous breakfast without having recourse to recall Mrs Pelforth's smudged makeup and Carmen heated rollers.

One of the school gates had again lost a hinge overnight. As Gareth Chivers turned into the school drive, he also noticed Mr Bailey, the caretaker, attaching a sheet of hardboard to the Biology lab window.

"Bloody hooligans," said Bailey. Chivers lipread this through the still defrosting windscreen as he passed, pretending not to notice. He briefly wondered why nearly all the caretakers laboured under the name of Bailey. Bob Bailey was the third he'd known by that name in his lengthy career.

With Philip Hart, his younger Deputy Head, chairing the Senior Staff Management Team meeting this morning, Gareth strode directly to his office, determined not to be accosted by either teacher, pupil, or Bob Bailey along route. Nine quickfire grunts of "Good morning" later, he entered the office, only to be confronted immediately by Valerie, the School Secretary. Like all school secretaries, Valerie knew too much for her own good, and barely tried to conceal her contempt when Gareth dismissed her urgent requests with a tetchy: "It can wait Valerie – later."

"No, it won't wait, Mr Chivers."

"Look, Valerie, I've just this minute got in. Any coffee on the go?" Gareth's South Wales accent grew more steadily pronounced when under stress and was already beginning to sound like a character from "Under Milk Wood."

"Too late I'm afraid" replied Valerie, taking the moral high ground. "I've been in since six-thirty typing those letters you dictated yesterday after school. You said they were urgent, so you'd better sign them."

"Oh alright, give them here," Gareth snapped, and began signing the letters in a rapid scribble.

"Well, read them first," Valerie instructed with scarcely concealed indignation.

"What's the point? I know what they say–"

"Well, if I were you…"

"Well, you're not me Valerie. Be grateful for small mercies."

"And…" Valerie smugly countered, "… fortunately, I'm not Mr Hart."

"Why's that?"

"He's livid."

"Because?"

"It's the new sign on his door."

"What about it?"

"Well – you obviously haven't noticed."

"Noticed what?"

Valerie suddenly became a little uncomfortable. She was a staid woman, with little sense of humour.

"He specifically asked you not to have the sign say: 'Deputy

Headmaster Mr P Hart'."

"Why ever not?" retorted Gareth disingenuously.

"Think about it." Valerie was determined not to be drawn into detail.

"No, you've lost me" Gareth said, with mock impatience.

"He wanted 'Philip'," announced Valerie emphatically.

"'Philip' would have cost another twenty quid."

"He considered it worth the cost."

"I still don't understand." Chivers pretended to sound a little exasperated.

Valerie took a deep breath: "P Hart, with no full stop between the P and H."

"So, he's angry about the loss of a full stop between the P and the H?" Gareth was becoming stubbornly resistant to the obvious.

Valerie finally snapped: "As a teacher, I would have thought you might have gathered that P and H together are pronounced 'EFF'!"

"Ohhhh! I see…!" Gareth feigned a revelation of St Paul dimensions. "Deputy Headmaster, Mr Far-oh-oh dear." He looked to Valerie for the faintest of smiles, but the secretary had turned on her flat heels and was out of the office, her neck revealingly flushed with acute embarrassment, and the door firmly shut in her wake.

Gareth Chivers permitted himself a rare chuckle before sinking behind his desk. Philip Hart, as far as he was concerned, lived up to his label. He was a grey-suited product of the post-eighties educational scene. In Gareth's early years as a teacher, state education was seen as 'progressive'. That epithet was now an insult. The profession he once loved had been driven by a misplaced and old-fashioned desire to turn back the clock to a less questioning time. Hart gave the impression of being organised, efficient, disciplined and diligent. In reality he lacked the character, personality and individuality that marked out some of the really great teachers Gareth had worked with in the past. Many of those had long gone, feeling persecuted and driven out by modern orthodoxies. Hart was the master of the career interview. Head Teachers unable to keep up with the demands of the National Curriculum, Ofsted inspections, Social Inclusion and league tables, were only too eager to help Hart up another rung on the career ladder. Hart had everything a Head Teacher could want in an administrator. He could do flowcharts, action plans and timetables in his sleep. What he couldn't do – was teach. Or relate to kids. But that didn't matter in the modern age. Hart preferred the term 'Classroom Manager' to that of 'teacher'. That is, indeed, what he was – a man who managed buildings and rooms – that just happened to be occupied by children in need of learning. Gareth thought Hart would have been a better manager of a vegetable warehouse. At least vegetables sit quietly and don't talk back.

"Mr Phart," said Gareth to himself with a chuckle, as he searched through his desk drawer for this morning's vital teaching resource: A 1960s volume entitled: *One Hundred and One School Assemblies*.

CHAPTER 2

# HEADMASTER'S ASSEMBLY: STORTFIELD ACADEMY

"Good Morning Sixth Form. Well, we're now into the first week in February. Half-term is on the horizon. After half-term there will be six weeks to Easter. Six weeks after that, the exams will begin again. That's less than fourteen school weeks in all. My goodness, doesn't time fly? And there's so much to cram in: the school play; Handel's *Messiah* – which is our the Easter concert at the local parish church; the public school Rugby Sevens – which we look forward to hosting, and, of course, the beginning of the cricket season – to name but a few. And while all of these proceed, the school moves ahead, expanding, developing, improving, in every respect."

"Today I shall be taking lunch with a very eminent

businessman, Mr Jack Wildblood CBE. Mr Wildblood's story is a great inspiration to us all. As a child, he knew poverty. That was until his father, a mere laundry delivery man, discovered a niche market for plastic moulded coat-hangers. A simple idea, yes, but would you or I have thought of it? Least of all, would we have had the courage to invest every penny of our modest savings into such a scheme? Well, Mr Wildblood's father did. And within three years he was able to transfer young Jack from his humble, backstreet secondary school to Winchester College, one of the most eminent schools in the country."

"But it wasn't easy. Jack was unhappy at first. He was bullied because of his East End accent; teased because his father was a mere tradesman. Yet, sometimes these things are the making of a man. They help to build character, resilience, the real qualifications needed for success."

"So Jack became determined. He wasn't simply going to hang onto his father's coattails – or should I say coat hangers… hah, yes… no, Jack decided, when the time came, to move the business into construction, providing drainage and piping to some of the most impressive buildings in the world. Magnificent monuments like the Gapau Dam in Malaysia, and the Jhalabad Nuclear Power Facility in Pakistan, bringing energy to these far-flung parts, and with that energy, greater amenities, greater opportunities and a greater education for the local people."

"Indeed, we are looking to Mr Wildblood to help us realise our own expansion schemes, in particular the creation of a brand new theatre and concert hall next to the lake. What better position for such a beautiful monument – not unlike the Royal Shakespeare theatre by the river in Stratford-upon-Avon. And though you all will have moved on to pastures new by the time we open the theatre, I hope you will pay us regular visits to see our marvellous concerts and plays in a setting that befits the high standards we have here at Stortfield."

"Now I would like you to join me in singing the hymn: 'Lead us Heavenly Father, Lead Us'."

Meanwhile, on the other side of town….

CHAPTER 3

# HEADMASTER'S ASSEMBLY: STORTVALE HIGH SCHOOL

"Good morning Year Twelve and Thirteen. Well, we're now in the first week of February. Half-term is on the horizon. After half-term there will be six weeks to Easter. Six weeks after that the exams will begin again. That's less than fourteen weeks in all. My goodness, doesn't time fly? It only seems like yesterday I was welcoming you back to what I fondly like to think of as the Sixth Form, and we were chewing over the successes – and failures – of last year's examination results. Well, it's all coming around again, and I, for one, am looking forward to seeing if we can't get Stortvale a little bit further up that County league table. We did drop two places last year and that did slightly take the gloss off the successes we had. Now you know, and I know, what with staff shortages, particularly in science, we might have done a little better – and that's not to undermine the sterling work done by our regular supply teachers at short notice. Also, if we'd been able to get rid of one or two notable troublemakers – now thankfully departed – we might have done a bit better in GCSE. But, I think you may probably have read in the local press that every time I kick someone out in the lower school – it counts against us in other ways, particularly funding. But that's not your problem, that's my problem."

"It's also my problem to catch whoever it is that continually comes up here at night and throws stones through the windows. It's my problem because the local police force, have, as they see it, more important issues to deal with. Now I don't want to go to the trouble, or expense, of having to install yet more closed circuit TV cameras on the school site, so I'm asking for your help. As the older, more responsible students in the school, I am pretty sure none of you would take pleasure from this kind of vandalism. After all, you're here by choice. You could have gone to the technical college, but you chose to stay here, and for that reason we give you a greater sense of freedom than the lower school. I think you and I have a good relationship on the whole. But some of our Year Elevens and Tens, perhaps, might not look at the school in quite the same way. Now, if any of you can help me by providing names – or clues as to who might be doing this, you will be saving the school a lot of money. Money that buys you textbooks and computers – and helps you pass your exams. You'll be saving us into turning this site into a fortress or into something out of George Orwell. I expect some of you have read *1984* and know what I'm talking about. So, names, clues, and evidence will make my life a lot easier."

"Finally, congratulations to our Under-18 rugby team who

made a terrific fist of our annual needle match with our old local rivals at Stortfield Academy. We only went down by 57 points to 10, which was a great improvement on last year. I think we could have done without the brawl that followed, however. Although, they were every bit as much to blame as us, in my book. So, I won't be banning spectators from next year's encounter. Well done to all those who took part – er – in the match that is… Alright, alright, it wasn't meant to be a joke.

Now, in accordance with legislation decreeing that we indulge in a daily act of Christian worship, let us pray:"

"O, Lord, grant us we pray, the opportunity to see a meaning in our humble lives; to take strength from small victories, and to be undiminished by defeat. Amen."

CHAPTER 4

# MARJORIE

Marjorie Pelforth sat alone at breakfast. She scanned the letters on the kitchen table. Only one was addressed to her, a circular. The rest were addressed to her husband. Usually, even if letters were addressed to Marjorie, it was in the name of "Mrs Adrian Pelforth."

Marjorie half-heartedly nibbled at the toast and stared through the leaded kitchen window of her mock-Tudor home. The Headmaster's House had been built in the 1950s in a design considered tastefully in keeping with the school's original building, a genuine Elizabethan manor house. In fact, the Headmaster's House stood out as sympathetically as a wart on the derriere of Michelangelo's *David*.

Marjorie had spent thousands of pounds of the school's money on refurbishing the Headmaster's House, redesigning the garden and recruiting a feng shui expert. No matter how hard she tried, the house was a tasteless heap and would take no disguising.

The Headmaster's 'Cottage' as some rather inappropriately called it, was also known by the name 'Johannesburg' in honour of one of the school's South African benefactors. Stortfield had enjoyed a fruitful relationship with South Africa over the years, and had reinstated its rugby and cricket exchange visits, following the fall of Apartheid, with what one local councillor called 'indecent haste'. Requests from certain members of staff to rename the Headmaster's dwelling 'Mandela House' had fallen on deaf ears, despite the previous school hierarchy having no idea that 'Mandela House' was also the name of a fictional block of Peckham council flats, in which resided a popular pair of TV sitcom brothers and their uncle.

'Johannesburg' though, was to Marjorie Pelforth, her very own Robben Island. Twice in the last five years she had fled captivity officially to spend time with her ailing mother. Rumours abounded that Marjorie was engaged in extramarital business, but a clearer interpretation of the truth emerged when a school coach, loaded with hockey teams on their way to Eton, had spotted a somewhat raddled Mrs Pelforth emerging from a pub in Slough at one o'clock in the afternoon.

In a damage limitation exercise, Adrian had let it be known that Marjorie had been 'unwell' and was attending a clinic in Buckinghamshire. He was naturally appalled that anyone should assume his wife had deserted him; but for her to have fled to Slough was unthinkable.

Marjorie crossed to the kitchen cupboard where she kept the detergents. She reached for a Fairy Liquid Economy Size bottle, tucked away behind the bleach. She squirted a large measure of the contents into her recently emptied coffee cup. Marjorie had grown used to the unusual bouquet of Napoleon brandy, gently suffused with a blend of residual Nescafe, and a faint, aromatic hint of lemon pine liquid. Indeed, she had nothing less than a craving for this early morning indulgence.

Marjorie's duty for the day was to attend lunch in the Sir Ian Botham Suite with Adrian's guest, Jack Wildblood. She had heard that Wildblood was something of a ladies' man. Sipping her Fairy Napoleon Gold Blend, her mind turned to which outfit would be most appropriate. She decided on the scarlet, low-necked dress with matching stilettos. It would infuriate Adrian, of course, but she wasn't going to let Wildblood see her in the Thatcherite, navy blue twinset her husband always seemed to think appropriate for any occasion. She found Adrian's Margaret Thatcher fixation deeply troublesome.

Marjorie topped up her measure with another squirt, and took the brandy with her to the bedroom. She was determined, this time, not to spill the evidence in the vicinity of Adrian's tie rack.

CHAPTER 5

# CARVINGS

Gareth could not quite conceal the smile on his face at the arrival of Philip Hart, his deputy. Hart's knock had been a mere token of politeness.

"Come in," said Gareth pointedly, as Hart stood agitatedly twitching before him. "Oh Philip, there you are. Everything alright?"

"Not really Headmaster." (Hart always insisted on calling Gareth "Headmaster" despite Chivers' preference for first names.) "It's the sign on my door, you see. Rather a delicate matter, I'm afraid…"

Gareth allowed Hart to stutter through the explanation in his usual pained and over-articulate manner. To interrupt, he thought, would spoil the moment. Hart couldn't bring himself to say 'fart' of course, choosing to use 'flatulence'.

"I must be very thick," said Gareth. What do you mean 'P. Hart alludes to flatulence?' I'm not quite with you." Gareth was reeling Philip in like a master angler. He was determined to draw the fart out of Hart. And he did.

"Oooohhhh, sorry!" Gareth said with a slight chuckle, clasping his hands together. "I'm a bit slow on the uptake where linguistic jokes are concerned. Well, not to worry Philip. If I can't work it out, not many others will."

Chivers could see Philip flushing with suppressed rage, and momentarily felt guilty that he was taking such delight in teasing him.

"I must insist we change it, Headmaster. I'm not inclined to make myself look a fool."

It was everything Gareth could do to hold back from expressing any number of sarcastic comments in reply: "Very well, but we can't afford a new one. I'll have Bailey take it down, saw off the 'P' and neatly put the rest back on again. How's that?"

Before Phillip could reply, Gareth held up his hand in anticipation of what might follow and emphasised: "I guarantee no one will spot the difference."

"Bailey? But –" Hart was lost for words. The thought of Bailey further bodging the job it had already taken him six months to accomplish was almost intolerable.

"No, no," interrupted Gareth, anticipating Hart's objection. "He'll find the time. If not. I'll do it myself."

The wind was fully taken from Philip Hart's billowing sails.

"Now then," continued Gareth rapidly. What's on the agenda today?"

Hart took a seat without being asked and opened his A4 double-page-a-day diary. He hated keeping anything other than an electronic diary, but Gareth refused to use it. The 'morning' page was full. The 'afternoon' page clearly ran into the next day. Gareth caught sight of the entries and heaved a sigh of faintly suppressed despair. His fun for the day was over.

Hart went through the schedule methodically, leaving nothing open to interpretation. He liked Chivers to know exactly how hard he worked, and to what effect. Gareth tried to look faintly interested but was just switching off when the words 'lunch', 'pig' and 'whistle' caught his ear.

Of course! That's why he didn't pick up his packed lunch. He'd faintly remembered, on waking, that he was dining out today – if a ploughman's lunch at the Pig and Whistle could indeed be deemed 'dining out'. There was no expense account for this sort of thing, but it was worth it just to escape school for an hour.

Gareth was entertaining the unlikely duo of Raymond Chater and Nigel Slot. Chater was an erudite, articulate, charming pillar of the community. Slot was not. Slot was an artist. A sculptor, to be precise. He had ingratiated himself into the inner circle of Lady Doulting, wife of the late Sir Arthur Doulting, and now Managing Director of Doulting Stone. Doulting Stone was the massive quarrying company which worked from a hole in the ground that used to be the village of Blackrock, two miles from Storton

Slot had won a commission to sculpt Lady Doulting and produced a work of such reverence and unctuousness, that a woman best described as looking like a 1950s suburban housewife was transformed into a Boudicca-like warrior goddess.

Lady Doulting was now a great admirer of Slot, and saw to it that she indulged every scheme he came up with to supplement his income, which was otherwise attained through benefit fraud. Her vast lawn was now littered with Slot creations. Fairies and elves danced incongruously with phallic-like erections.

Slot had now come up with a scheme so grand that it demanded the full support of her Public Relations department. Raymond Chater had been Head of PR at Doulting for twenty-seven years. He was the only reason Gareth could think it worth attending Rotary meetings, other than trying to screw a few quid out of local industry. Chivers suddenly brightened up at the thought of a lunchtime pint with Raymond. The thought suddenly brought him back to life in the middle of Hart's chronological monologue; half way through his rendition of appointments 15.30 to 15.45.

"Er – Phillip, sorry to butt in and so on… but what do you think about this project Raymond Chater's put forward? I could do with your views."

"I'd be pleased to give them Headmaster," said Hart, after a pause.

Gareth took the hint more quickly than Hart supposed.

"Yes, well, I'd invite you to lunch with us, only someone's got to run the school in my absence," he quickly countered.

"Quite, Headmaster," replied Philip with as little deference as could possibly be implied without offence.

"So… what do you think, Philip?"

"I'm surprised you should wish my opinion on the matter, Headmaster."

All this 'Headmaster' nonsense was guaranteed to get up Gareth's proverbial nose. He knew Hart only insisted on the epithet because he had, himself, grand designs one day to be a Headmaster and would insist on being addressed as such.

"Oh, don't be soft Philip." Gareth's annoyance could barely be tempered. "This is a big project. You've got a grip on the finances, what do you think?"

There was a considered pause before Hart replied, racking up the tension between the two men just a degree more.

"Well, as you know, I'm all for selling off those football pitches to a developer. I mean, we don't use them like we used to, and it would be nice to put a few private houses between us and the Ringwood Estate."

"Or as some of the staff are calling it: The Ringworm Estate," chuckled Chivers.

"Er, quite… quite." Hart was always quick to put an end to levity. "According to my statistics, even three or four middle-class families sending their children here could make the difference of up to two places in the league table results."

Gareth knew he was right but there were bigger cards on the table: "Yes, yes. But what about this sculpture park idea?"

"Well, it will placate the local press and the parents. I mean, if we sell off the land for recreational purposes, it won't seem quite so bad."

"Have you seen any of this chap Slot's work?" Gareth asked.

"Yes," came the surprising answer. Gareth hadn't put Philip down as an art collector. "I attended an auction at the Assembly Rooms recently. He was selling some items there."

"I suppose they called it the Slot Lot! Eh!" Gareth was most pleased with his little joke and giggled a little through Hart's description that followed.

"Yes very droll, Headmaster" he began, without as much as a flicker of a smile.

"So, what did you think of his stuff then?"

"In a word, Headmaster: Appalling. In the end he was practically giving it away. Nothing reached asking price except for this giant mushroom which an old lady thought 'might come in handy as a bird table'."

"Oh dear." Gareth looked genuinely disappointed. "So an entire park devoted to his sculptures might not be welcome, other than to the local ornithological society perhaps."

"Headmaster," said Hart, pursing his lips and lowering his eyelids in the way unfunny people often do when trying to appear ironic – "I think the quality of the work is immaterial."

"Meaning, Philip?"

"Meaning – that controversial art is better than no art. When was the Turner Prize last won by anyone who could paint?"

"Phil – you're right." Chivers couldn't agree so readily with Hart without resorting to calling him by the truncated nomenclature the Deputy Head so disliked. "Go to an art gallery these days and what do you get? A pile of old dustbins welded together with a Tesco shopping trolley on the top."

"Indeed Headmaster" said Hart just slightly warming to his superior. "The real question, I would suggest" he continued, "is not whether we like the work, but whether the Arts Council or the National Lottery Commission would approve."

Hart was once again doing Chivers' thinking for him, and he knew it. He leaned back in his chair looking at Gareth, longing for the day when he could inherit Chivers' position, and could think for himself instead. "Then we'd see who had the crummy nameplate on his door" he thought.

Chivers, though, was no fool. He had survived by delegating. Other headmasters he knew in state schools had retired in ill-health, been pensioned off early, or simply died in post, but Gareth Chivers, despite his bad back, high cholesterol, and chronic haemorrhoids, had remained, albeit uncomfortably, in the literal hot seat. Yes, he was worn out, tired, unenthusiastic and cynical, but no more so than any other head teacher. He sometimes dreamed of doing a reality TV show in which he could trade places with his counterpart at Stortfield Academy. "That'd show the bastard," he thought. But Gareth knew that such a reversal would involve him selling his soul. Having been a product of the comprehensive system himself, Gareth believed passionately in the principle. While his radical tag had faded more notably than his Swansea accent, Chivers was still politically astute enough to handle his superiors well. He couldn't always handle his staff, or the pupils, but that was no longer an important requisite for running a school. Gareth could also see the glimmer behind Philip Hart's spectacles. He knew the likes of Hart would never remain loyal, even to those who had shown faith in them. He also knew that Hart wouldn't advise him badly, just in case he inherited the ensuing mess.

"So, you're intimating there are resources to be tapped, are you?" he challenged Hart.

"Naturally, Headmaster. A sculpture park would not only bring in money for the land, but might earn Lottery support and give us leverage to apply for special status. That could bring in thousands over the years."

"Yes, but we'd have to buy-in to whatever hare-brained scheme the latest Education Secretary was dreaming up. It's a bloody minefield. And anyway, the money's earmarked. It doesn't repair windows or buy books, does it?"

"Yes, but that's where creative accounting can prove useful" Hart said, doing that supercilious eyelid-closing and lip-pursing thing Chivers hated. "I mean, if a window is broken in the toilets, repair work might be listed under an audiovisual upgrade."

Gareth could not but look a little impressed. Hart had his uses, after all. "So, I shouldn't worry too much about this Nigel Slot's dodgy sculptures then?"

"No, I wouldn't have thought so. These projects are commonly called 'art interventions' I believe" Hart advised.

"Art interventions, my arse!" Gareth laughed. "What a lot of pretentious bollocks!" He stood to indicate their meeting was over. "Well done, Philip. Don't worry; you'll only be missing a ploughman's. I'll bring you back a pickled onion."

"I'd rather you didn't, Headmaster" Hart replied, disdainfully.

"Why's that? Do you have a problem with f-f-f-flatulence, Phil?"

Gareth roared with laughter as he patted Hart firmly between the shoulder blades, projecting the deputy to the door in even greater haste than he would have wished.

CHAPTER 6

# WILDBLOOD

Jack Wildblood had dined with the Queen, yet still he held his knife and fork as if he had trotters for fingers. The cutlery handle seemed to disappear into his shirt cuffs, leaving only the tip of each implement visible. It seemed to Marjorie Pelforth that Wildblood was almost scooping mashed potato onto the back of his hairy hands and sucking it into his mouth. Frankly, to Marjorie, Jack Wildblood was a major disappointment. Tales of his attractiveness to women must have been, surely, a product of his own public relations department. For here was spin-doctoring so good, that she shuddered to think of how such a thing might be used by an unscrupulous government department, for example. She then realised of course, that it had been.

Wildblood was a big man. Not tall – but big. He had a

broad, flat forehead which looked as if it had been panel-beaten into shape. A widow's peak crept down to the topper-most furrow of his brow like descending bindweed. His eyebrows formed a double quiff, and it was difficult to ascertain where eyebrows ended and the thick, bottle-black sheet of greased back hair began. In fact thought Marjorie, if he receded, a combover extended from his lustrous eyebrows was distinctly possible.

Marjorie had time to notice these things. Whilst Wildblood and her husband crammed, talked and spat their way through lunch, she was relegated, as usual, to the role of consort. She became quite fascinated by this hairy, warthog of a man. In his youth he could never, surely, have worn a fringe? The hair would have stood at right angles to his forehead. Had he ever plucked his eyebrows? Or trimmed the copiously hirsute nostrils and ears? The nostril hair was so thick it looked like remnants of a moustache. The ear hair could furnish a modest plait. She sniggered at the thought, but quickly turned it into a cough, having caught her husband's eye.

Marjorie has also noticed the hair sprouting from beneath Wildblood's collar. At the front it sprang forth from his Adam's apple and looped up over the top of his tie. At the back, his hair was cut short, but still tufts protruded up over the collar. She shuddered at what he might look like in the shower. Like a man who had forgotten to take off a dark woolly jumper, she imagined.

Wildblood's facial hair could be witnessed almost growing as they spoke, being a tight, blueish grey stubble, from the throat to the eye sockets. Had Wildblood been ginger in his youth, it occurred to Marjorie, he would have been indistinguishable from an orangutan. She giggled again, this time enduring a withering stare from her husband, who knew all too well the meaning of that slightly forced cough.

At least Melinda Farnsworth-Rogers and Belinda Bellingham-Steele could be relied upon to maintain small-talk without letting the side down. Pelforth was deeply proud of his prize prefects and was relieved that Wildblood was far too preoccupied with Belinda's more evident assets to pay attention to Marjorie's nervous giggle or scarlet attire.

After lunch, Adrian dismissed the girls (including Marjorie who he thought could not be relied upon in such circumstances) and walked Wildblood down to the lake, which he hoped would be overlooked by the new theatre. They were accompanied by Simon Petherton-Pugh, the Chairman of the school governors, and Edwin Slater, the school Bursar. Wildblood's hunched and heavy frame carried him down the slope with such runaway momentum that the delicately proportioned Bursar could barely keep up.

"So, here we are," declared Pelforth. "This is the spot. We envisage a glass-fronted foyer overlooking the lake, which is, of course, beautifully lit at night. The public entrance would be just about where we stand."

"Pardon me for being pragmatic," cracked the gin-sodden voice of Wildblood. It has half Major-General, half cockney wide boy. "But surely a theatre needs seats. Those seats need to be raked, and this incline here…" (he gestured broadly) "… would make the ideal slope along which to set the building. That would mean moving the foyer to the other end."

"Yes, yes. Sound economic sense," cut in the Bursar with an insidious little laugh.

"Yes, of course," Pelforth intervened dismissively. "But why lose the beauty of the lake? I mean, if this theatre is to be a place, not only for the school, but the community, then people will be attracted by the setting."

"You see Jack," said the smooth Petherton-Pugh, "we have a vision. This building isn't just a theatre or school drama studio. This building will be a monument. We want people from miles around to flock to the Stortfield Academy Theatre. We want the best companies here, The Royal Shakespeare Company; the National Theatre. When people think of Stortfield Academy, they won't just think of cricket or rowing they'll think theatre, beauty and tranquillity – excellence for the arts."

Simon Petherton-Pugh was an 'Old Stortfieldian'. Now in his early forties, Petherton-Pugh was everything one could want in a Chairman of Governors. In his tailored beige suit, Petherton-Pugh glowed with health. Christmas in the Caribbean, followed in January by one of his regular seasonal visits to ski in Gstaad, had helped keep body and tan intact. The Bursar firmly believed that no one had the right to look so bronzed in February, but could not help but admire Petherton-Pugh's eloquence and charm. He always wore a buttonhole. Today a startling pink rose to match the handkerchief in his top pocket, offset the summery suit. His sandy hair was brushed in a floppy, boyish quiff, and his teeth were enviably straight and white. Marjorie Pelforth adored him, as did many of Stortfield's female staff. For some he was just a little too much of a dandy, but charismatic nonetheless. Adrian, though, loathed him. He hated the 'swanky' dress sense, and called him a 'fop', much to Marjorie's amusement. He hated Simon's inherited wealth, which meant, apart from serving as a director on the board of his father's pharmaceutical company, he hadn't really done a day's work in his life. This is why he had time to indulge in his old Alma Mater. He also knew damn well that 'Pugh' as he abruptly called him was also indulging much of his time with Viola McIntyre, Stortfield's Head of Drama and locally celebrated leading lady in the Storton Operatic and Dramatic Society – or SODS as it was known locally.

Adrian had been trying to get rid of Viola McIntyre before the theatre scheme came about. Now he became increasingly resolved. He didn't want Stortfield's prized new facility dropping into the lap of a woman renowned locally as the convincing principal in 'The Best Little Whorehouse in Texas'.

Mrs McIntyre was a free spirit who regularly failed to complete paperwork and once forgot to enter twenty-four pupils for GCSE Drama because she was "Emotionally drained. SODS have cast me as Lady Macbeth, you know. It's taking its toll. Everything seems petty by comparison."

Despite every attempt to covertly campaign against Petherton-Pugh, Adrian was dismayed at the latter's election as Chairman of Governors. The Reverend Harker-Smith had been his ideal chairman: old, frail, easy to manipulate, and profoundly deaf. Pugh had none of these attributes, but it had to be said, he was doing a good job on Wildblood. Too good a job, in fact. Adrian could see the elevation of Viola McIntyre to Theatre Director in Pugh's every sweeping gesture. "Still, we shall see," he thought.

Simon Petherton-Pugh was a man of many contacts. He had used Stortfield when running a summer conference for the Confederation of British Industry. Wildblood had been in attendance and Pugh had 'buttonholed' him on a tour of the campus. He knew Wildblood was swimming in money and that he was eager to find a worthy cause that wasn't, in his words: "Third World, ethnic, or inner cities." "I've done enough for the Third World" he told Simon. "And I came from an inner city myself. It doesn't seem to have held me back. And as for ethnic issues–" he spat the words out with such contempt, it was not necessary to complete the sentence. Petherton-Pugh was nothing, if not politically correct, and had pointed out that Stortfield had its share of ethnic-minority students.

"I'm not talking about Prince Abdul Salim of Saudi, or the sons of the Tiger Economy," barked back Wildblood. "I'm talking about throwing money at the 'Steve Biko Community Centre' in Clapham, or Croydon, or somewhere oooop north. People should learn to stand on their own two feet, not expect handouts from others."

Petherton-Pugh took in Wildblood's diatribe whilst being all too aware that it was public subsidy that had elevated Wildblood from 'The Coat-hanger King' to the elite of the British plutocracy. It was Wildblood's patronage of the Conservative Party that helped win him the contract to supply pipelines from his embryonic construction company to the Gapau Dam project in Malaysia. It was also subsidy in the form of British Foreign Aid that enabled the Malaysian Government to afford this massive investment. The conditions laid down were that British companies would be exclusively contracted to do the construction. The end result was a very healthy boom in the UK's Civil Engineering business. Of course, Wildblood saw to it that a small part of his immense profit was donated as a gesture of thanks to the ruling Conservative Party, for which he was duly rewarded with a CBE. He was told that a knighthood "might be a little too ostentatious."

Petherton-Pugh still genuinely believed he was doing a public service in getting Wildblood to part with his dubiously earned cash. Slater, the Bursar, knew something about the

Gapau Dam business, and didn't entirely approve, but wasn't going to look a gift horse in the mouth. Pelforth didn't know much about it, and didn't want to. Pelforth wanted Stortfield to be the best school in Britain, with the best theatre of any of them. That theatre, he hoped, would be called the Pelforth Theatre.

The three men were caught for a moment in reverie as they looked upon the lake. Whatever their differences, or motives, a mutual vision began to stir in this small corner of England.

CHAPTER 7

# SLOT

Nigel Slot was happily assuming that someone else would pick up the tab on an expenses account. He was now on his third pint while Chater and Chivers were only on their second half.

The Pig and Whistle was emptier than usual thanks to a party of eight teachers from Stortvale High School leaving suddenly, seemingly by coincidence, as Gareth Chivers arrived. The manager was less than impressed when he and his waitress appeared from the kitchens with eight steaming plates for their departed guests. Fortunately for the landlord, Gareth intervened, promising his truanting staff would return to make payment, suspecting the dinners would be recycled to more recent arrivals in any case. The incident was, however, a distraction he could have well done without before settling down to business.

Slot's plans lay spread on the table before them. On the most recent update, he had extended the ambition of the sculpture park to include a landscaped amphitheatre surrounded by huge Easter Island heads.

"Not sure about the statues," said Chater, when Slot was at the bar pestering for another pint on the tab. "He'll be showing us Stortvale's version of Mount Rushmore next. Having said that, I do like this amphitheatre idea. As he says, gives it a 'you know – interactive' vibe."

Gareth laughed at Raymond's impression of Slot. "Yes, I like that amphitheatre setting," he said, spitting a globule of bread on the plans, and flicking it away deftly. "This cheese is nice."

"Yes," continued Chater, "young Nigel's not quite the fool he looks. Make it a performance space too, and you can spread your bets, so to speak. More chance of lottery money; Arts Council funding and so on."

"Mmmn," nodded Gareth in agreement as he busily chewed on another bite of cheese. "There's also money for schools development projects too. This could be Stortvale's Millennium Dome."

"I'd rather it wasn't Gareth, old chap," Raymond replied in his familiar tongue-in-cheek manner. "But if your point is that we'll attract pots of public money to support a pretentious scheme dreamed up by one or two self-serving megalomaniacs, then it's very well made."

Raymond Chater was something of a dying breed. A latter day Kenneth More in style and manner, he was charming, inoffensive, community spirited and above-all, decent. Cynical perhaps, in his darker moments, but Raymond appreciated the opportunity given to him by Sir Arthur Doulting all those years ago. Even if Sir Arthur now resided beneath a large chunk of his own rock, Raymond saw it as his burden in life to placate, patronise and sometimes even put in her place, the old chap's whimsical widow. He had become less a Public Relations Officer and more a Personal Advisor.

Raymond also demonstrated great loyalty to Stortvale High School. He had attended the school in (as he saw it) the halcyon days when it was Stortvale Boys Grammar. He hadn't approved of the school becoming coeducational or comprehensive, and sent his eldest son Rupert to Stortfield Academy instead. Rupert however, was not of the Stortfieldian mould. What was initially considered 'solid bulk' and ideal 'prop forward' material, became simply 'overweight and lazy'. Rupert had stoically refused to cut his hair throughout his fourth year at Stortfield and had cited European Commission directives on civil liberties when suspension was threatened. He could frequently be seen parading around the school with his shirt unbuttoned, revealing an Iron Maiden T-shirt. Nobody else at Stortfield, liked Iron Maiden, least of all the Headmaster Adrian Pelforth, once he discovered the T-shirt was not an homage to Margaret Thatcher.

Somehow young Rupert managed to avoid expulsion, despite his best efforts, but when he was discovered in the lavatories with a group of cannabis smokers, Pelforth had every excuse to delete Rupert Chater from the register. The fact that Rupert had chronic diarrhoea and just happened, by chance, to be in the next cubicle, did not cause Pelforth to waver.

Gareth Chivers had persuaded Raymond Chater at a Round Table social evening that Stortvale was just the sort of environment for Rupert. Even though Raymond was contemplating sending Rupert to board at even more correctionally-minded institution, he gave Stortvale the chance, and was pleasantly surprised by the results. His son remained overweight, long-haired, and badly dressed, but happy. He managed to scrape a few GCSEs and two A-Levels before going off to study at the University of Luton. Ever the rebel, at university, Rupert took to wearing his hair short, adorned in smart suits, and began espousing the virtues of free market economics, mainly just to annoy his card-carrying contemporaries in the Socialist Workers Party. His father could hardly have been more proud.

Raymond, though not a malicious man, could not easily hide his grudge against Stortfield, and had seen in Slot's plans a way of upstaging the Academy. He was well aware of the school's theatre plans through his connections with the amateur drama scene.

Slot returned from the bar, spilling his pint on his scuffed Doc Marten boots…

So, er… like… what are you thinking?" said Slot. He used the words 'er' and 'like' and 'you know' gratuitously, and tended to nod his curly head from side to side as he spoke.

"We very much like the amphitheatre idea," said Raymond. "Very much."

"What about the sculptures?" replied Nigel, opening his tobacco tin, and beginning a roll up.

"Well, I'm no expert," said Gareth.

"Look, you don't have to be an expert," Nigel responded, just a little tetchily. "I don't, you know, believe in all that 'expert' stuff. You don't need to be an 'expert'. It's like, you know, do you like it, or not? Does it appeal to you?"

Gareth finished chewing and thought for a moment: "Well yes. Yes, it's very… nice."

"Nice?" Nigel laughed. "Nice? Nice is not the word. 'Attractive' is not the word. Is it striking? Does it create a simple, gut reaction? Does it have purpose?"

Raymond was blunt. He could see Slot beginning to irritate Gareth, who had more important matters to be dealing with, and might just tell Slot to clear off.

"Listen Nigel, whether we like the detail or not is immaterial. We like the idea. We think it will be a sensation. I'd like to recommend to Gareth that Lady Doulting buy these fields to save them from the planners, and that we recommend seeking matching funding for the amphitheatre and sculptures"

Slot smiled crookedly. He was unshaven, his dark, curly hair uncombed, and his Dr. Martens boots unlaced. That this individual had managed to ingratiate himself into Lady Doulting's trust could only be seen as a mark of her own latent vanity. He did, though, have a touch of the brooding gypsy about him, with dark, staring eyes and hooded lids. If not a modern day Heathcliff, there was a little of the impish punk about him, and he had quite a reputation for 'pulling birds' (as he would put it) ten or more years younger than himself.

"You er – like – happy with that Gareth?" said Nigel trying to draw something more profound from him.

Gareth, bloated and relaxed following his lunch, momentarily slipped into sarcastic headmaster mode and responded as if Slot was an inarticulate yob.

"Yea, like great, you know…" Chivers chided. Then, as if to make amends, gave Nigel a gentle punch on the arm as you would an old mate, and forced a laugh.

"Good. Cheers," said Nigel, whilst all the time wanting to say "wanker."

Raymond thought it a good idea to wind up the meeting:

"So, er… shall we split the bill three ways here Gareth, Nigel?"

"Oh… er, sorry" Slot interjected. "I naturally assumed it was on the company."

"Oh no, no" replied Raymond. "Gareth here doesn't have an expenses account. Schools like Stortvale can't afford such luxuries. And for me… well, I'm strictly limited to commercial clients. This doesn't count, I'm afraid. No matter, if we divide it three ways, you'll come out on top. After all, we've only had a couple of halves."

"Yeah, appreciated like, but er… you know, I didn't come out with any dosh. I'm still waiting for that cheque from the er… auction, you know and I… I, er…" Nigel stuttered, patting his empty pockets with well-rehearsed discomfort.

"Fear not dear boy" Raymond announced magnanimously. "I would hate to have deceived you. This one's on me."

"Oh, very decent of you Raymond" chipped in Chivers, with a nod and a wink. "My shout next time."

"Yeah, great," said Slot, nearly showing gratitude.

Gareth stood reluctantly and made his parting platitudes: "Got to get back. Mr Hart will be going frantic by now."

"Yes, time waits for no man," agreed Raymond, in his best Richard Briers accent.

Slot attempted to join in: "Yeah, got some, er… heavy stuff to deal with this afternoon, you know."

"What, concrete?" countered Raymond chirpily.

"Funny, yeah," said Nigel Slot – distinctly unamused.

Raymond turned to Gareth as Slot led the way out of the pub, and whispered: "Heavy stuff, my arse. Heavy sleep more like. After you, dear boy." Slot, by now, was too busy lighting his roll up in the car park to notice Raymond and Gareth's private conversation on the way out. Stepping aside for Gareth,

Raymond tucked the till receipt in his top pocket.

"Mustn't forget the receipt," he whispered to Gareth. "Accounts will need a copy. Mum's the word." And with a chuckle and a tap of the nose, he departed the Pig and Whistle in high spirits.

CHAPTER 8

# LADY DOULTING'S CARVINGS

Lady Doulting was taking tea alone in the drawing room of Blackrock House. The house was a pet project of her husband who had bought the mansion in a derelict state, and spent much time and money on its renovation. The house had been constructed from original Blackrock sandstone in 1768, and so the raw materials for the rebuilding were readily at his disposal. What Sir Arthur Doulting would have thought of Nigel Slot's anally retentive carvings on his lawn, Raymond Chater dreaded to think.

As Raymond entered the living room, Lady Doulting greeted him with the teapot held aloft. "Ah hah! Raymond, there you are. How did it go?"

"Fine, Lady Doulting, I'd say a promising start." Raymond was always guarded in his reports to the "Baroness of Blackrock" as she was inaccurately labelled by the staff.

"Did the Headmaster approve of the designs?"

"Absolutely. Loved the amphitheatre."

"Good. Tea?"

"Oh – I – very well, thank you."

"Do sit Raymond."

"Thank you," said Raymond squatting in a familiar wing-backed chair, and receiving the cup and saucer in a well-worn ritual of gratitude.

"What will they do with the money for the school land?" she demanded.

"Oh there are plenty of possibilities. To begin with, they have debts of something like a quarter of a million."

"Well! How on earth did a school get into quite such a state?"

"Too many staff, according to the powers that be. Not enough, according to Gareth Chivers. Something to do with falling numbers in the Sixth Form I believe. Their Science labs badly need renovation. They'll be no shortage of bidders amongst the school departments for any spare cash.

"Did you telephone the County Council?" Lady Doulting had acquired an aristocratic manner of speech since her late husband's elevation to a knighthood, rarely using common abbreviations like 'phone' or 'TV'.

"Yes, I spoke to the Chief Education Officer personally. Had to name-drop yourself, to get through the interminable automations on the switchboard. He gave me his verbal reassurance that the money from the sale would be entirely reinvested in the school."

"I should think so too!" interjected Lady Doulting. "If they think they can syphon off a single penny from the sale…"

"There's no danger of that, m'Lady," reassured Raymond. "The CEO chap said they'd be more than happy to see the school improve its image. It needs to attract more pupils to become solvent again."

"I'm very excited. So many marvellous ideas all contained within the space of two football pitches."

"A public relations triumph, m' Lady."

"And we certainly need that at the present." There was a pause as they each took another sip from the elegant china cups.

"I take it you will be personally attending the other council business on Thursday?" Lady Doulting insisted politely.

"Naturally" Raymond replied. The matter in discussion had changed to the serious business of Doulting's planning application to further extend their enormous quarry.

"What do our people think of the chances?"

"They're not too confident, I'm afraid. The environmentalists have got the upper hand. Apparently the opposition we've seen so far could erupt into a massive campaign if the planners approve our case."

"Are these people complete fools?" Lady Doulting was at her most agitated. Are they aware what the quarry industry brings to this area?"

"I've tried to explain Lady Doulting."

"Make no mistake Raymond, if we can't expand, then jobs will go. That's what I'd be telling them in no uncertain terms."

"It's been clearly stated ma'am" said Raymond, wearily.

"And another thing. There won't be room for any more local philanthropy. We'll have to put a stop to that. Let them put a housing estate on the school playing fields, and see where it gets them."

"I suggest it may be a little too early to be playing that particular card, Lady Doulting."

"These people need putting in their places – in no uncertain terms, Raymond."

"Well they have been" said Raymond, allowing his impatience to show just a little, "by the electorate. Which is why we must be persuasive, but remain diplomatic."

Lady Doulting recognised there was no further point in pressurising Raymond. "Yes, yes, I'll leave it to you." She placed her cup and saucer on the tray beside her, and moved to the window. She looked out over her garden.

"Ahh! Those delightful carvings. Can you imagine this on a grand scale Raymond?"

"Yes, indeed," Raymond replied, battling to suppress the faintest hint of sarcasm.

Lady D paused for a moment, as she surveyed her sculptures. "By the way," she continued, still looking through the window, "I've heard through the local grapevine that Jack Wildblood was taking lunch up at Stortfield Academy recently. What's that revolting beast of a man doing there? He doesn't have children at the school – as far as he, or anyone else knows. Never been married for long enough."

"I don't know ma'am. No idea what he was there for" said Raymond.

"Find out will you? You have your contacts."

"I'll do my best Lady Doulting."

"And – dear Nigel – such a glorious maverick. Was he well?"

"Nigel?" Chater was good at acting remote and aloof. "Oh, Nigel Slot? Yes, he enjoyed our hospitality greatly."

"Good. Look after him Raymond. He's a man of unique talent."

"He surely is ma'am" said Raymond Chater through gritted teeth. "Unique."

CHAPTER 9

# VIGILANTES

Darkness had descended on Stortfield Academy. From his bedroom, Pelforth looked out over the subtly illuminated lakeside. His tie rack tinkled in time to the winking of light on the gently moving water. He dreamed of his theatre standing there – reflected in the lake. His theatre – his landmark – his monument. The reverie was abruptly shattered by Marjorie removing her eye mask, and in no uncertain terms demanding the he "Close the curtain, get to bed, and turn off that bloody tie rack."

Churchill House was deemed fortunate to accommodate seven of Stortfield's first fifteen rugby squad, who, for reasons known only to themselves, were called 'The Vigilantes'. It was assumed by some that their stern and effective prefect-ship of the House had brought about the label. Churchill was certainly a more disciplined institution than it had been in recent years.

Each floor of Churchill House was designated to pupils of one year group, progressing from the youngest on the ground floor. The Sixth Form boys on the top floor were furthest away from the ground floor flat of the Housemaster Bernard Jenkins.

Had Pelforth dwelt a little longer at his bedroom window, he would have glimpsed, in the distance, a sudden shaft of light, breaking from the fire exit on the top floor of Churchill House. Seven figures in shadow slipped out from the exit and clumsily tiptoed down the fire escape. The creaking metal stairway of the modern, purpose built boarding house, was unforgiving. Alerted by the creaking on the steps, a Year 10 boy on the second floor foolishly opened the fire exit to immediately confront the last of the descending figures. He let out a girlish scream which was stifled by a black gloved hand covering his mouth. Another gloved hand then clasped his infertile testicles. The boy was pinned to the iron bannister and found himself peering into the eye sockets of what he took to be two balaclava-hooded urban guerrillas.

"We know you Timpson," said one of the figures. "We know you, and if you breathe a word we shall come in the night. We shall come to you in the night," he repeated. A second black-clad figure, his voice even gruffer and more menacing than the first added: "And we shall do you unspeakable harm."

The younger boy's eyes widened. Tears darted from beneath his spectacles.

"Oh fuck! Fuck!" One of the masked assailants exclaimed urgently, suddenly releasing his grasp of the adolescent testicles: "The bastard's pissed his pants!"

He ripped off the warm, wet glove, and crammed it into Timpson's gaping gob. "That'll shut him up." The two menacing figures then, in one swift movement, thrust the dripping boy back through the emergency door and into his dormitory. The dark duo then raced down the remaining stairs to catch up with their comrades.

The Housemaster, Bernard Jenkins, delicately tugged at his bedroom curtain. He caught a glimpse of the two errant figures catching up with their five comrades who crouched behind a distant hedgerow.

"What is it, Bernard?" said Mrs Jenkins, from her twin bed across the compact bedroom.

"Oh, it's only The Vigilantes," replied Jenkins, dismissively. "One of these nights someone's going to catch them."

"Well, it certainly won't be you," muttered Mrs J (as the boys called her).

"Don't be ridiculous!" said Jenkins defensively. "They could be expelled."

Mrs J momentarily raised her eyes from the pages of her Georgette Heyer novel. "There are more things in life than winning the House Rugby Cup, Bernard."

Jogging rapidly down the nearby country lane, The Vigilantes flashed their torches ahead of them. Suddenly, the leading member gave a shout: "Car!" The seven, as one, rolled down their woolly black hats in to balaclavas that stretched down to the top of their identical black polo necked jumpers, leaving not a glimpse of flesh. Torches were extinguished and each boy pressed into the hedgerow. The passing car swerved beyond them and screeched to a halt. The driver, stared, startled, into his rear-view mirror. Having confirmed what he thought he saw, the man then frantically tried to restart the engine. Realising that they'd been spotted, two of The Vigilantes ran back to the car and began hammering on the roof. They heard the central locking device activate, and the car screeched into action.

"Anyone we know?" said the tallest of the pack.

"Don't think so," said another.

The taller of the group also appeared to be the pack leader. He'll probably call the police, so plan B."

"Plan B" meant taking a more circuitous route, to avoid roads. At the end of the lane, the paramilitary unit turned left towards the Ringwood Estate in the northern suburbs of Storton. The troop went no further than was necessary into the estate, knowing that while they were a match for any of the local street gangs, a fight might expose their identity.

They slipped down the side alley between two houses and looked carefully to ensure all neighbouring lights were out. They then split into two separate groups. One group of three jumped the low fence to their left and cut across a back garden which was divided from Stortvale High School's playing fields by a high, chain link fence. The other group of four mirrored the exact movements through the garden on their right. Suddenly, the latter group was startled into panic. The long, low growl of a large dog was heard. Before they had time to register from where the menacing sound was coming, a large, dark dog barged between them, brushing and butting them aside, almost unsure which one to attack. They heard the rattle of a chain and rightly assumed the animal was tethered.

The rear fence was hardly wide enough for four bodies. The tallest Vigilante elected to wait: "Quick, you go," he instructed the other three. Backing against the fence, he flashed his torch into the dog's eyes.

"Fuck me, it's a bloody Rottweiler!"

This seemed to spur the others into an even speedier scaling of the fence. The dog paused in the torch beam before running, headlong, at the mysterious stranger in its garden, barking and baring its frightening teeth. The black figure brought the rubber torch down on the dog's head with all possible force. This bought him no more than three or four seconds in which to climb the fence. The others, by now, were safely on the other side. The Rottweiler shook its head and recovered, launching at the climbing figure. Its jaws opened and sank into black clad buttock of the intruder.

A light went on and a window was opened. The voice of an elderly woman cried out: "You hold him Jasper! Good boy! Mummy call the police!"

Thinking quickly, another of the mob prized a garden cane through the chain link fence and gave Jasper a sharp prod in the ribs. Still, his teeth locked onto the Vigilante who tried to continue his climb. A further sharp prod, this time in the dog's eye, and the beast retracted a moment. The intruder clambered up the fence, the dog jumped, but the chain attached to its collar became fully extended, and Jasper's jaws snapped shut in thin air as a trailing leg was withdrawn with relief.

The seven figures, one limping painfully, ran across the playing field with commendable athleticism. The tall limping leader yelled: "She'll be calling the police. Just do the front windows."

Ducking beyond the reach of the security cameras, the boys in black, in a well-rehearsed ritual, grabbed handfuls of large pebbles from the Stortvale Rural Studies Garden – ("Sponsored" as the sign declared "by Birch and Sons Garden Centre") – and began their assault on the Art Block. They heard three distinct crashes.

"That's enough," one of them cried. "Save a few for next week."

With that, they ran around the front of the building, sticking close to the wall and beyond the arc of the moving cameras. Lining up, backs to the wall of the school's reception building, the seven then made a rugby-style charge on the school's iron gates, leaping and clambering to the top. At this point, Bailey's untrustworthy repair work dealt them a bitter blow. The recently repaired hinge on the top of the left-hand gate gave way causing it to drop at an angle, broken only by the tarmac below, and so sending a breath-taking jolt through several pairs of elevated testicles.

The seven marauders raced along the main road, knowing they had to risk being seen by passing cars. They made it to the junction with the country lane out of town, and proceeded back to Stortfield at a jog. The round trip of some three miles had been accomplished in record time, but with limited impact and a troublesome injury count.

"Fucking old cow and her Rottweiler," breathily exhaled the one with the limp. "She's sussed us. We'll need to find another way through. And I'll need a bloody tetanus shot. I'll tell the school nurse I was bitten on a morning jog."

The Vigilantes hobbled across the lawn surrounding Churchill House and up the fire escape, seemingly unnoticed. Jenkins was relieved however, to count them all back again as he peeked discreetly from behind the bedroom curtains. In the general direction of the Ringwood Estate he could hear the sound of a police siren.

CHAPTER 10

# PLANNING

Pelforth, Petherton-Pugh, and Slater the Bursar, took their seats in the gallery of the Storton District Council chamber. The spectator's gallery was unusually busy for a Planning Committee meeting on account of Doulting's controversial quarry expansion scheme. A number of environmental protesters with banners had thrust leaflets in their hands outside the Town Hall, and were surrounding the Stortfield deposition on all sides.

"Oh dear" said Slater. "I hope we don't get confused for this lot."

"Bloody hippy dippy sorts," muttered Pelforth under his breath. "Wouldn't be campaigning if their own livelihoods depended on the quarry. Probably haven't got a job between the lot of them."

"Well, I've got some sympathy with them, I must say,"

Petherton-Pugh contradicted. “That quarry is an absolute monster. A massive, ugly cavity in the countryside. They’ve gone far enough.”

“If you say so,” replied Adrian disinterestedly. Storton matters were not terribly important to him. To Pelforth, his school was a little like a military barracks – it was self-contained and could be anywhere in England. Stortfield Academy existed almost as an island suburb of Storton. He interacted with local life as little as possible, which partly accounted for his reaction on seeing Raymond Chater enter the chamber.

“Oh, Christ.”

“What?” said Slater, looking around for clues.

“It’s Raymond Chater.” Adrian pointed him out discreetly. “I expelled his son. Gave me a bad time over it. Drugs. No choice.”

“Oh yes, I remember. He’s a big noise at Doulting isn’t he?” Slater looked mildly excited. He was a natural social climber and enjoyed being in eminent company. Slater had almost been too excited to speak to Jack Wildblood, during his recent visit, but Chater was a man he thought to be more on his level.

Edwin Slater managed Stortfield’s purse strings with attention to detail. His staff in the Bursary would probably describe him as meticulous and interfering. He had come to his job through the ranks following the retirement of Major Burnside. Burnside had continued a tradition of retired military men to the role of Bursar at Stortfield. It was widely recognised that Slater had kept the Bursary intact despite Burnside’s maverick approach to economics that threatened to heap fiscal catastrophe on the school.

Adrian was relieved to see the eventual departure of the

'Galloping Major', as Burnside was known. This had little to do with his title, and more to do with his penchant for taking afternoons off during the National Hunt season. Burnside had not so much cooked his own goose as cremated it, by taking a business trip to the Middle East on the pretext of "drumming up trade." Sultan Sali Al Hamman reported to the school governors that he found Burnside's requirement of a £4000 advance in fees for his nephew's education, somewhat irregular. Eventually the Sultan's cheque, which he thought was being paid to an educational recruitment agency, was traced to the account of a trackside bookmaker who had been operating at the Dubai Classic. Coincidentally, the Classic occurred at the time of Burnside's visit.

Pelforth had been unusually upbeat about Burnside's embarrassing dismissal. Viola McIntyre had put it around the staffroom "on good authority" that Adrian had always envied Burnside's military rank, having only reached the status of Captain himself. Pelforth caught wind of the rumour and knew its source, that is to say, the smooth, elegantly coiffured man in a beige suit sitting next to him.

Adrian reluctantly nodded across to Chater in the gallery, who returned a little wave and a stunningly insincere smile. He noted Chater had been joined by the Stortvale Headmaster, Gareth Chivers, who he regarded as "an over-promoted oaf."

The Chairman of the Planning Committee announced that the order of business had been changed to bring the quarry expansion application to the top of the agenda.

"Bloody hell," whispered Adrian to his colleagues. "I bloody rushed to get here. This quarry business will take forever."

And it did. The debate was as protracted as it was heated.

The Conservatives who had long held the majority on the District Council were naturally all for quarry expansion, as indeed they were "all for" the development of a regional airport, motorway extension, nuclear power station and any number of failed schemes which had promised to turn the Storton from a pleasant, modestly sized town, into an industrial time bomb. There was one Tory exception, Councillor Mrs Ranklin, representing what remained of the village of Blackrock, who opposed the proposal, not because it threatened to remove half her ward from the map, but because of the damage it would do to undercover fox hunting in the area.

The Labour Party, conscious of the green vote, was generally opposed, although some were anxious to preserve working class jobs. Ultimately they decided in a three line whip to oppose the proposal, for no better reason than to make life difficult for the Tories. The Liberal Democrats were generally opposed but "could see both sides of the argument" and mostly abstained from voting altogether.

Doulting's "good work in the community" was cited in the proposal, and their support of Stortvale High School's new 'Arts Environment' as it was grandly named, was also alluded to, softening up one or two waverers against quarry expansion.

The last point raised the well-groomed eyebrows of Adrian Pelforth in the direction of Simon Petherton-Pugh: "What bloody Arts Environment?" he whispered from the corner of his mouth. "They'd better not be planning a theatre."

"It comes up later on the agenda," said Edwin Slater discreetly. Slater could always be relied on to read the most tedious of documents from cover to cover.

Adrian spent much of the meeting trying to look as if he was taking notes. He was instead drafting letters to parents and members of staff, preferring to use the time more constructively. Virtually the last item on the agenda was passed, and planning permission granted for the proposed theatre at Stortfield.

After rapidly thanking the Head of Planning, the Stortfield deposition adjourned, with great relief, to the nearby Pig and Whistle. The celebratory beer had been soured however by two unexpected discoveries: The least problematical was Pelforth chancing upon his Head Girl and her Deputy as he passed through the Snug Bar on his way to the toilet. Melinda and Belinda were old enough to drink, but visits to the pub were strictly limited, and certainly not acceptable in mid-week. Melinda and Belinda had claimed to be discussing the prefect duty rota over a gin and tonic. Adrian preferred to interpret this as showing remarkable maturity, until, that was, the emergence of two bikers from the lavatory, with whom the girls seemed somewhat over familiar. Adrian was quietly furious discovering the girls had other rotations on their mind. Pelforth had time to utter a thinly disguised invitation to his study "first thing in the morning," before deciding to avoid confrontation with the students' leather-clad Lotharios.

As Pelforth stood at the urinal, the steam of his warm piss rose up. He breathed it out of his nostrils like a bull aroused. The Council had also approved of Stortvale High's plan to develop their sculpture park and amphitheatre. Indeed, the matter had been greeted with great enthusiasm in the chamber. The Council had seemed determined to talk up Doulting Stone's role in the "regeneration of the school playing field" to temper the civil unrest that had greeted their earlier decision to allow the quarry extension.

Stortfield's own plans, though approved, had hardly brought

more than a cursory comment from the Chairman, who maintained that "it seemed a shame to spoil the view over that lovely lake. But–" he concluded "– it is Stortfield's land, and providing it falls within regulations, it is up to them if they want to desecrate it."

As Pelforth pondered, the steam was drawn out through a draft, as the door opened, and in, through the mist, stumbled Gareth Chivers. Pelforth pretended he hadn't noticed. Chivers sidled next to him at the urinal. "Oh hello, Adrian," said Gareth. "Just come from the Planning meeting. Thought I noticed you in the gallery."

"Oh I didn't notice," Pelforth lied. "Yes, yes, delighted to have got our theatre approved."

"And ours," said Gareth, fumbling in his flies. "Bit of a coincidence, eh?"

"Yes. I'd almost have thought you'd been spying on us," said Pelforth.

Gareth could tell Adrian was feeling somewhat upstaged, and was determined to enjoy the moment.

"No, this sculpture park and outdoor theatre has been in the offing for ages," he exaggerated. "Lady Doulting's right behind it, you know. She's actually purchasing the land so it can't be flogged off for housing. I don't suppose you'll ever have that problem at Stortfield Academy."

"Highly unlikely, my friend," replied Pelforth, zipping his fly. He was keen to exit the toilet, but felt obliged to give his hands a cursory wash.

"Still," he shouted over the particularly noisy hand dryer. "We can't do this sort of thing on our own. We need to call in a few favours too – donations and so forth."

Chivers, completing his purpose, was intrigued. "Anyone we know?"

"Well, I'm not at liberty to divulge – fully," blurted out Pelforth, "but between you and I, Jack Wildblood's very interested." Almost immediately he recognised that he should have kept his counsel.

"Jack Wildblood? Isn't he the man who got caught up in the Gapau Dam scandal?" Gareth was enjoying this.

"Er… yes, there was some controversy surrounding that, but really that was just a drop in the ocean compared to his other investments," Pelforth retorted, whilst shaking his hands dry.

"Or perhaps, a drop in the dam," said Chivers, chuckling, with a little shake of his own.

Pelforth tried again to dry his hands under the noisy but feeble hand dryer.

"I wouldn't bother with that," yelled Chivers. "You'll be here all night."

"Yes, I take your point." Pelforth took his silk handkerchief from his top pocket to finish the job.

"I suppose you'll be looking for Lottery funding too?" Chivers queried cagily.

"Lottery funding? No wouldn't dream of taking money from the public domain. Besides I don't really approve. Don't have much time for gambling."

Chivers spuriously washed his hands and dried them indiscreetly on his trousers. "Not like your old Bursar then? What's his name, Major Bloodnok?" he chuckled.

"Burnside – actually." Adrian could barely contain his irritation. "And you don't want to believe everything you read in the papers."

"No, of course, but I think we'll get a good press this week," said Gareth Chivers, opening the toilet door for his arch-nemesis, with overdone politeness. "The Council seemed quite taken by our plans."

CHAPTER 11

# EXCLUSIVE

Chivers was wrong. The *Storton Courier* once again displayed inexplicable loyalty to Stortfield Academy. Chivers had a theory that the editor, a local man, had never forgiven Stortvale for converting from grammar to comprehensive.

The High School's new plans made the second story on page three under the headline:

"High School Shock as Fields Sold!"

The main story on the same page had been reproduced verbatim from the press release issued by the Academy's public relations office and was headed:

"Academy's Theatre of Dreams!"

The *Courier*'s editor had a harder than usual decision to make on his page one headline. Page two though was entirely devoted to the story:

"Workers Delight as Quarry Gets Green Light!"

This had also been flagged up under the masthead on page one to indicate its importance.

But there could only be one front page headline this week:

"Storton Under Siege!" with the by-line: "Masked Terror Gang on Rampage!"

Gareth Chivers sat at the breakfast table hardly able to digest either his lightly burned toast, or the story that confronted him. He read it aloud:

> A gang of masked vandals wreaked havoc on the Ringwood Estate in the early hours of Monday morning, before causing hundreds of pounds worth of damage to the windows of Stortvale High School.
>
> The gang, wearing black clothing and hooded masks, were spotted in Gypsy Lane, adjoining the Ringwood Estate, by motorist Reg Dearden, who was returning home from a social engagement.
>
> "It was terrifying," said Mr Dearden aged 73. "They were standing by the bushes in the lane. I stopped the car to take another look and they came after me. They were pounding on the roof of my car, so I drove off. They might have been armed, I can't be sure."
>
> Cissy Bunyan, aged 80, a widow, was also caught up in the ordeal and has since been recovering from the ordeal with relatives. She was awoken just after midnight on Monday when several raiders entered her garden and

attacked her puppy, Jasper. "Jasper was very upset and frightened," said Mrs Bunyan. "I could see them bashing him across the head with something that looked like a cosh or truncheon. When they'd finished they climbed over the school fence and ran off."

By the time the police arrived, the gang had escaped, but not before breaking several school windows and tearing a school gate from its hinges. (Continued on page 5)

Masked Vandals (Continued from Page 1)

Police hoped that the High School's newly installed closed circuit television security system might shed some light on the identity of the terror gang, but school caretaker, Bob Bailey, admitted that there had been some "teething troubles" with the twenty thousand pound installation, which they were "unable to rectify."

Janice Perkins, who manages the Newsmart shop on the Ringwood Estate, believes the gang to be pupils at Stortvale High. "We've had a lot of trouble around here" she remarked. "But it went quiet when the school and ourselves started using TV cameras a while back. These villains have just become more clever. I blame the school, I'm afraid."

Gareth almost spat his toast across the room:

"Jesus Christ! That bloody woman at Newsmart! She spends half the day selling fags to underage smokers and truanters, and half the evening flogging cheap booze to underage drinkers. Then she blames the school for the kids' behaviour. And as for that Reg Dearden-"terrifying" – my arse. He wasn't so terrified when we suspended his grandson. Threatened to punch my head in."

Linda Chivers emptied the kettle into the teapot. She was an attractive woman in her way, never beautiful, but "nice looking" as Gareth's mother used to say. She first met Gareth when both were training to teach at university in Hereford. Linda loved children, but her patience was fully tested whilst working in her first primary school in Newport, Gwent. Storton was a pleasant option by comparison, but in recent years, due to the demands of teaching, her engaging, youthful look was less in evidence, its absence more pronounced by the residual, pronounced folds around her mouth, where a smile had once been.

Linda spent a lot of time worrying. She worried about Gareth and his cholesterol levels. She wondered if he'd live long enough to retire. She worried about their grown-up kids. Judith was alright. She'd done well at school. One of Stortvale's noted successes with fourA Levels at grade A. Gareth had tried to persuade her to apply for Oxford or Cambridge, but Judith refused to be "a party to your vain attempts at one-upmanship with Stortfield Academy," and had settled for King's College, London. Linda too, had preferred to think of Judith in the more comfortable and cultural climate of Cambridge, but respected her daughter's independence. The idea of Judith walking home through the East End filled her with dread:

"Don't worry mum," Judith had reassured, Jack the Ripper left these parts some time ago."

Dominic, on the other hand, was wholly more capable of

looking after himself. Linda and Gareth's eldest had left home with no place at university, no job and no prospects. He eventually found work as a courier for a holiday company in Ibiza, and returned home only in the winter months to "crash" at his parent's "pad." Linda would always enjoy his annual homecoming, but after about three weeks, she secretly couldn't wait for the holiday season to start again.

Cleaning Dom's room was like a trek into a world of depravity for someone as 'straitlaced' as Linda. She would find a world of condoms, Rizlas, and tins with their exotic smelling contents. On one occasion, she was devastated to turn Dominic's mattress and uncover, beneath the bed, a large polythene bag containing hundreds of white pills. She replaced everything without saying anything to her son. Later spot-checks would reveal that quantities had disappeared from the bag. This would coincide with Dominic's overnight visits to clubs in the Midlands. Linda lived in expectation of a midnight phone call from a police station in Wolverhampton, Walsall, or worse, claiming that her son had been taken into custody.

Both her children were products of Gareth's obsession with education. Judith had risen to the challenge, having natural intelligence and a willingness to work. Dominic, on the other hand, could not compete with his father who, like his political hero Neil Kinnock, was the first in a family raised in the valleys of South Wales to receive a university education.

Dominic pleaded to be allowed to leave Stortvale High on account of "always having dad there." What could be more embarrassing to a pubescent teenager than having his father for a headmaster? Dom had made a mess of his Lower Sixth at Stortvale, but fared no better at the neighbouring college of further education. Linda always said she was "past worrying about Dominic," but Linda was never past worrying about anything.

Marjorie Pelforth had not seen the local paper. Adrian had it sent to his office – another perk of the job. As she searched the detergent bottles for her early morning shot, she listened to the news on Stort FM.

The news was, as ever, inane. A newshound began her report: "I'm standing outside the Storton and District Council offices where, last night, the District Council agreed to give planning permission for a new controversial amphitheatre and sculpture park."

Marjorie could never quite understand why a radio reporter should need to be standing in the rain outside a building to tell us something so uninteresting that it could be happily relayed from the comfort of the studio. She was greatly amused however, that Stortvale had upstaged her husband for once. She rather sympathised with "that nice Mr Chivers." Of her two sons, Charles and Jeremy, she rather thought the latter would have prospered at the High School, much to her husband's annoyance:

"Of course we can't take Jeremy away from Stortfield, woman," she recalled him yelling. "What kind of advertisement is that?"

She thought Jeremy who, according to reports was "somewhat nonconformist and independent minded," would largely go unnoticed amongst Stortvale's more notable ne'er do wells. Charles had been an exemplary son of his father. Tall, square jawed, the first team rugby captain, and justly so. Charles was largely forgiven by his contemporaries for being the father of his son. Not entirely academic, Charles had gone to Sandhurst and pursued an army career which enabled him to assert his authority without too much intelligence, and more importantly, allowed him to continue playing top class rugby.

Jeremy was not good at sports. He loved drama and was much cossetted by Viola McIntyre. Mrs McIntyre's patronage of the boy kept her from Pelforth's axe just long enough. Her affair with Simon Petherton-Pugh began as Jeremy was entering his final year, and so the volatile Head of Drama had an even better ally to call upon when faced with Pelforth's animosity.

Viola had quickly deduced Jeremy's problem. She hadn't spent three years at the Central School of Speech and Drama without instantly recognising when a young man was struggling to recognise his homosexuality.

That Jeremy was gay was disputed only by Adrian Pelforth. After graduating in Fashion Design, Jeremy was now living with a florist in Aberdeen. This is about as far north as any self-respecting florist would wish to travel, but by no means far enough for Jeremy's father.

Marjorie missed Jeremy. Jeremy who talked to her. Jeremy who asked her what she thought. Jeremy, whose life was not wrapped up in a box and labelled "Property of Stortfield Academy." He was a great comfort to Marjorie. Now he could only comfort her with guilty bottles of the finest Scotch whisky secreted in a delivery disguised as a budding pot plant.

Today, Marjorie had been instructed to dress well for another visit by Jack Wildblood. It was on these occasions she missed Jeremy more than ever. He had immaculate taste in clothes, and exactly matched the outfit for the occasion. Her dilemma was greatly increased by the fact that she had forgotten completely what she had worn on the previous occasion. She sensed the outfit may have been intentionally alluring, but recalling the hairy boar-like demeanour of Wildblood, she decided to opt for one of her pink “church service” twin sets with matching scarf. The scarf would have been Jeremy’s idea.

CHAPTER 12

# CONVULSIONS

Adrian Pelforth sat gloating over the *Storton Courier* in his oak-panelled study. His secretary Mrs Bingham had informed him that Melinda and Belinda were waiting outside.

It was to their good fortune that Pelforth had seen the newspaper. This gave him more ammunition to present to Wildblood, who still needed some persuading to head up fundraising for the new theatre. Pelforth had also decided that his Head Girl and her Deputy were far too impressive to relinquish. Demotion was out of the question. What's more, he could not deny to himself that their presence and charm often brightened his day, and gave rise to fantasies of intimate school camping trips. In these reveries, the three of them were marooned or abandoned on the moors, in a single, remaining tent, with only his expert army training standing between them and survival.

As Melinda and Belinda stood before him, he tried hard to concentrate on the disciplinary issue at hand, whilst images of the three of them huddled together for body warmth under a large sheet of Bacofoil, flashed before him.

Belinda breathed a great sigh of annoyance as he muttered about "conduct unbecoming of the two of you," and her well-appointed breasts heaved before him as he sat glancing beyond the rims of his bifocals.

"You know, I really must point out," he said unthinkingly, "that you are two of the bigger assets of this school. I'm very proud of you – both. You are a fine, upstanding pair. I mean, you've got everything going for you." Pelforth began to recognise his Freudian slips, and was now anxiously trying to conceal them.

"I can tell you, I've spent many sleepless nights thinking about you – I mean, when deciding which of you I should have made Head Girl. In the end I almost had to toss for it."

At this point Belinda suppressed a snort of laughter.

"Yes, Belinda, I found it hard to come between the two of you." Belinda now stood silently giggling, indicated only by the subtle tightening of her neck. Pelforth stood and wandered behind them, now flushed with embarrassment and excitement.

"There's nothing to laugh at. I certainly wouldn't be sniggering if I were either of you."

From behind, he noticed their shoulders shuffling, almost imperceptibly. He also noticed the sweet curls from Melinda's highly tied hair, which trailed around the nape of her neck like a Hardy heroine. He also noted that Belinda's bottom was as agreeably sculpted by her school skirt as were her breasts by the regulation blouse.

"Of course, I shall have to inform your parents. What they'll think of you riding pillion behind two bikers in leather, I dread to imagine."

At this point, Belinda snorted so loudly that Melinda was forced into emergency action. She disguised her erupting giggle into a heavy sob, and began talking through it:

"Please sir, we weren't riding with them."

Belinda, desperate not to explode into hysterical laughter also managed to turn on the tears.

"No sir," she blurted, "we just went for a drink. We don't know them at all."

"They just sat with us," Melinda emoted, catching her breath.

"They were horrible, sir," blurted out Belinda. "We'll not go to the pub again out of hours."

"Please don't tell our parents," Melinda mumbled through her handkerchief, as she wiped her nose in an affected manner. "It was only a quiet drink. We've been under such pressure lately sir."

"It's not as if we're underage, sir," said Belinda, recovering a little.

Pelforth sidled around to catch sight of their red, tear-stained faces and was convinced of their repentance and regret.

He found this exhibition of emotion somewhat unbecoming in these otherwise mature young women, but was also strongly overwhelmed by his own sense of power. Convinced that he had won them over, they were dismissed with no more than a quiet warning, and ordered to be at the Sir Ian Botham Suite for lunch, with the Chairman of Governors and Mr Wildblood.

"But we have netball practice before lunch, Mr Pelforth," said Melinda with a tiny, residual sob. "We won't have time to change."

"Never mind" said Adrian, imagining them flushed and perspiring in their short netball skirts. "Come as you are." He had developed a throbbing erection.

The girls stumbled into the corridor outside Pelforth's office, leaning on one another for support. They walked rapidly, heads down, still wiping away their tears, to the nearest toilets where, before the door had closed behind them they exploded into convulsions of hysterical laughter, holding onto thc wash basins and propping themselves against lavatory doors for support.

"Dirty old bastard!" Belinda blurted between breaths. "He couldn't take his eyes off my tits – did you notice?"

"Don't, don't, please!" pitched in Melinda. Her stomach was aching with laughter as she stumbled into a cubicle to rapidly hoist up her school skirt, and lower her rather less than regulation G-string, before slumping onto the toilet seat. "I'm wetting myself. Oh God!" she almost screamed, before kicking shut the cubicle door.

Pelforth, meanwhile, slid into the private bathroom installed in the office suite, dropped his trousers and similarly exploded into convulsions over the sink, following which he applied the air freshener liberally.

Belinda and Melinda sat astride lavatory seats in adjoining cubicles and regretted the lack of anything to disguise the evidence of cigarette smoke which threatened their reputations further.

CHAPTER 13

# NETBALL

Melinda and Belinda looked particularly fetching in their netball skirts, thought Pelforth, especially with their faces flushed from full-blooded exercise. Marjorie, on the other hand, looked pale and puce in pink beside them, and he made a point of ignoring her.

The girls left politely at the sight of the brandy, giving Pelforth much satisfaction at their new found discretion. A pity Marjorie hadn't done the same.

Wildblood was holding forth, bristling like an ensnared warthog:

"Listen, I don't mind heading up this fund raising business. I don't mind putting in a few quid of my own, but I'm buggered if I'm going to let some tuppenny-ha'penny comprehensive down the road steal all the glory from under my nose."

He paused to take a swig of the brandy, and growled on:

"I mean, what the hell does Lady Doulting think she's up to? They'd be better off building houses on the land. A sculpture park will only be vandalised by the locals. A waste of time and money."

"They're expecting to get Lottery funding too," chipped in the ingratiatingly irritating School Bursar. This proved a red rag to the already snorting bull.

"Lottery money?" Christ! Anyone'd think it was the Royal Opera House or something. What a waste!" Wildblood was almost choking on his brandy. "Lottery money indeed!"

"Well, yes," said Slater, "but we're equally entitled to apply for a Lottery grant."

"I doubt if we'd qualify," said Simon Petherton-Pugh dismissively. "As a private school, I don't suppose our application would meet with much sympathy."

"Eton got a Lottery grant," countered Slater, almost apologetically. "You've only got to suggest it's for community use."

"Eton?" Wildblood's shoulders grew more hunched, his eyebrows more animated than ever. The bull was about to charge "Eton? Good God! They've got more money stashed away than Fort bloody Knox!"

"Surely," Simon suggested, "Stortvale had stolen a march on us here. I met Raymond Chater last week and he was moaning about all the paperwork involved. They must have got it underway already. The National Lottery chaps are hardly going to stump up twice at the same time, in the same town, are they?"

"We've got to get the buggers on our side then," Wildblood urged. How much can we put in for?"

Slater, his confidence growing, was quick to respond. "Well, quite often they'll agree to matched funding."

"Meaning what?" interjected Pelforth, who had been listening intently to the debate.

"Meaning," said Slater smugly, revelling in his role of oracle, "we raise half, and they provide the rest."

Wildblood soon scotched Slater's message of hope. "Meaning their project is going to be up and ready long before our own. Whose idea was this sculpture park anyway?"

"Ah, I think I can answer that," said Petherton-Pugh. "He's a friend of a friend."

Adrian immediately guessed that the 'friend' in question was Viola McIntyre, who seemed to know all the Bohemians in Storton. He decided it better not to prompt Pugh beyond an inquisitive…

"Well?"

"Er-his name's Nigel Slot" Simon responded on cue. "He's been running community art projects in Storton over the years. He was the one who built the Easter Island statue outside the library."

"That bloody monstrosity!" retorted Pelforth, unable to contain himself. "And I suppose he got an Arts Council grant for it too?"

"Funding was provided jointly by the local council and the Arts Council, yes," corrected Simon. Doulting provided the stone at no cost. "Personally, I think Slot's work is quite arresting."

"Personally I think Slot wants arresting," chimed in Adrian, laughing at his own joke.

Wildblood would not be drawn into levity. "You mean this fellow, this Slot, can get paid to create that pile of rubbish?"

"Precisely," added Slater.

"And that he claims subsidies from institutional quangos for the privilege?"

"Absolutely," replied Slater.

"Then, there's only one thing for it," Wildblood asserted. "We need him on our side."

"What?" Pelforth looked uneasily across the table.

"Yes, if he's the key who can knock on the door to all this public money."

"Key to unlock the door, I imagine you mean," responded Petherton-Pugh, with a supercilious chuckle.

It didn't pay to make Wildblood more of a monkey than he already looked:

"Unlock it then. Unlock it. You know my meaning, smart Alec," he bristled.

"But Adrian just declared his work a pile of rubbish," Petherton-Pugh countered.

"So it is" replied Wildblood, burping. "So it is. But if we can get him to work for us, if we can find a role for him here…" Wildblood was gathering momentum. "All this public money slushing about. Why can't we get our hands on it? After all, Stortfield has stood here for 134 years. It has been a bastion of respectability and brought wealth, jobs, and prosperity to Storton. And what has it asked for in return, eh? Stortfield's parents pay their taxes too you know. And what do they get in return? Nothing but the scant satisfaction of knowing that, by paying school fees, they are indirectly subsidising lavish and exotic projects. All to be wasted on a local comprehensive that can't even keep its windows repaired. We need this Slot bod on our side." He thumped the table, rattling the cutlery.

"And," the normally diffident Slater was looking a little

pleased with himself, "and we happen to know that Nigel Slot is the primary reason for Lady Doulting's involvement. Perhaps if he were to be lured away…"

"… she would follow" concluded Adrian.

"Exactly," said Wildblood. "Perhaps, he could be lured away, but before he can do too much damage to our plans, we pay him off."

"Drop him you mean?" Adrian liked the sound of this.

"Absolutely," croaked Wildblood, swigging a large mouthful of brandy. "It's what we call in industry – consolidation."

Simon Petherton-Pugh looked very uncomfortable. "Really, I have friends with children at Stortvale. Decent, hardworking people. They'd love to send their kids to us of course, but not everyone can afford it. We really ought not to get involved in this sort of sabotage."

Wildblood was losing patience with what he thought of as Petherton-Pugh's bleeding heart liberalism, but he tried to sound conciliatory: "Look, I'm not suggesting we deny the school essentials like books, teachers, central heating. I'm simply proposing that we allow them to do what they do best – provide a decent, basic education. The sort that I found perfectly adequate before Winchester knocked it out of me…" He paused to chuckle nostalgically. "No, no, I jest. If schools like Stortvale want to build theatres and sculpture parks, surely they should get the basics sorted out first. At Stortfield you have earned the right to indulge yourselves with beauty and art. Great minds are forged in schools like this. Without these inventive, imaginative leaders of the future, this school would have, long ago, become some soulless, second rate, new-Socialist slum. I have no compunction when it comes to reasserting the legacy of schools like Stortfield. I don't mind putting a stop to the senseless drain of taxpayer's money on pet projects, dreamed up by civic worthies, and deluded old nutters like Lady Doulting. She was a damned shorthand typist when Arthur Doulting first met her, you know. More money than sense."

"Quite, quite." Petherton-Pugh was looking flustered. "I fully respect some of your views, Jack, but we have enough bad blood between us at Stortfield and the comprehensive."

"Then what have you got to lose?!" Wildblood spat the words at the Chair of Governors along with a small remainder of coq au vin.

Simon Petherton-Pugh wiped the remnant discreetly from his beige cuff, put down his table napkin and stood. "Well, I'm afraid I have another appointment, gentlemen. I'll have to leave you to draw your own conclusions as to where we go next with this project."

A moment of silence fell upon the room as Petherton-Pugh flounced out, barely disguising his distaste for the turn of the conversation. Slater, Wildblood and not least Pelforth, knew that the eminent and respectable Simon was withdrawing in order to keep his conscience clean.

Adrian Pelforth had watched the reaction of his Chairman of Governors with interest. He too had reservations about luring Nigel Slot from the Stortvale project, not least because he genuinely hated Slot's type and, in particular, his pretentious work. But, it was true, his dream was about to be rudely disrupted by that smug bastard Gareth Chivers, and radical measures may be needed to ensure Stortfield's plans were not overshadowed. Furthermore, he found Petherton-Pugh's sanctimonious stand unutterably vomit-inducing. Pugh was a man of substantial privilege. He knew nothing of comprehensive schools, and not nearly as many of Stortvale's parents as he pretended. It was all part of his desire to be seen as a local philanthropist, and maybe to get the safe Conservative seat he longed for, since chairing Stortfield's debating society as a foppish sixth former.

Adrian disliked Petherton-Pugh now, even more than before. In Jack Wildblood he had an ally he could cultivate. If Wildblood's idea was acted upon, perhaps Petherton-Pugh's sanctimonious principles would finally drive him to relinquish the coveted position of Chairman of Governors. And, with any luck, he's take that bloody McIntyre woman with him.

CHAPTER 14

# DRESSING UP

Viola McIntyre had again borrowed the keys to the SODS wardrobe. The Storton Operatic and Dramatic Society owned an impressive store house of costumes, collected over the course of seventy-five years. These were housed in a farmer's barn just beyond the village of Blackrock. The farmer had been compensated handsomely when Doulting's decided to detonate half his land without asking his permission. The barn and several outhouses were now perched precariously on the lip of the ever expanding quarry, and the farmer had no use for them, having retired to a life of indolence and luxury. The farmer's daughter had been a stalwart of SODS, and it was she who persuaded him to lease the society the barn on a peppercorn rent.

Inside the barn, the lower floor was filled with rack upon rack of historical costumes. The smell of mothballs did not detract from the warm cosy feeling Viola McIntyre felt every time she entered the dimly lit barn. Here was a world of pretence, of make-believe, in which she often sought refuge.

The barn had a mezzanine upper floor 'hayloft' which extended half the length of the roof. It was accessible from an outside staircase and, from the inside, by a ladder leading through a trapdoor. The hayloft was used to store old scenery flats, painted cloths, rugs and a huge pile of unsorted garments.

Viola had brought with her, as usual, a large velvet throw to keep the soft but dusty pile of costumes from contact with her soft, but slightly ageing, skin. The great thing about making love in a costume store was the limitless supply of erotic fancy dress with which to experiment. Viola soon discovered that Simon Petherton-Pugh's penchant had been forged in his early years. Deprived of affection, the eight-year-old Simon, like so many of his social class, was entrusted to the care of a boarding school, and spent many a night sobbing into the firm bosom of a soft-voiced matron.

Viola lay on the improvised velvet bed adorning the accoutrements of an old fashioned boarding school matron. She chose to limit the costume to essential basics-that is to say a nurse's cap, a full, starched apron, and nothing else. She raised a naked knee and looked up in expectation as she heard the ladder to the hayloft trap door creak ominously, as it was slowly propped open by the head of the incoming principal in this pantomime. Her first glimpse of her lover was the flash of a silver badge. The badge was pinned above the peak of a black cap. The stern peak partially hid the familiar cool, blue eyes which peered temptingly over the parapet:

"Oooh, Matron, I wasn't expecting you here." The voice

was low, teasing, and ever-so Leslie Phillips in *Carry On Doctor*.

"Hello, you naughty boy," Viola responded like a slightly sophisticated chat-line hostess. "You seem to have caught me taking the air." At this point Mrs McIntyre swivelled her hips and revealed a single, naked buttock, pinkily imprinted with the pattern of the velvet throw.

"I say!" came the silky voice from beneath the military cap. The lover continued his ascent and, in so doing, revealed shoulders and sleeves shrouded in leather. As he emerged, Viola recognised (from her acclaimed interpretation of Maria Von Trapp in *The Sound of Music*) the distinguished uniform of an officer of the Waffen SS.

"Simon!" Viola's voice was tinged with more than a little concern. "I'm not sure that I approve of your choice."

Simon was now fully visible to the fringe of his shiny coat. He looked at her, raised an eyebrow, and in a passable German accent made his excuses:

"You vill undershtand zat I hev been attending a meeting wiz ze Fuhrer, und hev had little time to change from zese, shall ve say, formal garments."

At which point, Obergruppenfuhrer Petherton-Pugh climbed the remaining rungs of the ladder revealing bony shins beneath the leather hem.

"You could, at least, have kept your boots on" said the matron, sternly.

"Matron," Simon said in his more familiar silky tones, "I have a great deal more yet to reveal."

Viola McIntyre found the postcoital conversation a little more intriguing than usual. Viola preferred not to indulge in the politics of Stortfield Academy in her private life, but her badly contained 'secret' liaison with the Chairman of Governors sometimes mitigated against it.

Viola was a woman who followed her passions. Teaching Drama at Stortfield Academy was a poor substitute for what she had most desired, which was to be a successful actress.

Viola had trained at the Guildhall School in London, where many thought she had the will, desire, talent, and most of all, good looks, to succeed in the theatre. Before completing her course however, Viola was drawn back to her home in Lincolnshire to look after her ailing mother. Her mother died within months of her return. Viola's father had long deserted the family, and so she naturally was seduced, in her distress, by the comforting proposals of Benedict Sanderton, and lured by the relative stability of being an army officer's wife. This seemed to happen to Viola before she really had time to take it all in.

For two years, Mrs Sanderton suppressed her artistic talents, but grew bored within the confines of various barrack postings. Having assisted voluntarily in the schools for military children, she decided to return to England and train as a teacher.

Benedict did not object. Neither did he entirely approve, but he could see that his headstrong wife would not be easily held back. Studying Educational Drama again rekindled Viola's passion for the theatre. It also rekindled other, more urgent passions. After two years on the course, it was clear she would never settle back as the dutiful wife of an army captain. She met Duncan, an actor, and moved in with him. Duncan struggled to find work and so Viola, upon graduating, took up teaching in a London comprehensive to support them both. She fully intended to get into acting herself, but this job was just to tide them over in the meantime.

Duncan eventually found repertory work in Dundee. He also found the pretty, waspish, Cecilia Redfern, who played Titania to his Oberon.

Viola, though devastated, and bitter at the sacrifice she had made for the charming, though devious, Duncan, was, at least, free to try her hand at acting. She tolerated nine months of auditions and applications, but was unable to secure a job.

Teaching eventually seemed an agreeable alternative, particularly when she was appointed as Head of Drama at the prestigious Stortfield Academy. Yes, she was the only one in her department, and was answerable to the Head of English, but that independence suited her well. In addition, she was offered and Assistant Housemistress post which brought with it a pleasant flat in a girl's boarding house.

Viola had forgotten though, that institutional life can be somewhat suffocating. Boarding schools and army barracks were not dissimilar in many ways. Soon she began sagging off duties to attend rehearsals with Storton Operatic and Dramatic Society, where she proved an instant hit-and revelled in being regarded as a 'professional' in the ranks.

It was during a production of *My Fair Lady* when, as Eliza Doolittle, she met her Freddy Eynsford-Hill, and the form of Vincent McIntyre. Vincent, like most solicitors, was a very credible actor. They married within a year, had three children within five years, and for a while, despite upsetting her Headmaster, Adrian Pelforth, with her frequent requests for maternity leave, Viola was happy.

That was until Simon Petherton-Pugh moved back to the town in which he had been schooled; joined the Operatic and Dramatic Society; became a governor at the Academy; and played Anthony to her Cleopatra.

Now forty-four, Viola was indulging in perhaps her final fling. She wouldn't dream of deserting Vincent or the children, but though she publicly denied it, she never fully took to teaching and needed the adrenaline rush of performing. Viola had seen some of her better pupils go on to drama schools, and some graduated into films and television. This would sometimes cause her more pain than pride.

Once, after a very dull production of *Pericles* at the Royal Shakespeare Theatre in Stratford-upon-Avon, Viola, having taken charge of a visiting coach party from Stortfield, got very drunk in the Dirty Duck, the well-known actors' pub by the theatre. To the immense embarrassment of the other staff, she berated the performers as they appeared one by one in the bar, following the matinee performance. In particular, she singled out a young actor called Emile Gladstone, who she remembered when he was plain, old Eric Gardener, a bit part player in the school dramatic society.

Having raised the school party simply to support Emile's Stratford debut, she shot the boy down in flames in a performance that upstaged any seen in the theatre that day.

"Emile! Darling! Or may I call you Eric?" Viola bellowed. "After all, that is your name, isn't it? Eric? I said it before, and I'll say it again…" Viola bundled her way up to him at the bar – obstructing all exit routes with a very deliberate invasion of body space. "You've done remarkably well for yourself. Really. I haven't the faintest idea how you got into drama school. But I take my hat off to you. To be brutally honest, I don't quite know how such an august institution as the Royal Shakespeare Company could also see fit to absorb your talents" (she mimed inverted commas around the word "talents" and, in so doing, spilt much of her wine down Emile's Jacobean red jacket) –

"that was until I saw you mincing about in Act 3, and realised that it is more than just your talents that are being absorbed. So who exactly are you sleeping with Eric? The director? No offence, but I've heard he's a bit of an old fruit."

If Eric had learned one thing in drama school, it was how to make a fast and cutting reply:

"No, Mrs McIntyre-er, you are still Mrs McIntyre I presume? Only seeing how little your own career flourished by sleeping with the Chairman of the Governors, I realised, at an early age, that prostituting oneself for personal gain, could never really enhance one's sense of self-worth."

And with that, Eric Gardener slammed down his brandy and lemonade, wiped what wine he could from the front of his jacket with a flick of the wrist, turned with ballet-like exactitude, and flounced off to another, more hospitable hostelry, where he could, again, safely assume the mantle of Emile Gladstone.

The episode gave rise to many repercussions. Firstly, Viola's affair was not common knowledge until that moment. Having skipped Acts 4 and 5 of Pericles, abandoning her charges and taking refuge in a bottle of sauvignon blanc at the Dirty Duck, she had forgotten why she helped Eric audition for drama school in the first place. It was entirely because the boy's mother was wardrobe supervisor for SODS and had chanced upon Viola and Simon 'role playing' in the hayloft. On that particular occasion, Viola later recalled to her enormous embarrassment, she had decided to be Joan of Arc to his Mother Superior of the Convent of Our Lady of the Immaculate Conception – a theatrical combination not always found in the scripts.

Mrs Gardener has been the soul of discretion but had used the incident to full advantage. Viola had even raised Eric's A

Level Theatre Studies practical grade, after the merest hint from the well-informed wardrobe mistress.

In attendance at the Dirty Duck were several members of staff, not to mention a host of sixth formers who had also sought refuge from *Pericles*. When Viola arrived, rather than chastise them, she insisted they refrained from escape, bought an enormous round, and proceeded to tell them how she, not Eric, "should have been up on that fucking stage!"

Needless to say, word got back to Adrian Pelforth. Viola never found out who spilled the beans, but she was pretty sure it was Peter Edwards' wife Sally. Peter was Head of English and had a soft spot for Viola. Sally knew this, and it infuriated her that Viola was allowed to get away with so many administrative and organisational cock-ups. Peter would always be there to pick up the pieces and, apart from rather fancying Viola, genuinely loved her school plays.

Pelforth, on the other hand, did not like Mrs McIntyre's school plays, far from it. He had often found them "too intense," "sexually explicit," "politically correct" and, above all "offensively intellectual" or "too clever by half." On one occasion, in a vain attempt to take a positive response to Viola's pro-feminist production of *The Tempest*, the only compliment he could utter before the assembled school was to say how "patient and well-behaved" he found the audience.

Simon Petherton-Pugh whispered postcoital sweet nothings as he gently nibbled Viola's ear lobes. "Oh, and by the way," he added, almost as if by chance, "I may have to oppose the theatre project after all."

"What?" Viola pushed him back by the shoulders so as to look at him hard between the eyes. "What the fuck are you on about?"

“Pelforth’s making it hard for me to get behind the scheme,” said Simon, almost laconically.

“But you’re supposed to be the biggest supporter.”

“I know, but Jack Wildblood’s started this crusade to sabotage the Stortvale amphitheatre project. Pelforth’s convinced him they’re stealing our thunder. He’s frightened they’ll get funding and beat us to it.”

Viola eased herself from beneath Simon, keeping him at arms-length. “But what does it matter? Stortvale are building an amphitheatre surrounded by Stotty’s hideous carvings. It’s just a monument. It’ll not be in use most of the year.”

“You try telling that to Adrian. He has this vision of the punters coming to Stortfield, picnicking by the lake, and sampling the pre-show delights of the terrace bar, like at Chichester, or Glyndebourne. He can’t stand the idea of Stortvale promising the bloody Proms with fireworks, not to mention scantily clad nymphs dancing dreamily around Slot’s sculptures.”

There was a pause. Viola’s nostrils flared like sailor’s trousers.

“What do you mean ‘sabotage’?”

Simon explained the whole ludicrous business as he saw it.

“You don’t seriously expect Pelforth to try to get a talentless old crack-head like Nigel Slot on board, do you?” Viola responded with rising incredulity.

“Oh, they won’t use any of his work. They just think Nigel has the knack of getting funding from all sides. Even if they eventually drop all his designs, they can, at least scupper Stortvale’s idea.”

“Well,” said Viola, standing with as much dignity as her

costume would allow, "I don't see why we couldn't have discussed this earlier."

"I just didn't want to trouble you with it," said Simon, peering directly at her pert bottom.

"Didn't want it to spoil your rather bizarre little ritual, I suppose?" challenged Viola, suddenly trying to look dignified.

Simon could see that Viola was suppressing a more intense rage, and was annoyed with himself that her delicate attempts to look demure against the odds, had given rise to another bulge in his leather greatcoat.

"Simon, you know how much I want this theatre. You know how much I'd give to ensure we get it built. Christ! I even did *Carousel* last year to keep Pelforth happy. Why can't you just swallow your pride and let them have their little games with Slot?"

"Viola, darling, it would be a PR disaster for the Academy. If Pelforth and Wildblood start screwing with the Stortvale plans, I shall have to consider my position on the Governors. My reputation would be in tatters."

"And, if you resign – who will stand between me and the sack? Is that what you want, Simon?"

"No of course I don't want to get you the sack." Petherton-Pugh paused before continuing slyly – "In the sack, perhaps."

"Don't fuck about," warned Viola, removing her matronly garb. Simon was now in possession of an erection as steep as a cathedral spire.

"Look, I'll tell you what." Simon was thinking quickly while his manhood held firm. "Why don't we get together with Slot and warn him off?"

"He doesn't strike me as a man with whom we can confide," observed Viola, shivering a little.

"I'm sure you can work your charms, darling," suggested Simon, seeing an obvious opening, so to speak. "Now come on, let's warm up a little shall we?" He opened his large leather coat and invited her in.

"Oh, alright," agreed Viola with pretend reluctance, and a hint of a smile. "But do take that silly fucking hat off."

CHAPTER 15

# BEELZEBUB

Nigel Slot had never felt so popular. Not only was the Stortvale sculpture park looking a certain runner, he had unexpectedly been invited by Adrian Pelforth to give a lecture on his works to the Stortfield Academy Sixth Form. This was despite the fact that he and Chris Parkes, Stortfield's Head of Art, were almost sworn enemies.

Last night's clandestine meeting however, with Simon Petherton-Pugh and Viola McIntyre, had put a new complexion on matters. Slot's mission in life was to fool everyone and be a fool to no one. Though moderately talented, Nigel long recognised his limitations as a sculptor and artist. He was the son of an East End market stall holder and knew a thing or two about selling people stuff they don't really want. His 'old man' did a nice line in cheap clothes. His 'end of line' pre-washed jeans were a specialty. Many were, in fact, not only pre-washed, but genuinely fresh off the end of washing lines in the suburbs of Dagenham. Nigel knew this because it was he who often created the diversion his dad needed to "have it away" with the 501s.

The popularity of the tumbler dryer did not stop Harry Slot who was nothing if not resourceful, and so he got himself into the photo and portrait framing business. Young Nigel's talent at "knocking out the odd Van Gogh" certainly came in handy, before the boy got ideas above his station and managed to 'blag' his way into the Central School of Art. He knew all too well that his humble East End background could be used to "get those mugs on the panel" to think that they were able to see through his limited file of work and find a "great, earthy, naïve talent." Much of his portfolio comprised photos of quite impressive graffiti art, most of which had hadn't actually painted himself.

Nigel enjoyed his student life to the full. In other words, he did no work, took lots of drugs, and failed the course. It didn't stop him adding 'BA' to his name though. Who would check up anyway? He also was assured excellent references from a lecturer at art school to whom Nigel had provided a regular supply of cocaine.

Nigel knew he couldn't "cut the mustard" in the London art world. He moved to Storton to be with a girlfriend who he rapidly dumped as soon as a comfortable squat could be found. Storton was just the place to appreciate Nigel's "talent." It was full of suburban, upwardly mobile, pretentious types, who had neither the excessive wealth, taste, nor confidence, to shop in the galleries of Bond Street. He soon found a couple of art shops willing to stock his overpriced forgeries and fripperies, and, with income from an evening class at Stortvale High, coupled with welfare benefits, he eked out a living.

Nigel hadn't been taken in by Pelforth. He knew the lecture invitation was a front for something. When Pelforth invited him for a sherry in his study, Slot instantly recognised the bastard was going to pump him for information on the Stortvale project. He hadn't, however, expected to be offered a sizeable sum to defect to the other side.

The subsequent meeting with Petherton-Pugh and Viola confirmed Slot's suspicions that Stortfield did not want him for his creative powers, but he was delighted, none the less, to be in a position of such influence.

Nigel mulled over the possibilities whilst breaking his fast with the remnants of last night's Chinese take away, and found himself in a dilemma. For most artists the matter would have come down to manna or morals, and they would have squirmed for days in indecision. Not Nigel. As he picked the tin foil tray of noodles, the cat leapt up on the table and stole a large slice of chicken. Recognising the cat as a kindred spirit, Nigel just laughed. He further tempted the creature with a full fork waved under its nose. The cat followed the fork from left to right, and then stared hard as Nigel slowly slipped the food between his nicotine-stained teeth.

"The thing is, Beelzebub," enunciated Nigel, staring back at the cat, "how to take the whole fucking lot of them to cleaners."

CHAPTER 16

# HEALTH AND SAFETY

An ambulance may have appeared and extravagance, but in these days of 'health and safety', it seemed the most sensible course of action.

Rosemary Jenkins had seen it all as the Housemother of Churchill House. At times, she thought it might be better to have an ambulance on permanent standby outside the front door.

Concussion from hockey balls; dislocated shoulders from rugby matches; choking on vomit from clandestine drinking sessions; boys' heads irretrievably stuck in waste bins; bottom burns caused by errant bangers in bed… the accident book bore witness to them all. But this was different. As she saw the quaking and shivering little frame of Timpson being hauled, stretcher-bound, into the ambulance, she felt an unusual sense of sympathy and foreboding.

Rosemary was sure that the boy's failure to talk was down to fear, rather than amnesia. He had been acting strangely recently. Bed wetting was not unheard of in the new intake, but it didn't usually start at Timpson's age. Timpson had seemed settled and secure when he first arrived, having boarded before at Prep School. He was a sensitive boy, no doubt about that, given to bursting into tears at the minor brutalities of a boys' boarding house, but he would soon bury himself in a *Harry Potter* epic and forget all about it. He was studious and quiet, but very supportive of the House and vociferous on the touchline when cheering on those who could play games that were beyond his ungainly and uncoordinated efforts.

Timpson had fainted in assembly recently. He had also developed a mysterious rash on his back which was eventually diagnosed as an allergic reaction. This was after various forms of antibiotic, administered by the school doctor, had proven not only pointless, but had induced severe diarrhoea and vomiting. He had become pale and thin, his glasses suddenly looked enormous on his tiny face, and seemed to be constantly sliding down his pinched nose. He was forever propping them up with a middle finger, and Rosemary had noticed that he seemed to blink wildly behind the looming lenses.

This morning he'd been discovered by one of his roommates curled up in a wardrobe, a tie fastened around his bare neck, but still in his pyjamas. He was shaking, and had wet himself again. Ordinarily, he might have been sent home, but his father was a senior diplomat and the High Commission in Nairobi was a long way to go for what his Housemaster, Bernard Jenkins, had described as "no more than an adolescent affectation." Privately he reported that "the boy's probably recognising certain homoerotic urges. Many do."

Rosemary had also observed an increase in the nightly comings and goings of the 'first team' boys. She was now inclined to mention it to Vera Lovett, her fellow Housemother, but knew that an indiscreet word could spread around the confined Academy campus faster than an outbreak of impetigo, and didn't want to raise alarm.

She watched Timpson's little frame pass through the doors of the ambulance, the faint twitch of a smile on his face. Once in the ambulance his taught facial muscles relaxed and he looked the tiniest bit relieved.

CHAPTER 17

# OLD SCHOOL

"He's what? The slimy little shit!" exclaimed Gareth Chivers down the phone, dragging from within the South Walian gift for musicality when angry.

Valerie sat back in her chair, notepad on knee, and looked distinctly ruffled. Gareth gripped the slightly battered, black phone even harder and signalled Valerie to leave the room, with a swift, sweeping wave. She went, tightening her neck muscles and setting her jaw in that tense, tetchy way he had noticed in Linda when she was silently annoyed.

"You can't be serious, Raymond. What would Stortfield want with an idiot like Slot? Even we don't really want him."

"Well whatever it is dear boy," purred Raymond, sitting back casually in his expensive leather office chair and throwing words in the general direction of the speakerphone, "it hasn't done him much good with Lady Doulting. She's convinced that Jack Wildblood's involved. Reckons they might have paid Slot off in order to scupper our Lottery bid."

"What's this Wildblood character got to do with it?"

"Lady D knows that he's been looking for a good cause to try and up his chances of a KBE. They go back a long way. The late Sir Arthur Doulting was opposed to supplying Doulting Stone for a rather dubious dam project in Malaysia. It was part of a government scam to filter foreign aid back into British business."

"Oh, I remember that. The Gapau Dam" said Chivers.

"That's the one. Well, Jack Wildblood had his trotters firmly in the trough, and Sir Arthur named him in an interview for the *Observer*. Sir Arthur was old school you see. Served in the Far East during the Second World War. Felt that Britain should be beyond that sort of thing. It made it terribly difficult to give Wildblood the knighthood he's been hankering after, once that came out."

"The thing is" countered Gareth, "I don't give two hoots about Slot anyway – or his horrible sculptures. He was just a means to an end. The question is: what do we do now?"

"Leave it with me. Lady D's so furious, she's prepared to raise the stakes. She's asked me to contact Burnley, Brace and Bridges for a chinwag."

"Who the hell are they? Solicitors?"

"No, no, they're the architects who redesigned the mansion's new wing. Top firm – involved in the restoration of Storton Castle a while back."

"What can they offer us?" Chivers asked.

"Possibly a slight change of approach." There was a little

uplift in Raymond's response. "How would you like an indoor theatre instead?"

CHAPTER 18

# SUMMER TERM

The summer term was a brief but magical time of year for Adrian Pelforth. Flowerbeds bloomed around the campus, the lake was alive with water fowl, and the tranquillity of the late afternoon was broken only by the distant echo of ball against bat. In Adrian's ideal world, the summer term would be the longest, extending well into August, mainly so that the cricketers could be given a "longer stay at the crease." If pupils were forced to take most of their holiday in the winter, the more vulgar game of Association football might be squeezed. This would also reduce the number of state school teams visiting the campus, slopping around in their ghastly sweat shirts and trainers, chewing gum, and making much amusement of their brief interaction with the world of privilege – or 'civilisation' as Adrian would prefer to think of it.

Cricket has been almost exclusively the province of the public school, and it was always a pleasure to receive boys from the type of school Stortfield Academy aspired to be. Pelforth was usually in evidence at matches and subsequent high teas, when the visiting teams happened to be Eton, Harrow or Winchester. State school visitors would rarely be given the courtesy of a greeting, when they brought their busloads of soccer playing 'hooligans' to tear up the playing fields and generally thump Stortfield's rather second-rate footballers. All the real athletes played rugby and cricket at Stortfield. Hockey also took priority over soccer. Stortfield proudly boasted a number of students who had won international honours during, or after, their time at the school. The fact that some of these sports (particularly those which involved a horse doing most of the hard work), were exclusively the province of the privileged few, mattered not a jot.

The summer term also brought exams for over half the school which took its pupils from the age of thirteen. Students locked in silent halls and gymnasia kept the campus and the corridors quiet and orderly for many hours at a time, giving the school the passive wistfulness of a monastery.

Pelforth wandered around the school anticipating the term ahead. It was the last week of the Easter term and he was already rather relieved not to be going with Marjorie to their cottage in Devon during the Easter holidays. He was determined to be around for the new proofs of his theatre scheme. If that gullible idiot Slot was about to turn the interior design into something resembling a junk yard in the name of 'art', he wanted to be on hand to throw the designs out of his study window personally.

Pelforth was also eagerly awaiting tonight's school play. It was something called *Our Country's Good* by someone called Timberlake Wertenbaker. When he enquired of Viola McIntyre "Who this Timberlake chappie was," she seemed only too smug to declare that Wertenbaker was in fact, a woman.

"Timberlake Wertenbaker? Tennessee Williams?" he had replied. "Why can't playwrights have proper names?" He almost instantly regretted it. Such casual comments get taken at face value and quoted around the staffroom.

Adrian Petherton Pugh had informed Pelforth that the play was "a savage indictment of our colonial past" and that it had "a few choice swear words in it."

"That'll have to stop when the new theatre goes up," Adrian had replied. "We'll need bums on seats then."

He knew that as long as Viola McIntyre remained in post, he would be doomed to the same old worthy, liberal, trendy and (worse still) earnest of school plays. One considerable silver lining to this pantomime cloud was the fact that the cast contained the brilliant, effervescent and absorbing talents of Melinda Farnsworth-Rogers and Belinda Bellingham-Steele. Both were, sadly, making their farewell performances on the Stortfield stage. With any luck, the only compensation for this costume drama might be both of his radiant principal girls parading their assets, each in a low cut bodice.

CHAPTER 19

# A BRIGHT NEW DAWN

Gareth Chivers was also anticipating the school play with some trepidation. If there were BAFTA awards for school plays, his Head of Drama, Irma Witherspoon, would have picked up the 'In Memoriam Award'. This was because few staff or pupils could remember what she looked like.

Irma Witherspoon had arrived at Stortvale as an assertive, hard-talking, dynamic, young teacher. Her interview for the post was exceptional. All too briefly, she breezed into the school with the air of a revolutionary, promising a "bright new dawn" for school drama.

Half way through her first term, however, Ms Witherspoon became victim to an insecure stage lantern that fell some twenty feet from the flies of the school stage, narrowly missing her head, but causing a glancing blow to her bottom and "irreversible trauma." A lengthy absence and litigation ensued. Word got back to Chivers that a bad back, sustained by slipping on a wet stage floor, had precipitated Ms Witherspoon's insurance claim against her previous school.

The irksome Irma returned to the her post in time for the new September term, but before you could say "Injuries 'R' Us" she tumbled again – this time falling pregnant, quite possibly due to a fleeting romance with the probationary history teacher Wayne Hallatrow, who promptly found himself the successful appointee to an English language school in Abu Dhabi, and was never heard of again.

For Irma, months of morning sickness were followed by the birth, and, in turn, by postnatal depression, which saw to what remained of the academic year. On her return, a brief altercation with a potentially violent pupil saw Ms Witherspoon crumble into an incurable demise, and another long lay-off ensued. She recovered her nerves well enough by the following summer holidays to act as freelance director of a summer school show in Torquay, but alas, after only one day into another school year at Stortvale, she was back on valium, and, having made a start to the term, fully within her rights to take off another three months sick leave on full pay. It was a right she was not about to waive.

It was during this time, that a little investigation on Chivers part unearthed the fact that Ms Witherspoon's career had followed a similar path in her previous school – a fact that had been conveniently forgotten in her references.

Chivers was becoming all too familiar with the rapid turnover of staff at schools like Stortvale. Graduate teachers could not be relied on to stay for more than eighteen months on average. The good ones were promoted to 'burn-out' positions in more reputable schools. The lesser talented simply left and walked into better paid jobs in industry. Some, often average teachers, defected to independent schools and wrote, in glowing terms, of their change in fortunes. Chivers loathed this, especially if the independent school in question was Stortfield Academy.

For Gareth, teachers like Maurice Hepplewhite were the salt of the earth, the bedrock of Stortvale High School. Now in his sixties, Maurice had joined the English Department over thirty years previously. He was loyal, uncomplaining, diligent, friendly, and supportive – just the man to step into the breach when a crisis loomed. Maurice had dutifully taken over directing the school play for the last three years in Ms. Witherspoon's stead. He dedicated hours and hours of preparation, thought, planning, and rehearsal into some very ambitious projects. There was just one problem: Maurice Hepplewhite was to artistic direction what Sir Kenneth Branagh was to road building. Directing air-traffic would have been far less a challenge. Put him in charge of forty pupils on a stage, and the result was the embodiment of helpless amateurism. Hepplewhite's *Midsummer Night's Dream* was so badly acted that the Mechanical's play-within-a play scene, where bad acting is being parodied, bore no distinction from the supposedly 'well-acted' bits.

Choice of scripts didn't help Maurice's cause. *West Side Story* was relocated, in the last week of rehearsal, because the director felt the accents "better matched *Neighbours* rather than New York." He was also persuaded to pull out most of the songs for fear of breach of copyright by the estate of the late Leonard Bernstein.

Given this track record, one may have thought that Maurice would have given deeper consideration to his current choice. Tonight however, it was a private joke amongst some in the staffroom that Jason Smethwick, of the Lower Sixth would be "giving his Lear." Gareth Chivers shuddered at the thought of this evening's ritual. The school play was one of the few events where the Headmaster's wife would normally be in attendance. Even the supportive, protective, sensitive Linda however, could not face sharing her husband's front row fate at this particular prospect…

CHAPTER 20

# TWO IN THE BUSH

Pelforth endured *Our Country's Good* thinking some parts rather well done, but spoiled by outrageous swearing. Fortunately this was one of Viola's 'small scale' studio shows, intended for her intellectual friends in SODS and a few of the brighter pupils. Parents were almost actively encouraged to avoid the presentation by Adrian, promising them "a good old-fashioned musical" the following year.

Heading for the backstage green room, Pelforth went to pay his respects, intending a salutary kiss on the cheek for the lovely Melinda and Belinda, who really came up to scratch in the low-cut costumes. In the corridor leading backstage, he noticed, through the glass emergency doors, shadows moving outside. Clearly someone was hiding from him.

Adrian launched himself at the emergency lever, and remembering his combat training of shock and awe, flew through the doors impressively before tripping on the door step. Fleetingly, in mid-flight, he made a mental note to have the Bursar check the doorstep first thing in the morning, before his fall was broken by some well-placed shrubbery.

Four figures looked down on him as he tried to extricate himself from the bush. He could see two young men in motorcycle leathers who appeared to be in deep embrace with two women in period costume. He instantly recognised the heaving bosom of Belinda Bellingham-Steele. Belinda though, did not recognise him. The flailing shape in the bush, coughing and spitting out buds and leaves, must surely be some stupid third-year boy, attempting to spy on Melinda and herself with their leather-clad consorts. The two couples, though startled, turned gasps into gales of laughter at the impromptu farce. As the figure clambered out of the clinging shrubbery, it staggered backwards and activated an automatic emergency light. Pelforth was illuminated in all his topiary-like glory. His carefully coiffed quiff stood up at ninety degrees from his head, allowing a halogen-halo to reflect on the thinly furnished scalp beneath. His tie knot had disappeared behind his collar, as if he were one of his own errant pupils, and a small branch protruded upwards from beneath the collar of his jacket and rose parallel with his left ear. His spectacles had slipped from the bridge of his nose and were parked precariously across his forehead at the angle of a rakish cap.

Despite their shock; despite the knowledge that they certainly were in more trouble than they'd ever imagined, the two girls, spurred on by their long-haired Lotharios, laughed harder than ever, hands over their mouths, desperately trying to stifle the uncontrollable mirth. This time, no attempt to turn on the tears would work.

Pelforth looked up and adjusted his glasses. Not only did he need reassurance that his eyes were not deceiving him, but he was quick to hide the tears that brewed in them. These were tears of pain, then of humiliation, then of envy. Above all, he could not reconcile himself to the idea that these most beautiful, elegant and sophisticated of girls could be wasting themselves on two Neanderthal-looking slobs, who, he suddenly noticed, had had the temerity to park their vulgar Harley Davidson motorbikes on the lawn behind the Performing Arts block.

"You two," he spat, pointing at the bikers, "get off this school site immediately, or I shall call the police. And if I see you on these premises again, you'll be prosecuted for trespass."

The bikers just sniggered in contempt. "Do I make myself clear?" Pelforth panted.

Before the bikers could reply, Melinda attempted to calm things down.

"It's our fault Mr Pelforth, we invited them."

"I don't care whether Her Majesty the Queen invited them!" Pelforth boiled. "They're trespassing on school property and I want them off."

"Alright, keep your hair on mate," said one of the bikers. The other just laughed again, seeing Pelforth's upended quiff.

"Don't Rory," Belinda butted in. "You'll only make it worse for us."

"Oh yeah?" said Rory. "If he gives you any grief, just let me know. We can deal with his sort."

"Get off this property immediately!" His voice was now high-pitched and hysterical.

"Go now," said Belinda calmly. "Go on." And as Rory

reluctantly turned away she whispered through gritted teeth – "Will phone you…"

"You sure you'll be OK?" intervened Ewan, Melinda's man.

"Yes. Don't upset him anymore" she replied.

The bikers collected their helmets from the verge nearby, and sidled off, looking behind them at Pelforth, like two gunslingers in defiance of the sheriff.

As soon as they disappeared into the shadows, Pelforth stared at the girls, his eyes rheumy and gleaming with menace. His voice became intense, quiet, and threatening.

"You two-get changed. My office – ten minutes – no more.

CHAPTER 21

# "A MAN MORE SINNED AGAINST THAN SINNING"

Jason Smethwick's Lear was a tour de force-for the prompter. The poor principal boy forgot half of his lines and dropped the lifeless Cordelia on her head in the final scene. Gareth Chivers was relieved that so few were witness the performance, which gave full value for money in terms of running time. Despite a 7 pm start, the play still managed to extend beyond the "last orders" call at the Pig and Whistle.

By eleven-thirty, having made a brief speech of thanks from the stage (which began with the rather tactless remark: "Phew, what an epic that was"), Gareth stumbled to the car park under the weight of his brief case. He still had thirty geography books to mark before the morning.

Just as he reached the car, Gareth heard a whisper. It seemed to be coming from behind the bush outside his office. He saw something move. Gareth put down his briefcase and tiptoed towards the bush. Just as he was upon it, two black balaclava-d figures leapt up to greet him:

"Stand back you old bastard!" whispered one in sinister, hushed, tones. Chivers had never considered himself old, and was immediately affronted by the insult.

"You what?" said Gareth affecting a dismissive chuckle, and with no thought for his own safety, leapt towards the four foot high bush, aiming his body weight at the silent and smaller of the two intruders.

The rugby fields of South Wales bred men with broad and solid shoulders. As the taller of the hooded figures fled, Gareth caught the shorter one around the neck. The figure threw a punch which caught Gareth painfully in the ear. Gareth gripped the top of the balaclava with his left hand and, as his assailant started to escape, the hood slipped off his head. As the figure turned to snatch his hood back, Gareth was able to evade his grasping clutches and take a long look at his face. As he expected, it was the face of a teenager. Gareth found himself stating the one thing you might not reveal in such circumstances:

"Wait a minute! I don't recognise you!"

At this… the dark figure, a frown of slight concern on his face, fled into the night.

CHAPTER 22

# DEAL OR NO DEAL

Melinda and Belinda stood motionless, heads bowed, before the dishevelled Pelforth. They had endured a ranting, hysterical and frightening performance. Had Stortfield Academy, rather than Stortvale High School, chosen *King Lear* as its school play, then Adrian Pelforth could have sustained the storm scene alone, without the help of sound effects and lightning. Never had these two worldly girls seen such a temperament in a grown man.

"To think I trusted you!" Pelforth's eyes bulged as he spat the words out. "I should have known, after that incident in the pub, what you were up to. I don't think I've ever been so upset, humiliated, let down, or deceived in my entire career. I realise that Easter is now upon us. I realise that you have examinations to take, but merely stripping you..." (At this point Melinda shuddered at Pelforth's emphatic use of the word "stripping")… merely stripping you of your positions of Head and Deputy Head Girl is not enough. You must apply to sit your exams elsewhere." He lowered his head as he quietly uttered his final words, like a Dickensian judge passing the death sentence: "You are expelled."

"What?" exclaimed Belinda, her eyes widening in barely contained rage. "You'd expel us on the brink of our exams? You'd ruin our future, just because we were seeing two guys from out of school?"

"Not just 'two guys'," Pelforth retorted. "Two loathsome, leather-clad, reptiles! The kind of abomination your parents have spent thousands of pounds trying to help you avoid! You know the rules in this school. The last thing we'd expect is two pupils – girls, at that – never mind the Head Girl and her Deputy, to be conducting relationships of a sexually charged nature with complete outsiders. Men, not even boys, by the look of it."

Belinda was nothing, if not bold. Had she been a little more contrite, and demure, it might have been she, not Melinda, who was Head Girl. Assertiveness had always suggested itself from her short, sharp, and spiky haircut down to her slender pointed shoes, not forgetting her pert and prominent breasts. She stepped forward with determination. Pelforth could not avert his eyes as she drew breath and pointed those nipples, like loaded hand guns, in his direction.

"Do you know what I think Mister Pelforth?" She wrinkled her nose as she spat out the 'Mister'. Melinda tried to calm her, fearing an outburst would compound their misery, "Ssshhh Belinda."

"No, I won't 'shh'. I'll tell you what I think: It's not the fact that you caught us breaking the rules Mr Pelforth. It's the fact that we've been seeing, as you say, 'outsiders'. Because in your closeted little existence, there is no room for those who choose to be different – who don't subscribe to your narrow worldview – who don't look, or sound, like you."

Pelforth looked aghast: "I don't have to take this kind of backchat from you or anyone, Belinda Bellingham-Steele."

Belinda though, was unrepentant. "If I am to be expelled, then like the condemned prisoner, you might, at least, give me the opportunity to make my case…."

"Belinda – no!" pleaded Melinda, her sense of propriety greatly compromised. She was a girl who always knew how to please and respect her betters.

Pelforth was unmoved: "That you should be presumptuous enough to attempt to judge me madam, only indicates your entire lack of integrity in this matter. I will not stand here and be lectured by one of your moral standards!"

"Moral standards? Ah well, if its low moral standards we're talking about, then we've certainly been given some bloody good role models in this school."

"What on earth can you mean?" Pelforth challenged contemptuously.

"What I mean sir, is the standard to which your own staff descends."

"I beg your pardon?"

"The things that we all know about. The things that go on. The things to which you turn a blind eye."

Melinda grew restless. Any hope she saw of a reprieve was being dashed by her bold companion.

"Belinda, I don't think you should…."

"No, no, come on. Let her speak!" Pelforth was suddenly

curious. "Come on, out with it! What great scandals am I apparently presiding over?"

Belinda looked him hard in the eye: "The Vigilantes"

"The what?"

"The Vigilantes. A group of students from this school, known to their Housemaster, who spend the midnight hours wreaking havoc in the local community – even destroying property at the high school. The pupils up there have been taking the rap for that all year. And yet nobody at this school dares breathe a word about it. And you know why?"

"I dare say you'll tell me."

"Because the Vigilantes are, to a man, all members of the first fifteen rugby squad."

"Names, Belinda, let's have names. I'm not interested in these scurrilous accusations without names."

Well, I suggest you ask Mr Jenkins for a start. He's the Housemaster."

"Well, I'll certainly do that. But I can assure you, it makes absolutely no difference to your fate, young lady."

"Doesn't it? And what if the papers found out?"

"Just how low are you prepared to stoop?"

"Not as low as your Chairman of Governors, it would seem."

Melinda could restrain herself no more: "Belinda! It's not fair, you shouldn't–!"

"Shouldn't what Melinda?" Belinda snapped back. "Shouldn't stand up for myself?"

Pelforth's manner suddenly became calmer and more curious: "And what kind of dirt do you wish to dish on Mr Petherton-Pugh?"

Belinda had noted his change of mood: "All I can say, sir,

is if you want to spy on some real action, some very hot stuff, if you want to see more than just a backstage snog with a bit of rough, then I'd advise you to check the costume barn belonging to the Storton Operatic and Dramatic Society – or SODS as I think they're better known."

Pelforth dismissed the gratuitous attempt at provocation. "I know what they're called, thank you." There was a reflective pause before he changed his tone to one of apparent concern: "So – where's your evidence for this, Belinda?"

"We caught them at it one day, Melinda and I."

"Caught who?"

"Oh come on. You know who. Everyone knows about the 'Chairman and the Broad'."

"What?"

"Petherton-Pugh and–"

"Don't tell him!" Melinda burst in.

"Fuck off Mel. Petherton Pugh and Mrs McIntyre. Happy?"

There was a pause. Adrian Pelforth slowly sat behind his desk and pressed his fingers together, raising them to his lips like a Bond villain "Tell me what you saw."

"Exactly?" questioned Belinda.

"Exactly" he affirmed.

Belinda paused and took a deep breath. "Mrs McIntyre took us to the barn to look at some costumes for the school play. Melissa and I thought the barn would be an ideal place to meet our friends."

"Boyfriends, I presume?" interrupted Pelforth.

Belinda was brazen and matter-of-fact in her reply. "Yes. We decided to meet them there a few days later. I knew where Mrs McIntyre kept the key."

"So – let's recap, shall we?" Pelforth was enjoying this.

"You steal the key, yes? Then you leave school without a signed exeat, and trespass on private property, in order meet up with two Hell's Angels, with the intention of making love?"

"They're not exactly Hell's Angels, but that's about the size of it," Belinda incautiously responded.

"Oh God Belinda, aren't we in enough trouble as it is?" interjected a now tearful and distraught Melinda.

"Can it get worse?" replied Belinda. "The point is, when we got there, we saw Mrs M's car parked up outside. There was another car, a silver Jag."

"Oh, really?" enunciated Pelforth in badly feigned surprise.

"Yes, we needed to know if she was still in there, so we went up the fire exit doors on the outside of the barn to the top floor. We looked in through a knothole in the wood. That's when we saw it."

"Saw what?" said Adrian trying not to sound terribly excited.

"Well, that depends," teased Belinda.

"Depends?"

"Depends on whether we decide to tell you, or go straight to the local paper as two very disturbed and distraught, not to say, vulnerable, schoolgirls."

"Right." Pelforth paused. He couldn't help but admire Belinda's brilliance at taking control of her own destiny. "And what exactly would persuade you to tell me – and not go to the paper?"

"Well – you can retract that ridiculous idea about expelling me–"

"And me," Mel jumped in.

"And her."

"So..." said Adrian, quietly sinister, "You're trying to

blackmail me now, are you?"

Belinda even surprised herself at her candid reply: "Look, we just need to stay here for one more term, take our exams, and fuck off."

"Belinda, you don't offend me with your foul language. I've lived in an army barracks, you know."

"Yea, right. So – deal or no deal?"

"I need hard evidence, not just your word for it."

"Evidence?" said Belinda

"Yes, the paper would need it too of course. You can't just make these accusations. Like an exam, you have to support your assertions with the right quotes. You still haven't told me precisely what was going on. I have to have the detail – sordid as it may be."

Belinda was quick to respond: "They were shagging on a pile of old costumes. Bloody filthy, moth-eaten old rags, most of them. It made me a bit sick, to be honest. And, of course, they couldn't resist using the costumes."

"Sorry?" said Pelforth naively.

"They were dressed up."

"Really? As what?"

"She was in a nurse's outfit."

Adrian was engrossed and curiously turned on by these revelations. He couldn't work out whether it was simply a case of second-hand voyeurism, or whether it was by being briefed on such intimate matters by Belinda Bellingham-Steele. "And what did Mr Petherton-Pugh choose as his preference in this little role play."

"Adolf Hitler."

"My God."

Pelforth was close to smiling. He bit into his knuckle to

stifle a snigger. There was a pause.

"You know, you'd being doing Stortfield Academy a huge favour by supporting this claim of yours. Is this costume barn protected by CCTV cameras by any chance?"

Melinda would never have risked a liaison there, if there was. "No," she interjected.

"What do you mean we'd be doing Stortfield a favour?" Belinda responded.

"I mean that, for many years, this school has had problems with both Mr Petherton-Pugh and Mrs McIntyre."

"What sort of problems, sir?" said Melinda trying to sound concerned.

"Well, I can't go into details, of course, but they've formed quite an alliance politically, as a well as… er, socially."

Melinda looked over to Pelforth, face now illuminated only by a reading lamp, making him look even more sinister in the shadow. She'd never been in the oak panelled office at night. She swallowed hard and mustered a little defiance:

"I've always liked Viola. She doesn't mind us calling her Viola."

"Quite," replied Adrian, tersely.

"She's dynamic, considerate, amusing."

"Oh yes, of course. It's a shame your admiration is not reciprocated."

Melinda was perplexed: "What do you mean?"

Pelforth was the master of the 'divide and rule' method of man-management.

"Well, if she was that fond of you, why did she decline to act as your referee?"

"For university? But she did."

"No, Melinda, I did. Her reference implied considerable

doubts as to your academic abilities. Fortunately, I stepped in and made the right amendments. You see, Viola has something of an envious streak where talented girls are concerned. She lacks fulfilment in her own life, you see. She seems hell bent sometimes, on creating disasters for others."

"I find that very difficult to take on board Mr Pelforth" said Melinda, without trying to sound as if she doubted Pelforth's word.

"I understand Melinda, that this is a side of her you've never seen. But then, there has been more than one side to her that has been revealed of late. The point is, if we have a deal, I want the evidence that she and Petherton-Pugh are up to no good. Can you arrange that?"

"What, you mean photos, recordings, that kind of thing?" cut in Belinda.

"Whatever you may suggest," said the Headmaster slyly.

"And you'll not expel us?" Melinda asked.

"I won't."

"And you'll not tell our parents?" Belinda added.

"Not unless you let me down."

"And we get to stay as Head Girl and Deputy?" responded a now, more confident Melinda.

"I will, of course, have to issue you with a formal reprimand to placate those who may have witnessed our earlier, embarrassing scene. But it will remain an internal matter entirely, not for your parents. That's if I can trust you to say no more about this ridiculous Vigilante nonsense..."

"Yes, of course" replied Belinda in a business-like manner.

"And we'll be seeing no more of the leather-clad Lotharios?"

"No, sir" said Melinda. "It really wasn't serious."

"Good. Then you may leave."

They turned to go. As they reached door, he stopped them with a parting shot: "And remember… evidence."

The two girls, relieved, and at the same time perplexed, left the room. Pelforth rapidly engaged his private lavatory.

CHAPTER 23

# BRUISED

Linda Chivers looked down despairingly as she stood over her husband. Gareth was sitting on a dining room chair, naked from the waist up, with his back to her. She gently tried to apply an ice pack to his shoulder.

"Ow! Shit, Linda! That bloody hurt!"

"Then you need to go to casualty. You might have broken something."

"I haven't broken anything. I played rugby for long enough to know a break from a bruise."

"There's a massive lump there. You'll look like the Hunchback of Notre Dame in the morning," said Linda, vainly attempting to bring humour into the proceedings. "Why did you have to take them on?"

"Hey, don't worry about me. It's the other bloke you should feel sorry for."

"And there's another swelling on your ear. You could have been killed."

"Don't be daft woman."

Linda hated it when Gareth reverted to his Welsh Wales leanings: "I'm serious. And don't call me 'woman', thank you very much."

"Well, you worry too much."

"What about that Headmaster in London? He took on some yobs and they stabbed him, didn't they? That could have been you?"

"They didn't look up to it Linda."

"What do you mean, 'They didn't look up to it'? They were wearing masks! They were dressed like Al Qaeda bloody terrorists! You must be mad!"

There was a pause. He knew she was right. Linda massaged some ointment into Gareth's shoulder.

"What did the police have to say about it?"

"Not much. They said they'd keep an eye on the school. I told them I'd give them a statement in the morning. I've got all these bloody books to mark."

"Don't be ridiculous!" Linda was now becoming more assertive. "It's nearly two o'clock in the morning! If those yobs don't get you, you'll end up killing yourself! Come on, to bed."

She said the last line with a tenderness he hadn't heard in a long time.

"Oh, alright. If you insist."

Linda helped him up, kissed his stubbly cheek, and looked hard into the eyes of the only man she had ever really loved. She could see how much he'd aged. He looked pale and tired. But deep in his eyes, there was an unchanging glint which took her back to the good-looking young man she first met at teacher training college. She just hoped Gareth might make it to retirement. Then she could properly look after him.

CHAPTER 24

# UNMASKED

"You look like a bloody bomb went off," said Marjorie, peering out from under her eye mask, as Adrian stumbled into the bedroom.

"And there's a bit of twig sticking up by your ear. You haven't been at it in the bushes with the Head Girl, now have you?" Marjorie was trying her best not to sound too amused.

"That's all I bloody well need. Sympathy!" spat Adrian, as he unfastened a button with such vigour it became detached from his trousers and flew half way across the room.

"Bugger! That's my best bloody suit buggered. Bugger!"

"Oh dear" said Marjorie. "Had a bad night have we?"

And before Adrian even had a chance to explain, she drew down her mask, plumped the pillow, and went back to sleep.

CHAPTER 25

# THE HEAD THAT WEARS THE CROWN

Philip Hart had briefly assumed the mantle of Acting Head Teacher, when it was revealed that Chivers had been urgently admitted to the local hospital. After taking assembly, Hart had installed himself behind the Head Teacher's desk, and was busy covering his colleague's early morning calls, when Chivers suddenly strode in, arm in a sling, and acted mildly surprised to see his deputy prematurely assuming a headmasterly role.

"Ha! Philip! 'Uneasy lies the head that wears the crown', eh? Shakespeare, you know."

"Yes, Headmaster, I am familiar with the quote," Philip responded disingenuously.

"Shame you weren't at the play last night. It was a

Shakespeare I'll never forget."

"I went on the first night, Headmaster," replied Philip defensively.

"Yes, yes, but I could have done with you last night. I had to take on a gang of masked intruders single handed. Got a cracked collarbone for my sins. Two hours it took me to get out of casualty this morning."

Gareth knew that Hart would find his heroics unpalatable. He also laughed inwardly at the thought of Hart being any use in a scuffle. Hart was not a man who liked physical contact. "Anyway, I got a glimpse of the bugger who did this to me."

"Did you recognise him?" Hart had been briefed on the circumstances of the night previous, and knew that Chivers was about to turn the whole thing into a soap opera.

"That's the strange thing, Philip. No, I didn't recognise him, at first. I thought I should have. I assumed it would be one of our little bastards, past or present… maybe an old boy. The thing is… there was something recognisable about him. He had the sort of face which is all too familiar to a man like myself." Gareth was beginning to adopt the mantle of a private detective.

"How do you mean?" said Hart, raising himself out of Gareth's chair.

"No, no, remain seated, Philip. It rather suits you." Gareth continued, sitting down opposite Philip, making his would-be successor even more uneasy. "The thing is, this lad looked no more than a sixth former. He was stocky, had good bone structure, nose a little flat, but healthy looking. Fit. Very straight teeth. Square jaw.

"So…?" replied Hart.

"He looked like your stereotypical public school rugby player. He was certainly strong for his height. He had a touch of Johnny Wilkinson about him. Then it came into my mind this morning, as I sat there in the A and E, I could envisage this lad taking a conversion."

"Sorry?" Hart was not familiar with rugby terminology.

"A conversion that sealed the defeat of this school in last year's Under 16 Storton Cup match. He's the Stortfield fly half, I could swear to it!"

There was a slight pause.

"Er… Gareth, Headmaster… you didn't, by any chance… er, take a slight knock to the head, last night?"

"I certainly did. The bastard clumped me right around the earhole. Look at that for a bruise." He turned his head towards Hart. "No, no. I'm sure of it. The more I think about it, the better I recall. It was his arrogance that really got to me after the match."

"Are you going to report this to the police?" enquired an unconvinced Hart.

"I don't know Philip," said Chivers. "We may need more evidence…"

CHAPTER 26

# CHILD PSYCHOLOGIST

Janine Jeffries looked across at little Timpson with a mixture of deep sorrow and strange self-satisfaction. Timpson's wizened face and large glasses reminded her all too much of herself at the same age. Janine was the bespectacled 'swot' of her particularly unforgiving girls comprehensive in south London, and so was often bullied. She became a natural child psychologist with her empathy for the underdog. Janine was though, fashionably idealistic, and little Timpson's predicament only served to confirm her conceit that boarding schools were horrible, nasty places, where children were deprived of affection and attention. The paradox of all this was, as far as Janine was concerned, that boarding schools also gave pupils nothing more than an inflated sense of their own worth.

Janine's ideals, though broadly Socialist, were greatly challenged however, when it came to the education of her own children. After all, the local state primary was in 'Special Measures', and it would have been unreasonable not to have accepted her ex-husband's offer to set up a trust-fund for the children's education. She didn't get much else from him.

Boarding school though, was not to be contemplated, and if she needed further proof, the case study presented by Timpson could not be more conclusive. The little boy with his *Harry Potter* books stacked up by his bedside cabinet, stared at his feet as he sat on the edge of his hospital bed. Swinging his legs nervously, Timpson seemed to want to talk, but held back. He knew that Mr Pelforth might not like him talking to a psychologist. Pelforth had dismissed the school's Welfare Officer a year before, maintaining in a letter to parents that this service would now be undertaken by house parents and senior staff. Even Timpson recognised that it was the house parents and senior staff who drove most pupils to the Welfare Officer in the first place.

It was nice though, for Timpson to be encouraged to call a grown adult 'Janine', and he thought it even better that she wanted not to call him Timpson like everyone else, but Jamie. Only his mother ever called him Jamie and she was in Kenya. He hadn't seen her for nearly three months. His father called him James or 'Speccy', which he didn't much like. He hadn't seen his father for over six months. The Diplomatic Service had made urgent calls on his father's time during the last school holiday, and in half terms it was too far for him to travel to East Africa, so Jamie had to lodge with a surrogate parent who he barely knew.

"You see Miss–"

"No, call me Janine. I'm not a teacher, remember."

"Well… erm, Janine, it's like this… I c-c-can't sleep very well. I keep having these n-n-nightmares."

"What about?"

"All sorts r-really." Timpson stuttered. He couldn't recall stuttering much until recently. "But worst is the b-boys who come in the night."

"I'm sorry?" Janine anticipated a different kind of problem altogether. "What boys?"

"They wear masks and black jumpers, like t-t-t-terrorists. That's who I thought they were at first. They go out past my door. They make me stay awake to let them back in."

Janine looked at him intently, almost disbelievingly: "Terrorists, you say?"

"Yes. That's what they remind me of."

"Carry on Jamie… I'd like to hear all about it…"

CHAPTER 27

# SHORT CUTS

Belinda Bellingham-Steele lived up to the last syllable of her hyphenated name. She had the mettle to see out her time at Stortfield, no matter what the consequences.

Belinda's father, Major Timothy Bellingham-Steele, had, by his single-minded and unblinking determination, instilled in his daughter a sense of self-preservation. There was no way, therefore, that Belinda was ever going to let him hear of her disgraceful conduct. Melinda Farnsworth-Rogers was of different stock. Her parents had brought her up to be ambitious but honest. Her father was an art historian who detested fakery in all its forms. Melinda was less afraid of her parents discovering her 'crime' than she was of the charade she now undertook to betray a teacher she genuinely liked, despite Ms

McIntyre's sometimes irritating petulance. She knew the Head of Drama could be a bitch, but she had a determination and talent that had helped Melinda become something of a star at Stortfield. Melinda's stomach churned loudly as she nervously lay in wait at the top of the barn, armed with only a video camera, and her mobile phone.

Belinda had much of her father's grit but it was steered more towards provoking anarchy and disorder than keeping the peace. Since being caught by Pelforth, she knew that she had gained an advantage over the Headmaster, and sensed that he would be reluctant to challenge her until she had provided the evidence he desperately craved. In the days following her altercation with Pelforth, Belinda had begun to flout the school rules, almost defying Pelforth to confront her. Her school skirt seemed to have risen by an inch or two, and her fair, feminine, pixie cut had been shorn back into a mat of bleach-blonde spikes. A couple of impressionable younger girls in Belinda's boarding house had been reprimanded for copying the Bellingham-Steele look, but the House Parents were told to "loosen the reins on Belinda" by Pelforth.

Belinda peered out from behind a trunk of costumes. Her intellect, skill in languages, military background and acting ability made her the perfect spy. She had covertly harboured the desire to enter the secret service after university, but was unsure about following her father's footsteps in the military, as she really didn't want to give him the satisfaction. As the eldest of his three girls, her father had begun to look to Belinda to achieve the kind of things he had hoped for in a son, and a tom-boyish attitude was encouraged. This was never more evident than in her choice of hairstyle. Surrounded, in her teens, by elegant, pony-tailed, and carefully coiffured school friends,

Belinda remained defiantly wedded to a confrontational crop. She knew that her cheekbones and delicate ears also turned the potentially aggressive look into something altogether more alluring.

Belinda adopted the style one summer at their home close to her father's military base on the edge of Salisbury Plain. Her mother, who had too much time to consider at length the matter of her daughter's hairstyles, had taken Belinda to an upmarket salon on Salisbury in advance of attending a family wedding. Dictating every curl and twist of the elaborate, long, backcombed, bob to the clearly agitated hairstylist, Belinda's mother made the girl feel totally humiliated and fussed over. At the age of thirteen, she was already conscious of her developing sexuality, and wasn't prepared to be treated as if entered for a children's beauty pageant. Neither was she willing to be groomed in the image of her mother.

Belinda at least had the decency to wait until after the wedding was over before taking drastic action. Trying to convert the style into something less elaborate, Belinda threw the hairbrush in frustration at her reflection in the mirror. The crack of the mirror could be heard in the kitchen, where her mother was attempting to look busy by adorning an over-elaborate designer apron.

Rushing up the stairs, she saw the anger in her daughter's eyes, and in a foolhardy moment that she instantly regretted, blurted out: "Well, if it really is that bad, why don't you just cut it all off!"

Thirty minutes later, Belinda was sitting amongst bewildered squaddies in a nearby barber shop.

Her mother cried when Belinda returned home sporting what would nearly pass for a military short back and sides.

"Oh God, mother!" said Belinda in a moment intended to provoke. "I've lost my hair, not my virginity!"

"Well – I certainly won't have to worry about you losing the latter looking like that!" replied Mrs Bellingham-Steele tearfully. "At least it will have grown a bit before you go back to school."

Belinda though, had other plans, and saw to it that she began the next term with an even closer pixie crop that would have happily seen most girls through the school year.

As Belinda's clipped head peered up from behind the costume trunk, she looked all the more stark as she had also gone to the trouble of covering her face with army camouflage paint.

Melinda Farnsworth-Rogers had considered her attire with an even greater desire not to be revealed. Politely declining Belinda's offer of some "war paint" and screaming "No!" emphatically at Belinda's insistence at "getting rid of that bloody pony-tail," Melinda had borrowed a black balaclava, whichwas in the possession of one of the sixth form boys.

The two girls lay in hiding amongst the costumes and remnants of straw on the barn's mezzanine floor. They had staked the place out now for three nights without success, but had brought with them some revision aids in order to pass the time constructively.

On the fourth night, at nine o'clock, just as they were about to leave their watch, they heard the sound of a vehicle approaching. It was the rich, throaty growl of an expensive sports car. The girls ducked for cover amongst the mothballed costume debris at the back of the barn. Shortly afterwards they heard the outer wooden steps up to the top floor creaking, accompanied by a little flirty giggling. The outer door opened and the unmistakeable voice of Viola McIntyre cut through the darkness.

"I can never find the fucking switch in here."

"Leave it off," said a male voice.

"Are you kidding?" responded Viola. "We'll fall off the fucking mezzanine. End up calling an ambulance. Then the game will be up."

The male laughed. "Oh alright then. What's it to be tonight?"

"I came prepared," said Viola. "We had this little number in the school costume collection." At which point she unbuttoned her raincoat, and slid it to the floor revealing the skimpiest of schoolgirl outfits. "It's from 'Daisy Pulls it Off'," she announced.

"I bet it is," said the male voice.

"And what have you in mind?" said Mrs, McIntyre suggestively.

"Well," said the voice. "If you're going to be the naughty schoolgirl. I guess I ought to be the headmaster.

There was a pause while Viola made herself comfortable on a pile of costumes, throwing a mock-velvet gown over the top to give some semblance of dignity. She then switched on a fan heater to "take the chill off this bloody barn." Then the swish of a cane cut through the dusty air of the old farm building.

From under another pile of dirty costumes the faint whirr of palm-sized video cameras was imperceptible as the game began.

"I thought you were supposed to be the one who wields the cane," said Viola to her companion who could now be identified in close up as Simon Petherton-Pugh.

"Don't you know?" he replied. "Behind every cane-loving

headmaster there's a mere whipping boy waiting to be exposed. Ask Pelforth, it's pretty obvious where his preferences lie."

CHAPTER 28

# SHORTER CUTS

Melinda Farnsworth-Rogers was almost physically sick as she watched the playback on her camera. Belinda Bellingham-Steele giggled nervously, replaying her favourite moment of the footage:

"Oooh thir!" lisped Viola McIntyre like an errant schoolgirl. "You weally shouldn't have shown me that gweat big lollipop! What will the other girls thay?"

At which point, her straw-hatted head leaned down towards the missionary Petherton-Pugh and took a long, steady lick of his Jumbo Woppa.

"Ugh! Just stop it, Belinda!" cried out Melinda, shielding her eyes. "I'm going to go blind! It's disgusting! I never want to have sex again as long as I live!"

"Really?" replied Melinda. "Didn't you find it in the least bit horny?"

"God no!" replied Melinda. "Particularly between two old crusties."

"Didn't you feel even the slightest impulse to jump between them and join in?"

"Belinda! What are you saying?"

"There's nothing wrong with a threesome. It's quite common actually," said Belinda, unashamedly.

"You've been in boarding school for far too long, Belinda" said Melinda maternally. "You've never recovered from that incident with Polly Jessop."

"Perhaps we should just get back to the house" retorted Belinda, unabashed. "You're obviously feeling a bit frail."

Belinda led the way out of the old farmyard and along the narrow, unlit country road that emerged at the southern edge of Storton. It had been raining heavily and they were showered by dangerously close-passing cars.

Wet, tired, and emotionally confused, Melinda and Belinda took the shortest route they knew back to Stortfield Academy. Trying to avoid the Ringwood Estate, they jumped the fence of Stortvale High School's playing field. Both girls were fit from Stortfield's dedication to sports and found the fence no problem. They skirted around the back of the rival school's gymnasium, trying to cut a diagonal through the campus that would lead them back to the relative safety of the main road.

Philip had been set back by recent events. Just when he thought that Gareth Chivers had begun to lose his grip, and perhaps be forced into early retirement, his superior had suddenly been elevated to the status of 'Have-a-Go Hero' by the *Storton Courier*. Gareth was once again the darling of the school governors.

Philip was determined to play his part in bringing the

criminals who had been terrorising the school to book. Making a number of excuses to work late in the office, Philip hoped to catch the intruders in the act. Of course, he wasn't attempting to match Gareth's daring assault, but at least he ought to be able to get close enough with a camcorder to capture admissible evidence on film. The kind of evidence that might have been available had the schools CCTV system not been in a state of permanent disrepair. It was now 11 pm. Hart had completed his marking in his study. His regular breaks to patrol the site had once again, turned up nothing. He flicked the light off as he was about to leave to room, when his eyes were drawn to a circle of light about thirty yards away, crossing the school field. In the shadows, he could vaguely make out two figures. One was wearing a black balaclava, just as Chivers had described. The other was clearly less concerned about concealing identity. Hart fumbled in his briefcase for the camcorder and moved into the corridor. He gently pushed down the bar on the emergency door that gave access to the school field. He left his briefcase propping the door open, and began following the shadowy figures. He drew within ten yards of them, tracking to the rear, before either noticed. Suddenly, the crewcut figure carrying the torch spun around and flashed it in his eyes.

"What do you want? You a stalker?"

The voice sounded higher than he expected. If this was a schoolboy, then he could have been no more than thirteen. Philip plucked up the courage to stand his ground, even though avoiding confrontation was his usual policy.

"Certainly not! And what are you doing on my school field?" he responded proprietorially.

"Taking a short cut. What does it look like?" returned a second, more nervous, girlish voice.

The figure in black was motionless, but Philip suddenly became aware of a hint of a pony-tail protruding beneath the balaclava. Also there was shapeliness within the black jumper. He raised the video camera and looked into the viewer:

"Well, we've had a lot of intruders around here, so you won't mind if I just take a little evidence, now will you?"

The crop-headed figure then approached him. "I don't think that's necessary, do you?"

Hart continued filming until the figure was upon him. He had just enough time to realise that this trespasser was also a girl before he felt an excruciating pain between his legs and his body folded, flopping forward like an untethered puppet. He spilled the camera and clutched his testicles, just to ensure they had not penetrated his intestinal tract.

"Well, thank you" said the tough-looking girl. "We'll take that." The assailant snatched the camera from the ground, planted another firm kick between the legs of the prostrate Deputy Headmaster, who lie on his back wriggling like an upturned stick-insect, and ran off at high speed.

Melinda stood, half thinking that she should help the writhing soul. He didn't look the type who would actually hurt anyone. She stared at Hart whose body was still contorting on the ground.

"Melinda!" shouted a voice in the distance. "What the fuck are you doing? Hurry up!"

The figure in black was suddenly startled, and dashed off towards the circle of torchlight some way off.

The only evidence Philip Hart could gather that night was the word 'Melinda'. But how could he lay claim to the heroics of his Headmaster? He had just been beaten up by a teenage girl. The story would need a little spin, he decided.

CHAPTER 29

# EVIDENCE

Pelforth thought the day had begun well. After assembly, he returned to his study to discover two tired, but slightly triumphant students waiting to see him. Well one, at least, looked triumphant, the other, a little ashamed. Dear Melinda, he thought. This whole messy business must be upsetting her.

"Ah, girls. Do come in" he said with forced pleasantry. "Please, no calls thank you, Doreen" he called down the corridor to one of his two private secretaries. "Shut the door behind you, would you Melinda?"

Belinda, as ever, took the lead. Contemptuously, she threw a small DV tape onto the desk:

"There, Mr Pelforth, is your evidence. I suggest you don't watch it in the company of your wife. She'll think you're into hardcore porn."

"Really?" replied Pelforth trying to ignore Belinda's contempt. "I thought you were provided with two cameras?"

"We'll keep the other film. Just in case," Belinda replied.

"In case of what?"

"Insurance. In case you choose to get rid of us anyway. I'm sure the *Sun* would love to see this stuff, almost as much as you would. I don't think that would be in the school's interests, do you? Especially if they know you were the commissioning editor."

"You're a devious little devil, aren't you Belinda? Do you support this course of action Melinda?"

Melinda was distinctly uncomfortable:

"We'll hand you the tape on the last day of term, not before," Melinda muttered self-consciously. We don't want to damage the school's reputation any more than you. I shall be glad to be rid of the whole wretched business!" Melinda blurted out the last sentence, and her voice cracked as she broke into a sob.

"Melinda, really. There, there, don't cry, my dear." Pelforth gently approached as if to lend a comforting hand.

"Don't touch me!" Melinda said, rather too loudly, or so Pelforth thought, bearing in mind the proximity of his secretaries.

"You make me sick, all of you!" Melinda wouldn't easily be calmed by Pelforth's gentle "sshhhh!"

"I've seen and heard things in these last few days that have completely sickened me. I can't believe adults are capable of such degradation. And you, Mr Pelforth, are responsible for putting me through this. Something for which I will never forgive you!"

Adrian was hurt by this. Melinda had long been his

favourite pupil. His reaction though, was typically defensive.

"Really, Melinda. I don't see how you can lecture me on my actions. You brought this upon yourself, along with your entirely unsuitable choice of boyfriend."

"Who are you to decide who is suitable for me? It just so happens that Ewan is one of the nicest, sweetest, most sensitive people, I've ever met. He simply chooses to ride a motorbike, that's all. Compared to some of the self-righteous, stuck up prigs you've groomed at this school, he's a saint!"

"And Belinda?" said Pelforth, attempting to impose a sense of discretion on the proceedings by speaking in a tense whisper. "Are you going to leap to the defence of your leather-clad Lothario?"

Belinda brazenly raised her voice in response.

"No, Mr Pelforth. I just enjoyed the sex. I've got a thing about men in leather."

"Right! That's it!" Pelforth yelled between clenched teeth. "End of interview! I trust you to keep the film until the last day of term. We'll say no more about the whole nasty business. You may leave. I wish you well in your exams. We shall not meet again until the end of term."

Belinda nonchalantly opened the door, gave Pelforth a defiant look, and left, followed by Melinda, who was trying hard to stop sobbing.

Pelforth sat back in his swivel chair and turned it to face out of the window. He looked out over his empire, and sighed. Melinda's words had cut into him as if he were a jilted lover. A sudden knock on the open door woke him from this moment of indulgence. He spun around and tried to look composed. It was Doreen.

"Em, sorry to disturb. I hope everything's alright

Headmaster. I couldn't help but overhear raised voices."

"Yes, yes, yes, Doreen. It's simply that those two girls have been behaving very badly recently, but I don't want it to spoil the end of their time here. They've both outgrown this school, I suppose. I'd be obliged if you wouldn't mention this anyone. It's the girls' reputation I'm keen to uphold you understand."

"Yes, of course, Headmaster" said Doreen, who had not survived as the Headmaster's principle secretary without also being the soul of discretion.

"I thought you might like to see the local paper, Mr Pelforth. I've taken the trouble to outlinc the article on page 5 for you."

With that, Doreen left, almost before Adrian had issued a perfunctory "Thank you."

Adrian briefly hoped that the *Courier* might be heralding another great triumph for the Academy. The headline on page 5 caused him to reach for the DV tape on his desk, which he stowed safely in his pocket, before thumping the table in frustration:

"Stortvale Lottery Success!"

If the headline had hit Pelforth like a sudden headache, the by-line almost reduced him to a cardiac arrest.

"New Indoor Theatre Gets Green Light!"

CHAPTER 30

# CHAMPAGNE

Gareth and Linda Chivers were not used to this kind of reception. In the mayhem of the school intruder scandal, and the usual attempts to spin the latest school test results into positive news; Gareth had forgotten the school's Lottery application. This responsibility had been taken on by Lady Doulting, who inevitably, handed it on to Raymond Chater and her expert team of advisers. The whole ugly, bureaucratic process had been fast-tracked by "someone who could pull a few strings" at the Lottery Commission. Gareth had merely signed the application forms.

Burnley, Brace and Bridges had come up with some exciting, modernist, plans and the required matching funding was guaranteed by the Doulting Trust, a charity set up by the late Sir Arthur Doulting. The Trust was almost emptied by this outlay, but Lady Doulting was only too happy to prevent "the likes of Nigel Slot leeching on our goodwill."

Gareth and Linda stood at the French windows of Doulting Manor and looked out on the fabulous view over the surrounding hills – a landscape that Doulting Stone had in fact, done much to destroy. Despite this, it remained alluring. As he drank champagne, Gareth took in, for the first time, the magnitude of the project and felt grateful for once, at being the recipient of the kind of privilege normally reserved for his public school counterparts. All that spoiled his view was some particularly ugly looking sculptures previously planted in the garden by Nigel Slot.

Gareth looked decidedly smug, having persuaded Linda to drive them home. He reached for another glass of champagne from the tray of a passing maid. If he could only find a decent drama teacher to direct his school plays, life would be almost perfect.

CHAPTER 31

# THE SYMPATHETIC VISITORS

Little Timpson had rarely been so happy. He found the other children on the ward generally friendly, apart from one exceptionally large girl who had threatened to eat his hardback copy of *Harry Potter and the Prisoner of Azkaban* with only partial success. The girl, like one of Harry's own foes, had been spirited away after tea time one evening, never to be seen again.

Timpson's parents had sent him flowers and insisted on a private room. It seemed odd to Jamie that they could pay so much money to send him to a boarding school where he shared a large room with twelve other boys because "it was good for him"; yet when he had the opportunity to mix with (what seemed like) more normal children in the psychiatric wing of the local hospital, his parents were determined to separate him. Still, he had ample time to read and, despite Janine's regular requests to the school to provide him with 'homework' (which he took to mean 'prep'), none had, so far, been sent.

One evening, just a little tired of reading *Harry Potter and the Philosopher's Stone* for the fourth time, Timpson switched on the small television set at his bedside and watched something called *Supermarket Sweep* which comprised apparent shoplifters filling trolleys full of unhealthy produce, whilst presided over by a man with an orange face. It was on a channel he'd never heard of before called UK Gold. He rather wished they were allowed this channel at boarding school.

His amusement at this bizarre diversion was to end abruptly. There was a forceful knock on his door, and before he could muster the breath to bid a polite "Come in," he saw two eerie but familiar shadows in the doorway. The first was the slightly hunched figure of his House Master, Mr Jenkins. The second, more upright and even more disturbing figure, was that of his Headmaster, Mr Pelforth. It was the first time he'd been in a room with the Headmaster without the company of his school fellows. He stood uneasily.

"No, no, sit down Timpson," said Jenkins in an unfamiliarly sympathetic manner.

"Yes, no need to stand on ceremony, young man," chipped in Pelforth, almost chirpily. "You're amongst friends now."

"Do you mind if we take a seat?" said Jenkins as he sat, before giving the boy a chance to answer.

"No, no. please do sir" said Timpson, rapidly pointing the remote at the television guiltily, almost as if he had been caught reading a back copy of *Razzle*.

"Oh and er, Mrs Jenkins thought you might like something

to cheer you up" He reached into his battered briefcase and handed over a box of chocolates and a book. The book, judging by the cover illustration, was some kind of adventure about a girl who wanted to be a footballer. It was not in the least the kind of novel young Timpson enjoyed. Furthermore, it was printed in large type, suggesting suitability for a ten-year-old. He opened the book jacket. If the slightly dog-eared appearance of the book had not given the game away, the inside cover page certainly did. It was labelled and stamped: "Property of Stortfield Academy Library."

Jenkins saw a slight disappointment on the boy's face and quickly explained: "Er-Mr Molesworth in the library says you can keep it until you return to school. No need to worry about the fine."

"That's very generous of him" said Timpson, restraining himself from trying to sound sarcastic.

"Anything we can do for you, young man," said Pelforth, "anything you need – just ask."

"Thank you sir" came the timid, somewhat unconvinced reply.

"You see," said Jenkins, "Mr Pelforth and I are here to help."

"Yes – er, Jamie – it is Jamie, isn't it?" Pelforth continued.

"Jamie, sir, yes."

"Well, we're very sad that you've been feeling poorly." Pelforth was clearly winding up to something of a speech, thought Jamie. "And if there's anything we can do, we owe it to your parents to help you back on the road to recovery, and out of this nasty place as soon as possible.

"Oh but sir, it's not nasty. I like it here. Everybody's so kind compared to – er, well apart from one girl, but generally, everyone is being very nice to me."

Pelforth overlooked Timpson's unintended implication and continued:

"Yes, but Jamie, it's all very well sitting here, watching television, or reading, but you need to be back in school, making the most of your talents. We need clever chaps like you at Stortfield. It's not just the rugby lads, or the cricketers we appreciate. Good academics like you, keep us up there amongst the very top schools. We have high hopes for you Jamie. High hopes. We wouldn't want you to be tempted to go to another school, oh no. We're not like some third-rate football team that has to sell its best players. No, if you're loyal to us, we can be more than loyal to you."

"But, of course-er Jamie," jumped in the slightly anxious Mr Jenkins, "loyalty comes with a price."

"Yes, indeed," Pelforth continued: Mr Jenkins is right. Loyalty works both ways. Now, if we're loyal to you, we need to know if you're being loyal to us."

"Of course, sir. I never thought about going to another school."

"Ah, but Jamie," said Pelforth trying to sound slightly distressed, "the trouble is, you may have to."

"Why, sir?" Timpson replied in a totally detached and unemotional way.

"Well, it's about some of these things you've been saying to your psychologist, Mrs Jeffries."

"What things, sir?"

"Well, she's been to see me. She says you've been saying quite controversial, not to say hurtful things about other boys in the house."

"Oh. Yes. Well, I er…"

"No, no, we understand. Mrs Jeffries is a very clever lady. She has drawn you into her confidence, and she might be exaggerating some of the things you say. She's made it quite clear she doesn't like Stortfield you see."

"So" interjected Jenkins, "It's very important you don't tell her you're unhappy at school."

Pelforth was slightly irritated by Jenkins agitated interruptions, and quickly took control once again; "Yes, the stories about boys going out of the house at night, just play into her hands. Now she's suggesting that we have a problem at Stortfield, and that some of the older boys are causing trouble in the town at nights. Well, we've spoken to some of the older boys in Churchill House, and they admit to having sneaked out, in disguise, so to speak, on the odd occasion, for a pint at the local. All pretty harmless really – though, naturally, we don't approve. We've given them a thorough telling off, and they've promised not to do it again. They've also said that, when you get back, they will throw a little party for you, to make up for asking you to be their 'night-watchman' so to speak. They're very, very sorry that you were a bit sensitive to their fun and games. So we want to draw a line under the whole episode, and say no more about it.

"Most of all," Jenkins added with ill-conceived tetchiness, "we really don't think you should be using words like 'terrorists' to describe some of our top pupils."

Timpson was surprisingly defiant. "I only said they looked like terrorists, sir. Not that they were terrorists."

Pelforth was quick to diffuse any growing tension between the boy and his defensive sounding House Master: "Yes, yes, good point, young man, but you see, 'terrorist' is and emotive word in this day and age. Even when said as I kind of joke. Mr

Jenkins can show you why."

Jenkins reached down to his briefcase, producing a copy of the *Storton Courier*. The headline dazzled Timpson. He hadn't been tipping off the papers. What were they thinking? Timpson was a fast reader, and his bespectacled eyes darted across the page, picking out the salient points:

> Following last week's savage attack on Stortvale High's Headmaster, Gareth Chivers, his Deputy, Mr Philip Hart, was also assaulted on the school playing field after apprehending two masked raiders. Mr Hart, 37, refrained from defending himself when he realised his assailants were both female:
>
> "I would have used my training in restraint, but was greatly concerned at the damage I might do" said the Deputy Head. I managed to get a good look at one of them. She was very boyish looking, with short-cropped hair. Both were covered, head to toe, in black. I noticed the other had a ponytail, and her accomplice called her by name, which I can't reveal for legal reasons."

Timpson's eye was caught by a later paragraph:

> A confidential source, working with young people in the town, revealed to the *Storton Courier* that evidence has arisen to suggest that these 'terrorists', previously thought to be pupils or former pupils of Stortvale High School, are possibly attached to a rival school.

"You see," said Pelforth, pointing down the page. "Where it says 'a rival school', they have carefully avoided saying the Academy, for fear that we might take legal action. But it doesn't take much imagination to infer who they mean."

"But sir, these are girls. I didn't say anything about girls."

No, of course not Jamie" Pelforth replied. "And I'm sure those girls didn't come from our school – but once the people start to…"

Timpson couldn't help it. He interrupted the Headmaster as he would a classmate: "But sir, look!" He had followed the instructions at the foot of the page and turned to page three. "It looks a bit like Belinda Bellingham-Steele." Timpson pointed wide-eyed at the photofit of a young lady, who (as presumably described to police by Philip Hart) bore a slight resemblance to the Deputy Head Girl, whilst also being reminiscent of both Sinead O'Connor, and Moors Murderer Myra Hindley.

Yes, yes, yes, Timpson, that'll do for now" said Pelforth, swiftly taking the paper away from the boy. "An unfortunate coincidence."

"The point is – young man" Jenkins asserted an increasingly 'bad cop' manner, "we can't have you telling tales on members of the house."

"Or the school," butted in Pelforth.

"It's just bad form. Your psychologist has no right to be interfering in the business of Stortfield Academy." Jenkins was now dropping any pretence of humouring the boy.

Pelforth measured his tones more kindly: "I'm behind Mr Jenkins fully here, Timpson. If our pupils have stepped out of line, we will punish them. What we don't want is any unpleasant business discussed by busy bodies from the local authority. The local authorities have no say in how we run our school, as I was quick to remind Mrs Jeffries, when I saw her recently. So if she tries to get you to dish the dirt, or tell tales on any of our pupils, you must say 'no.' We're clear on that, aren't we – er Jamie?"

The boy nodded. His head dropped down and he stared at the bed cover. It was worn, but bright with TV cartoons dancing over it. They had cheered him up, unlike the drab, uniform covers of his dormitory bed. He addressed the headmaster but his eyes fixed instead on *SpongeBob Square Pants*: "Yes, Mr Pelforth. I didn't mean to. She was just so nice and I..." Timpson suddenly burst into tears.

"Yes, of course she was nice" said Jenkins, a little more placatory in tone. "Just as Mrs Jenkins and I would be nice if you came to us with your problem. But we would make sure that what you said to us remained private and confidential."

"Now, now, Timpson, chin up, eh?" Pelforth wasn't good with emotional little boys and rather took a dislike to Timpson for being 'a bit of a pansy'. But, nonetheless, he placed a consoling arm around the shoulder of his wet-cheeked charge and, like a parliamentary candidate kissing the proffered baby, turned on the transparent charm.

"Let's get you well again, Jamie. What we're going to do when you get back, is move you to a lovely new house we're building by the cricket pitch, where you can make a fresh start."

"I don't want (sniff) to (sniff) move Mr (sniff) Pelforth," Timpson replied. "I want to stay here."

"Well, you can't stay here forever, you know. You'll be right as rain soon, and mark my words, itching to get back. We'll talk about this when you're better. Boys are queuing up to be moved to the new house, with its lovely twin rooms. Like a hotel."

There was a pause as the two men stood and looked down on the pathetic little boy. Both were keen to leave in time for a pint at their usual watering hole close to the school. They each made their farewells to Timpson, shaking the boy's flaccid, flimsy, hand and patting him on the back. A parting, but kindly sounding warning from Jenkins, only made the boy feel more sorry for himself. When the door closed, he picked up the ridiculous library book and hit his teddy bear across the head with it several times before sobbing into his pillow.

After a minute or two, Timpson recovered his composure, and turned the TV back on again. The man with the tangerine face was still imploring his contestants to run around the supermarket. One contestant, a vastly overweight young woman with tattoos, steered her trolley into a freezer, sending the vehicle on its side. In trying to retrieve it, the plump young lady lost her balance and fell amongst the contents of her trolley, lying on her back like an upended dung-beetle. Timpson laughed. And laughed. And he continued laughing uncontrollably until he was finally heard by the Ward Sister and, mercifully, given a powerful sedative.

CHAPTER 32

# INVESTIGATIONS

Pelforth's membership of the same Masonic lodge as the Chief Constable had ensured that the police would proceed no further with their enquiries into the 'mystery teenagers' who stalked the streets of Storton deep into the night.

A nominal visit from two local officers armed with the photofit of Belinda Bellingham-Steele brought no formal recognition from the Headmaster. Belinda and Melinda were "confined to barracks" for two weeks with "severe food poisoning" so as to avoid recognition from locals. Belinda was ordered to grow her hair "as long as possible" in the meantime. Staff and pupils were informed that the police would investigate the case no further, due to "insufficient evidence." Philip Hart, for one, was secretly relieved that this wholly inadequate response to the event wouldn't be raised in court, and encouraged Gareth Chivers to "let the matter be."

Within the Academy, the matter of 'urban guerrillas' had become something of a joke, and passed off as 'hijinks'. Everyone knew that Melinda and Belinda were the guilty duo, but public schools, like parliamentary enquiries, have mastered the art of "closing ranks."

The British press however, are not easily shaken off the scent of scandal. As a loyal reader of the *Daily Telegraph*, Adrian Pelforth was mortified to discover that, just as the controversy was beginning to subside, the 'Teenage Terrorists' had resurfaced on page eight of that august journal. This time a "school insider" was quoted as citing "a cover up," coining the term "Stortgate" into the bargain. Worse still, the photofit of Belinda Hindley-O'Connor was reproduced and subsequently led to an encampment of press photographers outside the school waiting to snap the first crop-headed girl to emerge through the iron gates.

Adrian was intrigued to know which insider had "squealed like a rat" to the *Telegraph*. There were, of course, several possible candidates. Pelforth prided himself on the fact that "success will breed enemies as well as friends." Uppermost in his mind though was Simon Petherton-Pugh. Relations between Adrian and Simon PP (as he was fondly known by the female staff), had reached an all-time low. The two were barely on speaking terms, and Adrian knew that the well-connected Simon wouldn't hesitate to make him squirm before the nation's press. Petherton-Pugh was particularly well known to the Education Editor of the *Telegraph* and this had ensured Stortfield some very good publicity in the past. Indeed, only three years ago, Adrian had taken advantage of this fact when submitting an article entitled: "How to Reform the Comprehensive System." The feature had been published, evoking a written response in the letters column from his counterpart, Gareth Chivers, containing the lines: "Mr Pelforth has only ever conducted his business in a private school. He has operated on a budget ten times that of a comprehensive, and has not endured years of Government interference. What right has he to pontificate on the State system?"

The response had further damaged relations between the two schools. When Pelforth had asked his Chair of Governors to write a repost on his behalf, Petherton-Pugh had declined, even going so far as to say "Chivers does have a point."

Pelforth wanted Petherton-Pugh and his prima donna consort out of the school, but he could not present evidence of their "vulgar and seedy affair" without it becoming apparent that he had used his Head Girl and her deputy as unwitting spies, who had subsequently committed acts of trespass and assault. He decided first that he had to remove Belinda Bellingham-Steele from the glare of the press. "The stupid girl" in his view, had defied his instruction and continued to shave her hair down to a brisk crop of half an inch all over in "acknowledgment of her captive status." No other girl in the school dared match this style, and so she would be instantly spotted by the paparazzi. He decided that 'extended study leave' might be in the girl's interest. With exams fast upon them, Belinda was unlikely to complain. Her parents had already seen the photofit in the press and had contacted Pelforth concerned that Belinda was the "mystery terrorist" in question. Pelforth had cleverly calmed their concerns by saying that Belinda "was indeed" one of the girls in question, but that the whole thing was a just a prank amongst the upper sixth form to see who could escape the furthest on foot from school, which had "got out of hand." "They couldn't resist a challenge from the boys," Pelforth had explained. "Belinda's a great competitor, as you know." Pelforth even laughed about the enterprise and shared with Major Bellingham-Steele a few similar anecdotes that both could recall from their separate careers in the military.

In order to get Belinda away from Storton, a disguise would need to be adopted. Pelforth quickly ascertained Belinda's agreement in the matter, and brought in Melinda to assist.

Melinda looked very uncomfortable, standing as far back from the Headmaster's desk as she could, and refusing to make eye contact with the man she had once respected.

Pelforth was unperturbed: "Melinda, I need your help. Our little escapade has got out of hand. I don't need to tell you the consequences for both of us, if it were discovered that you and Belinda had committed an act of trespass and assault whilst operating under my guidance."

"I think, sir, the consequences for you would be worse than for me."

"That may be so, but I'm in the twilight of my career, Melinda. You have a bright future ahead of you. It would grieve me that it was compromised. All I'm asking is one small favour."

"No more favours, no more spying, Mr Pelforth. I don't care if you do expel me."

"No, no, no Melinda. I want nothing so untoward. No, you were unrecognised by the press in this escapade. Belinda though, has done nothing to maintain a low profile. We have half of Fleet Street camped around the school, and in the town, trying to get photographs of anyone looking remotely like Belinda. I want you to play a little visit to Mrs McIntyre's costume wardrobe."

Melinda was about to refuse, but Pelforth jumped in: "We need a convincing disguise for the girl."

Melinda saw sense in this. Belinda's defiant, rebellious presence around their house was beginning to wear her down. "I can't do this alone. It's too far out of town and we'd need a car to carry the stuff back. Besides, it means stealing the keys again. Why don't you just ask Mrs McIntyre? It can't do any harm..."

CHAPTER 33

# REVELATION

Pelforth at first objected to bringing Viola McIntyre into the business, but realised Mrs McIntyre's cooperation might be better for the time being. For her part, Viola thought the matter to be "something of a hoot," being only too happy to protect two of her star performers.

It was arranged that Melinda would go with Mrs McIntyre to the SODS costume barn that evening. Viola had intended paying a little visit anyway, and had texted Simon to postpone their liaison in the barn until a later hour. When no reply came, she just assumed he was in a meeting.

Melinda and Viola chatted like old friends in the car on the way to the barn. Viola was keen to know "why on earth" Melinda and Belinda had gone out on their little nocturnal adventure. Melinda passed it off as a "dare" and rapidly changed the subject.

The nights were getting lighter. As they approached the farm, the sun was setting over Doulting Quarry on the lip of which, the barn seemed to perch precariously.

Viola and Melinda climbed the outer stairs to the mezzanine floor of the barn. As usual, Viola fumbled to find the keys to the assortment of locks on the door. She placed her handbag at her feet as she sifted through the bunch of keys that contained her school, house and car keys in a random order that caused daily irritation and impatience. Finally, she opened the door, asked Melinda "bring my handbag" and switched on the light. Suddenly, she jumped backwards, as under the glare of the dull, single bulb hanging from the roof, stood a familiar figure. It was Simon, unrecognisable from the neck down, being, as he was, clad in a large Macintosh.

"I thought it a bit damp in here, so I put this on. What do you think?"

Viola had barely time to blurt out "Simon, no!" when the over-eager Petherton-Pugh ripped open the popper buttons on the mac. Simultaneously, Melinda, bending to collect Viola's handbag raised herself to full height to be confronted by the lower half of a body, naked, except for tights and suspenders. She screamed and ran back down the stairs, Viola instinctively in pursuit.

"Wait Melinda, we can explain! Just get back in the car." With remarkable speed Viola found her car key and remotely triggered the lock.

Melinda had little choice but to obey. She climbed into the car, taking sharp breaths and trying to collect herself. Viola slumped in beside her.

"It's not what it looks," Viola panted desperately.

"Oh don't try to fob me off with excuses Mrs McIntyre. I

know what's going on."

"Well, it is what it looks, I suppose. The point is, can you be trusted?" enquired Viola urgently.

"Look, I already know" came the response. "There's something I have to tell you..."

Melinda felt an enormous weight lift from her shoulders as she explained how she had become tied up in Pelforth's game of espionage. Viola sat staring at the steering wheel, looking, at any moment, as if she was going to sink her teeth into it.

Eventually, Petherton-Pugh appeared, fully dressed, but with the outward disposition of a sheep, fully shorn. He stood at the top of the steps and leaned over the handrail looking into the deep quarry. Momentarily he almost felt like jumping into the massive pit, but instead descended the stairway and moved to Viola's car.

Viola was not in the mood for Simon's attempts to smooth things over with Melinda, and knew the girl would be better off out of the way.

"Look, Melinda, would you mind trying to sort out this wretched disguise while Simon and I have a chat?"

Melinda stepped out of the car and passed Simon, without so much as an upward glance. He slid, shamefully into the seat she'd vacated and stared at his feet, as Viola explained Pelforth's intention to blackmail them.

"The bastard!" he blurted out, almost in tears. "The duplicitous, cunning, bastard!"

"Yes, but what do we do?"

"I don't know. I need time to think" replied Simon. There followed a pensive pause. "You're saying that there are two copies of this video?"

"Yes, Pelforth has one. The other is with Belinda. She

insisted on keeping a copy. I suppose she realised that it was evidence that Pelforth had corrupted her into filming an indecent act."

"So, Pelforth will obviously use the footage to get you and me to resign, on the assumption that we won't know who filmed it?"

"Yes. I imagine he'll wait until the girls have left, to keep them out of it."

"So, we have to prove that in getting the footage, he ordered pupils to witness an act of … er indecency…he would not only have to resign, but would face criminal prosecution."

"I'd love to see that bastard behind bars" growled Viola through gritted teeth.

"Tempting, isn't it?" replied Simon, brightening a little.

There was a pause. Both stared out through the car windscreen as if looking for inspiration.

Viola broke the silence: You know, if we got Melinda on our side, I think she'd shop Pelforth like a shot, if she could. He threatened to expel them both if they didn't conform. He'd got some dirt on them regarding secret liaisons they'd been having with a couple of local bikers."

"No, really? Melinda as well? Gosh!" Petherton-Pugh was momentarily distracted by the thought of the elegant Head Girl writhing about under her leathered-up 'bit of rough'.

"What we need is hard evidence," said Viola, in Miss Marple tones. Simon's reverie about Melinda was also providing hard evidence, which he hid by means of a strategically placed hand.

Viola was too distracted by her own thoughts to notice: "We need hard evidence that Pelforth commissioned that video. We may have to pay off Belinda."

CHAPTER 34

# AN INAPPROPRIATE SLOT

Pelforth and Wildblood were unanimous. Nigel Slot had to go. His defection from Stortvale had completely failed in its purpose. He had brought with him no artistic integrity and had not attracted public funding. In fact, Stortvale High School's fortunes seemed to have greatly improved without him. Stortfield would need to fall back on their own resources, and those of their influential friends in industry, if they were going to better their rival's theatre project.

Wildblood had been seconded to the Governors of the school at a recent meeting and Pelforth was only too happy to encourage the snarling, bullish industrialist in his designs on becoming Chairman of the Governors at the earliest opportunity.

Expecting a more positive outcome, Nigel Slot had compromised his usual dress code for the meeting, finding a grey lapelled jacket for the occasion, complemented, not by his usual paint-stained jeans, but a pair of crumpled chinos. Even so, the very sight of his collarless shirt and dangling earring as he entered sent a mild shudder through Wildblood's thick frame. Pelforth though, was slightly amused by Slot. Slot constantly reminded him of a younger Keith Richards of the Rolling Stones. Pelforth had once spent an agreeable night watching Mick Jagger and company from his friend's hospitality box at Twickenham Stadium. Naturally, he was rather affronted that the Stones had appropriated the hallowed turf of England's temple of Rugby Union, but it provided him with a rare opportunity to sound "young and hip," when recounting the experience in an assembly for school pupils, most of whom were not even old enough to be married to a Rolling Stone.

Pelforth took a back seat, mentally humming 'Honky Tonk Women', as Wildblood relentlessly showed no 'Sympathy for the Devil' when laying into Nigel Slot:

"Mr Slot, I have to say, on behalf of the School Governors, that it has been decided not to incorporate your designs into the school theatre development.

"You what?" Slot looked up in amazement. "Like…why?"

Wildblood was almost gleeful at being given the chance to gore the wounded beast.

"Because, frankly Mr Slot, despite being given appropriate references for your creative work, we considered your designs at length, and we are astonished that you have ever been employed as an artist. Some of your suggestions are, to my way of thinking, quite ludicrous."

Trying to be clever, Slot pressed for a more artistic analysis of his work. Wildblood took the opportunity with relish, spitting derogatory words that tumbled with spittle from his thick, rubbery, tongue:

"Banal," "anal," "facile," "fumbling," "flatulent," "reckless," "obscene," "shambolic" and "juvenile" were just some of the adjectives he applied in response.

Nigel Slot may have dressed for the occasion but, on hearing this barrage, he wasn't going to disguise his emotions:

"Why the fucking hell I thought you were genuine, I really don't know. Fancy being taken in by a ruthless pair of old pricks like you. You'll be receiving a bill for my designs and if you don't pay it, I'll be seeing my solicitor."

"Well, Mr Slot it will, no doubt, be a novelty to see you in court as the plaintiff" warbled Wildblood, sounding rather pleased with this comeback.

"Fuck off fat face," came the less than urbane answer. "I want my cheque by the end of the week, otherwise the papers will be on to you." Slot stood and noticed Pelforth was badly hiding a supressed grin at this exchange of verbal unpleasantries. "And as for you Pelforth – I always knew you were a jumped up, tasteless moron from the start. Fuck off the pair of you." And with that he ambled out in a louche manner, slamming the door behind him so hard the pictures nearly fell of the adjoining wall.

Striding along the school corridors, Slot decided to take his farewell of Viola McIntyre, who he had known before his brief association with Stortfield. Still simmering, he paced across the quad to the old converted cloakroom, which for years had served Viola as a drama studio. The studio door was slightly ajar and hearing Viola's voice, he peered in to see what looked like a costume fitting taking place.

"Hello, like er – what's this then? Slot said slyly. His sinister tone clearly touched a nerve as Viola, Melinda and Belinda turned and gasped. Belinda was wearing the dress and coat of a mature woman, whilst holding, by her side a long, red, wig.

"Oh costume fitting, Nigel," replied Viola. "That's all. What are you doing here?"

"Well, I thought I'd have a word. You got a minute?"

One minute turned into fifteen, as Slot spilled out his betrayal by Pelforth and Wildblood. For her part, Viola took him into her confidence and explained that she and Melinda were actually helping Belinda escape from school without being recognised by the paparazzi. She didn't, of course, explain that she and Petherton-Pugh effectively had to buy Belinda's loyalty due to their own personal indiscretions.

For a significant honorarium payment from Simon, Belinda had, the day before, made Pelforth a visit on the pretext of returning the video tape prior to departing on enforced study leave. In fact, she was returning the film files in order to engage Pelforth in conversation that was intended to incriminate him. Having got the taste for espionage, Belinda was easily convinced to wear a 'wire' in order to record the whole conversation. The wire was a remote tie-clip microphone, normally used to amplify teenage tenors in the annual school musical. Simon and Viola heard the entire exchange on headphones from their base in the Green Room, behind the school stage. This was easily within signal range of Pelforth's office. To ensure the perfect job, Belinda was also carrying a small digital recorder in her school bag.

Both recordings had worked. Pelforth, in his usual verbose way, had overstated his case to Belinda in a vain attempt to win back some of her respect. Belinda played along brilliantly, coaxing self-incriminating comments from him that had Viola and Simon "high fiving" in delight in the Green Room, as their heads were romantically pressed together, sharing a single set of headphones. Pelforth anxiously enquired of Belinda when he might receive the other DV tape. Belinda duly obliged by giving him the copy saying: "It wouldn't be safe with me at home, so I'm handing it in now." Pelforth, a digital ignoramus, had no idea how these things worked, took her word for it. The DV tape she handed Pelforth certainly contained lurid sexual activity, but the characters bore a remarkable resemblance to Jack Nicholson and Jessica Lange in *The Postman Always Rings Twice*.

The original, genuine copy of *A Romp in the Hay* as Belinda had titled it, was handed over to Simon, as requested, although not before Belinda had downloaded the footage on her computer.

Nigel, on hearing of Belinda's need for a disguise, offered to escort the Deputy Head Girl out of school as his 'partner'. Indeed the disguise certainly gave Belinda a look of far greater maturity. She donned the wig and a pair of large sunglasses. Nigel persuaded them that the sunglasses were too obvious, particularly given the dullness of the weather.

Belinda had with her a small case of essential clothes and study items. She was intending to take the train, not wishing to enact the charade in the company of her distraught parents who would normally have driven to Storton to collect her.

Belinda had met Slot on several occasions, when he visited the school. He had been at the play on the fateful night when all this had started. He had complimented her effusively on her performance, she recalled. She took Slot's arm and the two casually ambled through the school gates and past the unsuspecting newspaper reporters who were hanging around, smoking, whilst awaiting the exodus that followed the lunchtime bell.

"Where's your car Nige?" asked Belinda when the two had moved out of earshot of the reporters.

"What car? I'm like a bike man meself."

"You got a Harley? Where's it parked?"

"It's a push bike, you daft bint, and it's parked at home. Do I look like a bleedin' Hell's Angel?"

"No, you look more like an old punk rocker."

"Old? I'm only thirty-three."

"No, by old, I mean you remind me of someone like Joe Strummer."

"I'll take that as a compliment," replied Slot, raising the slightest of smiles I used to love all that stuff – The Clash; The Stranglers; Sex Pistols. I bit before my own time, but I can like, you know, relate to it."

"Yeah. I'd love to dress the way they used to," revealed Belinda. "I hate all this conformity. What I'd really like is a Mohican."

"Bit old fashioned – but it'd work on you."

"So, you walking me to the station then?"

"Can if you want."

"No, I don't want" Belinda confirmed categorically. "What I mean is, I don't want to go home. I don't want to have to explain all this shit to my parents."

"I really don't know what you've done," said Nigel, trying to sound slightly disinterested.

"I'll tell you another time."

"What time train you on?"

"Didn't book the train. I'd hoped stay in Storton. I tried to stay at a friend's house. She's a Day Girl. Her parents thought I'd be a bad influence. You can't stop rumours getting out in a school like this. I have to change trains in London, so I was thinking of looking up a friend and staying there.

"What about your mum and dad?"

"They don't even know I'm supposed to be coming back today. It was all pretty last minute."

They stopped to cross the road. Nigel reached out to press the button on the pelican crossing. Belinda looked at him. He wasn't a bad looking bloke, she thought. She found his lazy, uncouth manner quite attractive. He had that laid-back attitude affected by rock stars. Pete Doherty came to mind. It was an appealing manner for a girl of orthodox upbringing.

"You er – you can – like – er stay at my place if you like," said Slot, scratching his neck in as casual and unconcerned way as he could. Belinda took his arm again as he crossed the road.

"I don't know about that."

"It's a right dump, I warn you. Full of my paintings and stuff."

"Where is it?"

"Over by the allotments, round the back of the football club. Not far. It's a two up – two down."

"Would there be room for me?" Belinda asked in a matter-of-fact manner.

"Yea – I've got a spare bed. The cat usually sleeps there, so you'll have to fight him for it. There's two bathrooms though. You could have your own."

"I don't have any money for rent. I mean my parents would refuse to pay."

"I'm not bothered about that. Just help with the food."

"I don't know, Nigel. Can I trust you?"

"No."

"I can stick up for myself."

"Good. 'Cause I'm likely to get drunk and ravage you."

"You're joking, right?"

"Look Belinda, you're a lovely girl, but you're too young and, to be honest, you're not my type." Nigel Slot was nothing if not good at lying. "You can stay in my house until your exams are over, then you can fuck off somewhere else. Take it or leave it."

"Well, maybe I could come back and take a look."

"Sure."

Belinda, still in role, continued holding his arm. In an unusual and unlikely moment of chivalry for Nigel Slot, he took her case and carried it for her. They walked for ten minutes to his rented Victorian terrace in an old fashioned, but quiet, part of town. Slot led Belinda down the alleyway between his, and the adjoining house. She noted there was no real back garden, just a hard standing with an outhouse and Nigel's push bike leaning up against the hedge.

They entered the kitchen which was overcrowded with dirty cups and plates. The black cat, Beelzebub, slid along past her legs. For Belinda, being brought up by a mother who believed in cleaning up before, and after, her house cleaner, this was all so attractively Bohemian. Slot put down her bags.

Belinda took off her coat, revealing the tightly hugging stretchy black dress beneath. It was clearly a Marks and Spencer item which, despite the intention of modesty, outlined that shapely figure to considerable effect.

"Here, give us your coat," said Nigel, hanging it on the kitchen peg. "That dress suits you, but I hope you've got something to change into."

"Yeah. Don't worry. What shall I do with this?" Belinda reached up to her hairline and removed the long auburn wig.

Even though he'd seen her before, Nigel Slot was quite shocked by the stark difference between the woman he'd walked home with and the blonde, cropped, tough but angelic looking girl with strong, blue, eyes and angular cheek bones, standing before him. He took the hairpiece. "Don't let the cat see that, he might try to give it one."

"Lucky cat," purred Belinda, looking up at him. Suddenly, taking on Beelzebub's feline, feral instinct, she attacked. Beelzebub looked on as Belinda Bellingham-Steele bit and chewed at Nigel Slot's neck and shoulders, until he forced her to stop with a kiss. Within minutes they had committed intense, powerful sex on the kitchen table. "*The Postman Always Rings Twice*," thought Belinda.

CHAPTER 35

# CAUGHT IN THE CREASE

It was the last day of the summer term. The exams had been taken; the press reporters had gradually given up on their 'Stortgate' story, and Adrian Pelforth looked forward to a brief holiday in Scotland, before returning, with new enthusiasm for the start of the next academic year.

"It's always bloody Scotland," muttered Marjorie, as she searched through her wardrobe for a suitable Parents' Day outfit. "Who do you think you are? The Duke of Edinburgh?"

"Well, I hardly match that description," countered Adrian, as he fixed his regimental tie. "After all, he married above his rank."

"Touché" returned Marjorie drolly, quite amused by Adrian's unusually witty riposte. The only reason Marjorie had ever countenanced Scotland at all was because it would enable a flying visit to see her son Jeremy. The meeting was always on neutral territory however, as Adrian refused to enter the Aberdeen florist shop, under any circumstances. "Seriously though Adrian, I want to go somewhere warm for a change."

"We'll have plenty of time for the Caribbean when I'm retired."

"You'll never bloody retire. They'll be carrying you out of this place in a box."

"We'll see," replied Adrian, thinking it actually might be quite a noble way to go.

Parents' Day was when the school was 'on parade'. Pupils, their parents, teachers and guests meant that upwards of 2000 people were on campus.

Undeterred by the failure to thwart Stortvale High School's theatre project, Adrian had chosen Parents' Day to unveil plans for the new Stortfield Academy Theatre during his assemblies. These assemblies proved tiresome performances owing to the fact the school had long outgrown the 300-seat capacity Old Hall, which meant Adrian was forced into addressing pupils and parents in repeated performances, so as to give everyone a chance to hear (as Marjorie would put it) his "pearls of wisdom." Even then, many parents were forced to listen in the corridor outside the hall. With his new theatre of 600 raked and padded seats, Adrian could reduce this gruelling ordeal and so, to prove the point, he had implored pupils to bring their parents along to "this important address."

But first, there was work to do. Whilst Marjorie was playing consort in the Pimm's marquee with the early arrivals, and staff were preoccupied setting up the School versus Old Boys cricket match and other side shows, Adrian had decided that it was time for a showdown with Petherton-Pugh. He had invited Jack Wildblood in for support, but was determined to take the lead, demonstrating to the industrialist that he too could wield the sword.

Petherton-Pugh was used to Adrian's early morning meetings, but was not expecting such a call on Parents' Day. He knew something was up. As he parked his Jaguar in his especially designated space, he wondered if it might be the last time he was able so to do.

Simon walked slowly past the cricket green as the groundskeepers were making their final preparations. It was a glorious day in the height of summer. A day that took him back to his youth, and his time as Head Boy of a school he never wanted to leave. He saw himself as one of the last remaining links between the old Stortfield Boys Academy and the modern coeducational, international school now stretched out before him. The new boarding house close to the cricket pitch symbolised, for Simon, the growing reservations he harboured about Adrian Pelforth as the school's Headmaster, He had reluctantly agreed to the proposals for the new boarding house despite deploring the design. To Petherton-Pugh, it was too modern and far too much like a Travelodge motel. Yes, the facilities within were second to none, but he didn't believe boarding schools should offer twin rooms with en suite bathrooms. It was only by sharing dingy dormitories did some of the overindulged and pampered Stortfieldians learn a sense of community and cohabitation. It certainly did him no harm. Besides, he found the building tasteless and vulgar, an attitude which immediately conflicted with the nouveau riche inclinations of Pelforth, who was always envious of SPP's sense of breeding.

Even more objectionable to Simon was the house's position overlooking the cricket field. It had obscured the most tranquil view of the gentle fields that sloped beyond the school perimeter, across the countryside to a nearby village, discernible only by the church spire edging its way out of the valley and into view.

He had decided to go along, at the governor's meeting, with the general consensus supporting the building of the new house, but could not hide his objections when the location was proposed by the unctuous Bursar, Edwin Slater.

Having lost that particular argument, he soon put a stop to the momentum that was gathering for the name of the new house. It was clear to Simon that the original suggestion had come from the Headmaster's office. He could think of no one else who might conceive the name "Pelforth House" other than Adrian himself, through the mouthpiece of Slater. On that occasion, Petherton-Pugh put down an unbeatable alternative, and did so without consulting Adrian. He suggested to his fellow Governors naming the house after the late, much loved, Head of Games, Richard Burke; who after thirty-five years of loyal service, had died suddenly following a 'late night' at a rugby club reunion. Dicky Burke was certainly much admired, having an unorthodox, roguish and relaxed manner, which would not be easily tolerated in the modern, accountability obsessed, society. Pelforth hated him.

Burke openly ridiculed Adrian, often in staff meetings, drawing daring sniggers from impressionable young teachers. Of course, like the best of satirists, Burke found more fun in his own foibles, and so this former prop forward with his cauliflower ears and flat nose that seemed to zig zag down his endearingly flattened face became politically 'untouchable'.

Pelforth's address at Dickie "Bison" Burke's funeral was full of platitudes like "loyal"; "dedicated"; and "much loved." It was very similar to the oration he had given at the former caretaker's funeral the year before; a point not lost on Dickie's widow, Wendy, who publicly thanked the Headmaster for his "carefully considered speech."

When considering the case for naming the new house after the 'Bison', Pelforth had pointed out that that the title 'Burke's House' might give "rise to ridicule." Petherton-Pugh was quick to point out that Dickie Burke would have certainly approved of that; and that 'Burke's Peerage' didn't seem to undermine that particular institution.

Pelforth was angered by that riposte, but certainly wasn't going to let Petherton-Pugh stand in the way of giving the theatre a more 'appropriate' name.

Simon waited to be called into the Head's Study, much as he had waited as a schoolboy, to be admonished for hoisting 'Bertie' Blenkinsop's large, white, underpants from the top of the first team rugby posts. There followed a confrontation with the liberal, kindly, but firm Charles Myrtlewood, the old school headmaster who was given to wearing carpet slippers in his study and smoking a volatile briar.

Dr Myrtlewood had extracted a tentative confession from young Simon, staring at him over pince-nez, narrowing his eyes sternly, and with a tightening of the lips that made Simon certain that, at the very least, he would serve a dignified suspension. As Simon completed his account of his 'flag-raising' affair, Dr Myrtlewood's lips stretched slowly into a wry grin. A giggle escaped, and unable to resist, the Headmaster began chuckling guiltily.

"Simon, you really ought not to be doing this kind of thing.

Blenkinsop will be mortified. The poor chap can't entirely help his size. To suggest that his underpants might make a suitable ensign was a cruel, if amusing, prank. The thing is, Simon, you are on course to be Head Boy of this school. A Head Boy is allowed one major indiscretion. That is considered a sign of character. You have had your indiscretion. Don't have another."

What a contrast was Myrtlewood with his current successor thought Simon, as Pelforth ushered him in to the Headmaster's study.

"I'm afraid Simon, that we have some very uncomfortable matters to discuss. Do take a seat," said Pelforth, taking the upper hand. Simon sat, studying determinedly the faces of his counterparts, for signs of betrayal.

Pelforth began: "Er – Parents' Day is usually the customary time for the Chair of Governors to declare his plans for the forthcoming year. You appear to be intent on remaining in the seat, I take it?"

There was a pause. Pelforth shuffled uneasily.

"I have not, as yet, considered the alternative," Simon replied smoothly.

"No. I had assumed not. Jack and I have been considering your position however, in the light of some information that has been relayed to us."

"Information, Adrian? What kind of information?" Petherton-Pugh was determined that Adrian should give him chapter and verse, partly to watch him squirm, partly for the benefit of the small voice recorder lodged in his suit pocket.

"An incident has come to our attention," continued Adrian.

"Oh yes?" Simon acted mildly quizzical.

"An incident involving yourself and Mrs McIntyre."

"How do you mean 'an incident'?"

"I mean, that it was reported to us that you and er… Mrs McIntyre have been er…" Pelforth stuttered whilst trying to find the right words. This was turning out to be more delicate than he imagined. He continued with a sigh: "That you and Mrs McIntyre have been er… exercising er – relations in a public place."

"Exercising relations?" Simon responded sarcastically. "Taking an elderly aunt for a walk in the park. That sort of thing?"

"I think you know what I mean" re-countered Pelforth, who was used to more cooperative suspects. He then decided to throw caution to the wind: "I mean that you and Mrs McIntyre have been conducting an affair, and that you have been caught out."

"Caught out? Where, and by whom?" said Simon remaining calm.

"Caught in the act by a member of the Storton Operatic and Dramatic Society, who saw you in flagrante in the costume store."

"Really?" Simon smirked, "And how do you know that this person is a trustworthy source? Viola, as a leading light, has acquired one or two unjustified enemies in the SODS."

"That I can believe" ventured Adrian.

Wildblood shuffled on his seat in the corner like a walrus with haemorrhoids. He knew Petherton-Pugh was being bloody minded, but was anxious, as the Chairman-elect, to say nothing that might inflame the situation. He simply snorted through his nose from time to time, like a horse trying to evacuate a troublesome fly from his nostrils.

"Are you refusing to accept the accusations levelled at you?" pursued Pelforth, rather seeing himself as the prosecuting counsel.

"I'm not prepared to accept accusations made without foundation of evidence."

"We have the evidence" butted in Wildblood.

"Oh yes, caught on CCTV was it?"

"As a matter of fact, yes" Adrian smugly replied. "Well not CCTV as such... but the person concerned did have a suitable mobile phone recording and was able to present some incriminating evidence."

"Yes" growled Jack Wildblood. "Very incriminating. Involving the use of costumes in an inappropriate manner."

"So this person to whom you refer – how did she come to see this alleged act, without our knowing?"

"Through a window, I believe," Adrian replied dismissively.

"I do know the building in question and there is no window. Only a skylight. She wasn't on the roof at the time, I take it?"

Pelforth was barely containing his impatience. "You'll have to ask her how she managed to take the film, not me. All I can say is they verify it was you and Mrs McIntyre."

"Then, I'll have to see the evidence."

"I don't have it in the room with me. It is with the lady in question."

"Are you sure Adrian? Aren't you spinning this story somewhat?" Petherton-Pugh's calm was unnerving to Pelforth.

"How do you mean?"

"I mean," said Simon, at his most sanctimonious, "there was no anonymous lady as such. There were, in fact, two very young ladies armed with video camcorders and hiding in the barn under instruction from you."

"What!?" interjected Wildblood with false ferocity. "How can you attempt to turn the table on the Headmaster in this fashion? This is slander!"

"Oh do shut up Jack" Petherton-Pugh calmly responded. "We know what's in it for you. Chairman of the Governors; a large donation to the school theatre fund, and finally, that knighthood you so cravenly covet. If you're in on this it won't be the Palace, it'll be the Scrubs for you."

Pelforth was becoming very agitated: "Since we are discussing evidence, where's yours?"

"We have a copy of the digital recording. Belinda Bellingham-Steele gave it to us."

"You don't believe that little hussy, do you?" Pelforth leapt in. "She was acting on her own accord – trying to find something that could be used to keep her from being expelled."

"Actually, it wasn't even Belinda who told us. It was Melinda Farnsworth-Rogers who spilled the rather unpleasant beans. Belinda came on our side after that."

"You've thought this through, haven't you? You scheming dandy. You've thought through exactly how to attempt to make this look like my doing, in order to deflect the blame from yourself. A court of law would hardly believe the testimony of the guilty party, and two schoolgirls with a grudge, especially when they consider the consequences for such an eminent school as Stortfield."

Simon was inwardly gleeful at seeing Pelforth so rattled. "You're right Adrian, which is why we made sure we had the proof. When Belinda Bellingham-Steele came to hand in her copy of the video to you before she left, she was wearing what I believe those of you of a military background might regard as a 'wire'. In your vain attempt to win back her respect, you said more than enough to incriminate yourself to an honest jury."

There was silence. Pelforth sat back in his chair and turned to the window. He could not look at Petherton-Pugh. There was a long silence. He pursed his lips long and hard, thinking the matter through. Still facing the window, Pelforth, at last, found the right words.

"So you're implying, I take it, that if we forget about this incriminating footage of you and Viola McIntyre; and Mr Wildblood and I continue to acknowledge your position as Chairman of the Board of Governors, we will hear no more of Melinda and Belinda's information gathering?"

"I think that's about the size of it."

"Then I see no further need to continue this conversation. The matter must be forgotten."

"In which case, I'll take my leave" said Simon, standing. He felt the hawkish eyes of Wildblood and Pelforth upon him as he crossed the room, and so could not resist a further parting shot, as he opened the door.

"And – er, do enjoy the rest of Parents' Day, both of you. Ciao!"

Almost as soon as he foppishly made his exit, Pelforth was planning his next move on Simon.

"Cunning bugger," said Wildblood – almost in admiration.

"Yes, but no one can prove that I suspected them of having sex in that barn. I might have thought they were up to something else."

"Oh don't be naïve Adrian. You've been caught hook, line and sinker. You were still involving those girls in what might be regarded as blackmail. I'm quite used to industrial espionage, but this is not the sort of thing a public school should get involved in."

"Well, it's good to hear you taking the moral high ground

Jack" Pelforth cynically replied. "Petherton-Pugh's not as unruffled as he makes out. If this gets out his reputation would be ruined. He'll never be offered a winnable seat. We'll get him somehow."

"Will we Adrian? Wildblood warbled disdainfully. "Will we?"

CHAPTER 36

# TOTAL EXPOSURE

In the short time between Belinda Bellingham-Steele unofficially leaving Stortfield, and the end of term Parents' Day, the Deputy Head Girl had changed remarkably.

By day, she chose to continue her auburn disguise when about town, realising that it might be better to go unrecognised by former school friends. By night, however, knowing that neither teachers nor pupils of Stortfield Academy would deign nor dare frequent Storton's more Bohemian quarters, Belinda, having shaved the blonde crop to leave nothing but a pink-dyed carpet strip of a Mohican, felt free to hang out with Nigel in the dope dens and music clubs. Now heavily punctured by nasal studs and earrings, Belinda was bondaged in a black belt-like mini skirt, topped off with a loose fitting black vest, looking every bit a refugee from a travellers' convoy. The vest allowed her to display a tattoo so new and shiny, the ink barely looked dry. The tattoo was a spear rupturing a dove's heart-the motif beneath reading 'Vengeance' in Gothic script.

Even Nigel Slot felt a little uneasy amongst friends, with his newly acquired "punk princess" – as his friends referred to her. Her upmarket manner and ability to dominate him in company, showed Nigel in a different light to his militant friends. He couldn't resist her though. She was like a perfect sculpture.

Having been forced to take her exams wearing a headscarf to avoid (in Pelforth's words) "upsetting the other pupils," Belinda decided to adorn the auburn wig one last time for the end of term. She had told her own parents that she was flying off early to complete a summer acting course in New York, in an attempt to put them off attending Parents' Day. The acting course and flight to New York was paid for by Belinda's father who was all too ready to discourage her from coming home for too long. The course did not exist, and with the help of Nigel Slot's talent for forgery and deception, the tuition fees and air fares were paid into a holding bank account, accessible only to Nigel and Belinda. When she finally returned to her parents, Belinda planned to blame her radical hairstyle on the sacrifices made to honour the Stanislavski Method. Her parents surely would not object to their daughter having been cast as Joan of Arc.

Belinda breathed a heavy sigh of relief when her father and mother, undeterred (perhaps even encouraged) by her absence, walked past her in the main quad on Parents' Day without so much as a second glance. She hurried to the Old Hall where she would rendezvous with Nigel. She had also persuaded Nigel to wear a suitable disguise, and laughed aloud to see him hanging around outside the hall, looking uncomfortable in a white shirt and tie, all top quality, and purchased for a tenner from the Oxfam shop. Nigel had parted and slicked down his usually curly ball of hair, and wore a pair of heavy-framed glasses.

"What are you laughing about?" Nigel hissed through clenched teeth. "You dressed me up like this."

"I know. I just can't get used to seeing you looking smart."

"Smart? I look like a ponce."

"I rather like it actually. Promise me you won't take it off when we get home?"

"Get stuffed. I'm not into all that dressing up bollocks. I've seen too much of it lately."

Slot was referring to the many hours he'd spent carefully editing video footage in preparation for Belinda's parting gift to the school.

Belinda knew that the honour of engineering the lights and sound projections for the Headmaster's address would fall to a Lower Sixth boffin called Leslie Parks, or 'Sparks', to those who begrudgingly admired his electronic wizardry. Leslie was the archetypal techno-geek who had no interest whatsoever in art, but loved pressing buttons to illustrate a play, or create sound effects. For Leslie, lights and sound were far more important than the actual play, the action of which often got in the way of his technological display.

Belinda had not forgiven Sparks for leaving the front of house speakers on by accident whilst cueing up a later sound effect during a major scene in a previous school play. Belinda's big moment had arrived as Lady MacDuff, observing the brutal murder of her children, when the murderer's line "What you egg?" was greeted by the unexpected, if not entirely inappropriate sound of a cockerel crowing, several times. The scene descended into farce, and the rest of the play was punctuated by tittering from an otherwise tolerant audience. After the show, Belinda had ascended the vertical ladders to Leslie Parks' projection room overlooking the rear of the hall, and demanding Viola McIntyre (who was quietly chastising the boy) turn a blind eye. She then took off the geek's glasses and punched him firmly in the face. Belinda then held her hand over his mouth to stifle his squeals and announced like a gentle matron: "Not tomorrow night, Leslie. There's a good boy."

This episode had been the culmination of much of Belinda's frustration with her 'career' at Stortfield. Throughout her school life she had always been regarded as a little too maverick and always played second fiddle, vice-captain, supporting actress, and Deputy Head Girl to the immaculate Melinda Farnsworth-Rogers. In the casting of *Macbeth*, she knew she was a natural for Lady Macbeth, and resented Viola's decision to maintain the tradition of casting Melinda in the lead. A quiet resentment had been building in Belinda's final Stortfield year towards her blue-eyed chum, and to Viola McIntyre, who was enough of a maverick herself to appreciate Belinda's individuality. This resentment had manifested itself in her increasingly hardened image, and she had mulled it over rather too much in the company of Nigel, who was quick to encourage her anti-establishment ways.

Sparks was a little bewildered by the red-haired woman appearing by degrees through the trapdoor of his lighting box. She was followed by a familiar looking man, who looked uncomfortably smart and gave the appearance of being a used car salesman.

"Hello, Leslie" said Belinda emerging into the projection box. "Do you recognise me?"

"Er… no, sorry" said the confused Sparks, "Should I? You do look familiar."

Belinda had passed the first hurdle. She knew Leslie Parks would only recognise a face if it was in a computer game.

"Have you ever seen the television programme *Surprising Lives*? I'm the presenter Simone Singleton."

"Er…no…can't say as I have seen the programme. I sort of recognise you though."

"Well, I'm surprised, we are on the Dave Channel, you know," said Belinda, almost laughing at her own sense of irony. "This is the producer, Duncan Polanski."

"Hello," said Nigel Slot, in a badly affected posh accent, whilst sliding his index finger between his neck and the uncomfortable shirt collar.

Belinda continued (trying not extend Nigel's appalling acting skills any more than was necessary). "The idea is that the programme honours an important person or celebrity by throwing a kind of surprise party for them, and highlights the amazing things they've achieved. Well, today, believe it or not, we're going to surprise your Headmaster, Mr Pelforth, and this is where you come in…"

"Really?" replied Leslie. "But where are the cameras?" He looked terribly excited at the thought of cameras.

"Er… well" said Nigel, jumping in to cover as Belinda looked a little uneasy. "We've got people in the audience with hand-held cameras. Quite a few members of staff know they're there."

Sparks wondered why this man was speaking through the side of his mouth and trying to sound like Prince Charles.

Belinda quickly interrupted Slot's pantomime performance: "Then, when we've surprised him, we whisk him off to the studio. What we need you to do is play this piece of flashback footage we've compiled on Mr Pelforth's life. It's all on DVD. You only need to press play, when we give you the cue. Can you do that for me Leslie?"

"Well yes, but are you sure Mr Pelforth won't mind?"

"Look at the audience Leslie" said Belinda peering discreetly through the window of the projection box and looking down on the auditorium. "Many of them are already in on the secret. Mrs Pelforth's there, and the Governors, they all know. You're the first pupil to find out. Isn't that fantastic?"

"Well – I suppose so," replied Leslie, wrinkling his nose, and pushing his spectacles up to the wrinkle.

"Now here's the DVD. Load it up. Make sure it's all connected for me. Don't play it by accident though, will you? Wait for the cue." Belinda spoke the words with unnecessary sternness, momentarily recalling Leslie's inept timing.

"What about Mr Pelforth's DVD? I'm supposed to be projecting his plans for the new theatre."

"Ah well. This is why we left it until the leaver's assembly. You see none of these people will be terribly interested in Mr Pelforth's address. Unlike the parents of other year groups they won't get a chance to see the new theatre. The Chairman of Governors suggested this would be the ideal moment." Belinda seemed to have convinced the boy, but was slightly unnerved by the way he kept glancing at her, his blinking eyes looking as if he was trying to decipher something.

There was a respectful hush as Adrian Pelforth took the stage. He tried to sound enthusiastic as he introduced for the fourth and final time that morning, his end of year address. He was even able to work up a laugh about the repetition required on this occasion, which segued neatly into the need for a bigger and better hall, " Indeed, a purpose built, state of the art theatre, enabling Stortfield Academy to compete in the arts, much as it does in sport and academic achievement." He concluded: "I'd now like to show you a short film of our plans."

Leslie dimmed the lights and looked to Belinda nervously.

"Now!" she hissed assertively.

Sparks pressed the button. The screen at the back of the stage flickered. The soundtrack began in darkness. The familiar staccato guitar of 'Every Breath You Take' by The Police cut through the speakers. Sting's mellifluous voice chimed in as the footage commenced. The film had been edited to blur the features of the couple involved. One appeared to be a school master, the other, a pupil. Even with the facial detail blurred, it was clear that the schoolgirl was probably a little too middle-aged to be hoisting the pleated, grey uniform skirt almost to her bikini line. Her tight blouse, generously open, almost to the waist, came into close-up from the viewpoint of a very shaky camera.

Pelforth sat in an upright chair downstage. He smiled benignly at first at the wobbling footage. This was obviously a prank of some sort, typical end of term stuff, he thought. He expected a little skit, or sketch was to be played out. At first, Pelforth peered up at the projection box over his glasses, trying to catch the eye of young Parks. He then briefly looked across at the screen and furrowed his brow comically to the audience, raising a knowing eyebrow, as if to say, "I've seen it all before."

And, indeed, he had seen it all before. Realisation of this suddenly gripped Pelforth, and his playful gurning turned into frozen anguish. His eyes widened, his jaw dropped. "That barn"... he thought... "those costumes."

As he rose from his seat, Adrian removed his glasses and

stared like a bald eagle towards the nesting figure of Leslie Parks up in his lofty lighting room. As Sting intoned the line "I'll be watching you," Pelforth, desperately trying to maintain a semblance of calm, called up to the projection room.

"I think we'd better stop there, don't you?" He shielded his eyes but still couldn't see the face behind the viewing window.

"Do you hear me?" he shouted over the music. Quickly, he glanced over his shoulder at the screen to see a figure in a mortar board and gown swishing a cane playfully in the air, narrowly missing the uniformed schoolgirl, who jumped away from each strike, in balletic fashion. Unsure of his next move, Pelforth panicked, ran off stage, and fumbled in the wings for the red button marked 'Curtains Closed'. He hit the button with his index finger to activate the front of house tabs. The ancient mechanism cranked the curtains along their tracks so painfully slowly that Pelforth could not prevent his audience witnessing his on-screen alter-ego bending his schoolgirl victim over to commence "six of the best." The grey skirt rode up the 'girl's' thighs as she bent double, revealing a bottom that stretched a pair of flimsy, pink, knickers to breaking point. All of this was seen in glorious widescreen close up, exposing a small tattoo on the 'victim's' buttock. The tattoo was that of the classical comedy and tragedy masks, smiling and frowning, as it spread more widely across the offending cheek. The reaction amongst the audience, could be generally categorised into three classifications: Gasps from the wives and mothers present; childish sniggers from the prefects; and outright belly laughs from most of the half-sozzled husbands and fathers.

Pelforth panicked again. As the curtain crawled in slowly, he impatiently untied his academic robe, slipped it off, and ran towards the screen, desperately attempting to use the gown to veil over the offending flesh. Adrian reached up with the gown, standing on tip-toe. As he reached, he leaned against the screen, which hanging from the stage fly tower, simply hinged backwards, and so Adrian slid down the rippling canvas, clutching wildly at the weighted lower edge. This caused the top of the screen to loosen from its moorings and fall on top of the now prostrate Pelforth. Adrian was enveloped. Indeed, his legs protruded down stage from what looked like a large, vanilla envelope. He was, momentarily, in both senses, stationary. This was the final, humiliating, view, before the red curtains creaked to a close across his polished shoes, like the sad conclusion of a production-line funeral in a civic crematorium. And still, the film played on in shadow, across the fading red curtains. The hall descended into uproar.

Belinda could barely believe her luck as she restrained Leslie Parks, who had tried to spare his Headmaster further humiliation by switching off the projector. Belinda though, firmly gripped his hand before he could reach the button. The surprising strength of the grip, the glacial stare, and the calm, but determined tone of voice as she said "Now, now, Leslie, let's not interfere!" took the boy back to the last occasion he was assaulted in the lighting box.

"Fuck! It's you!" he squealed almost under his breath. With his free hand, he grabbed at Belinda's wig, managing to slide it askew, before Nigel intervened.

Bernard Jenkins was never going to be a headmaster himself. He was perfectly happy as custodian of Churchill House, and so long as he kept in Pelforth's good books, that's where he would stay. Besides, Pelforth knew more about the antics of some of Jenkins' boys than the Housemaster would wish. Seeing the Adrian Pelforth in desperation on stage,

Jenkins slipped out of his seat, past the preoccupied and hysterical audience. He opened the door at the back of the hall marked 'Projection Room – Entry by permission only' and began to ascend the upright ladder, just as Belinda and Nigel were about to make their exit. The ladder led to a loft-hatch trap door at the top. No longer able to judge his own balance, Jenkins propped the trap door open with the top of his head whilst gripping the frame. There his eyes met the black stockinged ankles of the incognito Belinda Bellingham-Steele. For a brief moment, he looked directly up the dress of the woman before him, and secretly wondered what he had done to enjoy so many such spectacles in a single day, firstly on screen, and now in real-life. His brief moment of pleasure was abruptly brought to an end as Belinda stamped down her stiletto on his fingers, forcing them to release their grip. Jenkins' high-pitched yelp turned into a groan, as she followed through by slamming the door down on his exposed, near hairless head, creating the percussive sound of cricket bat on ball.

Jenkins slipped down the ladder and landed in a heap, his academic gown splayed out beneath him. He writhed a little and started to get up when Nigel descended the ladder, his feet sliding on the side rails as if they were greased. He jumped off and stepped on Jenkins' torso in the process. The teacher heaved an asthmatic wheeze as his lungs emptied in one enforced rush. Belinda saw her moment and climbed quickly down the ladder. Not daring to stop her, Parks awaited his moment, and just as the top of her head was about to disappear from view, he made a second clutch for the wig and wrenched it off Belinda's head, then slammed the trapdoor shut. He stood on the trapdoor, wig in hand for several minutes, wondering if he really was correct in his brief observation that Belinda

Bellingham-Steele was almost bald.

Belinda and Nigel, their cover blown, left Jenkins gasping for air, and escaped into the rear of the hall, out of the doors, and into the quadrangle beyond.. They were clearly seen by parents who were leaving the hall in the embarrassment of the recent scene. Fortunately, staff and pupils felt duty bound to remain with the Headmaster in his moment of need. Most of them had enjoyed this little episode far more than they were admitting. The exception to this misplaced sense of loyalty was Viola McIntyre, who had moved discreetly from her seat, and escaped from the hall into the sunlit quad where she recognised the now loosely disguised figure before her. She reached out her hand and spun Belinda around by the shoulder.

"Thanks for keeping the faces out of the frame Belinda," she spat through gritted teeth. "Trouble is, the tattoo was a bit of a give-away." Viola pushed Belinda aside, and headed, tearfully, towards the car park. A tall, slightly careworn figure who had followed her out, stood and stared at Belinda and Nigel. He held his hand out to Belinda, who he knew from his many visits to see her in school plays: "Thanks Belinda," he said, as she just stared at the outstretched hand. "We have met. But to remind you, I'm Vincent McIntyre. I thought that not too many people knew about Viola's tattoo… until now."

# PART 2

CHAPTER 37

# AN APPOINTMENT

Gareth Chivers could hardly believe his luck. For years he had put up with a progression of inappropriate, uncommitted, or just plain poor drama teachers. Now, as his dreams of raising the Stortvale High profile with a new theatre about to be built, he had found the ideal Head of Drama.

Viola McIntyre sat before him with a sense of determination and dignity, despite her very public humiliation. Belonging to SODS and Stortfield Academy, two of Storton's most eminent institutions, made her embarrassment a source of gleeful, local gossip.

The *Storton Courier* gradually awakened to the school for scandal on their doorstep, and had begun giving Stortvale High a better press at the expense of its wealthy rival. The years of deference to the public school was giving way to barely concealed cynicism. An ambitious young journalist, Jed Crane, had reluctantly accepted the post of local reporter to Storton, moving there under sufferance, from the parent newspaper group in London. Though trapped in the parochial climate of the self-regarding town, Crane was determined to make his mark on the *Courier*, and move out of Storton as rapidly as possible. If Crane could dig out few exclusives that might sell on to the national tabloids, the stepping up to the door steps of the rich and famous on behalf of the *Sun*, could be a dream fulfilled.

As the subject of Crane's intense, investigative reporting, Viola's tattoo produced one of the Courier's more memorable headlines:

**TATTOO CLUE TO TACKY TWO**

Viola and Simon Petherton-Pugh were all but named in the subsequent report, proving the final straw for the proud, but put-upon Vincent McIntyre, who gave Viola the ultimatum to resign or risk divorce.

Viola was in no position to go through another messed up marriage, especially having three children depending on her, and knew that in view of the loss of respect amongst colleagues, she had little option but to leave Stortvale Academy. Viola had expected to be a woman of leisure for a term or two, but an unexpected phone call from Raymond Chater had presented a new challenge. Chater had, on occasion, trodden the boards impressively with Storton Operatic and Dramatic Society, and had his commitment to Lady Doulting been less demanding, there was every chance he might have become a regular leading man.

With the summer holidays well advanced, Chater was

concerned that all his work securing funding and planning permission for the new theatre would be a waste of time, if Stortvale could not attract a capable Head of Drama. Risking rejection from the woman who once played Eliza Doolittle to his Henry Higgins, Raymond took the liberty of asking Viola if he could recommend her for the vacant drama position.

Irma Witherspoon had threatened to return to Stortvale after three years of litigation, maternity leave, and severe depression, but the absentee Head of Drama had recently discovered the whereabouts of former history teacher Jason Hallatrow, father to her Annunziata (aged two). Rapidly resigning, Irma had flown out to the British School of Kuala Lumpur in the hope of Jason making her an honest woman. International schools are renowned amongst teachers as places of refuge for the desperate, disillusioned, and morally dubious of the profession, so it should not have been quite such a shock to discover that, on hearing of Irma's intention, Jason had suddenly received "an offer too good to refuse" in Beijing. A forwarding address "would be sent on" – eventually.

Gareth Chivers and Adrian Pelforth shared one thing in common: Both had accepted the resignation of their respective Heads of Drama with barely contained enthusiasm, and had waived the usual terms of notice with exceptional good will and understanding.

Returning to his desk in late August, before the beginning of term, Gareth was still casually attired and mentally imbibing the vin rouge and Camemberts of Provence, when Viola was presented before him.

"Of course, under the usual rules, the post can only be temporary at this stage, Ms. McIntyre, but we are looking for someone with commitment in the long term, who can bring stability to the department."

"Well," replied Viola, with measured enthusiasm, "this is an exciting time, and I hope my arrival will help move things in the right direction."

"But tell me" continued Gareth, feeling rather at ease in his Hawaiian-style open-necked 'holiday' shirt, "you've been lording it a bit – if you don't mind me saying so – up there at Stortfield" (Stortfield was always referred to as "up there" even though it was on barely higher ground than anywhere else in Storton), "Do you think you can handle the rough and tumble of a modest comprehensive?"

"I taught in North London, before Stortfield–Haringey. If you're a good teacher, you can teach anywhere. The private sector's not perfect, you know.

"No – absolutely er –Viola. May I call you Viola?"

"Of course, Headmaster."

"Oh, we're not quite so formal here, call me Gareth."

"Very well, Gareth."

"And may I say, my wife and I thoroughly enjoyed your Maria in *The Sound of Music*."

"Thank you" replied Viola politely, trying hard not to recall nuns and Nazis again.

"We don't get much time to go to the operatic shows. Shame that the Storton players don't have a better home than the Town Hall."

"Absolutely, Gareth. The facilities are so outdated."

"What chance do you think of Storton Operatic and Dramatic So–"

"SODS," she interrupted.

"Sorry?"

"Call them SODS – everyone else does," she laughed.

"Absolutely. What chance of getting er – SODS up here when the new theatre's built?

"I would certainly be using my influence to see it happen."

"Well, that's very reassuring, Viola. We really want to play our part in this community. We've been overlooked for a long time in this town."

"I couldn't agree more."

"Well Viola," Chivers said whilst standing and offering his hand-"Welcome to Stortvale High School. Nothing would give me greater pleasure in the full course of time, to be able to make this appointment permanent."

"A little permanence would be good for me too Gareth." Viola took his hand, but couldn't quite look him in the eye. She really had fouled things up… and this, she thought, was the price she had to pay.

CHAPTER 38

# THE CANDIDATE

For Simon Petherton-Pugh, there was no other obvious substitute in his life after vacating the Chairmanship of the Governors. His wife stood by him, in the way well-bred wives do. He knew Joanna would use the grudge as currency for the rest of their lives, but with a little penitence, and greater attention to her material needs, things might, eventually, get back to normal. Shoes would probably help – lots of them. Obviously the children would never be able to go to Stortfield. That, more than anything, upset Simon.

Simon deliberated on approaching Raymond Chater who he had found to be most agreeable, to see if Stortvale needed a new Governor. Helping a real, community school, might help rekindle his reputation and, given time, that Parliamentary Prospective candidacy would come around again.

Then, quite out of the blue, Denzil Braithwaite died.

Braithwaite was not a great friend of Petherton-Pugh's and had long cast doubts on Simon's eligibility for a parliamentary seat. Braithwaite was the archetypal working-class Tory, all bluster, self-righteousness, and with a corpulence that always threatened to strangle the life out of his slithery heart. Denzil's eventual demise occurred when bending down to pick up the very last bottle of Black Stump for a favoured customer in his 'Select Off-Licence', proving a stretch too far for the former mayor and Storton Borough Councillor of twenty-five uninterrupted years' service.

Simon had never considered cutting his political teeth as a local councillor. Prospective parliamentarians rarely do. All that messy business debating planning permissions and public lavatories was not what the Stortfield Debating Society and the Oxford Union had prepared him for.

Braithwaite's death left a substantial gap in the Council chamber in more than one respect. The subsequent byelection, normally a ritual ignored by the general public, and won by the candidate with the most friends, took on a greater significance. The Tories had a one seat majority. The election would be hotly contested. The winning candidate would determine the town's political manifesto for the remaining three years of office.

Petherton-Pugh could not deny to himself that he was also motivated by the thought of wielding influence over Stortfield Academy, albeit from a distance. Pelforth's empire could not grow without Council planning approval. Any significant changes to the theatre would have to be submitted too, and Simon could exact cold revenge on his old Alma Mater if he so desired. Outwardly, by standing in the byelection, he was hoping to win back the approval of his Conservative colleagues.

First he needed to win the nomination to stand. It was then that Simon really began to recognise the paucity of talent waiting to serve the Conservative cause. Even the discredited former Stortfieldian could hardly fail against the likes of:

1: Mrs Edna Dollimore, Housewife, 61. Former Chairwoman of the Storton Women's Institute, who resigned from that august body after her 'homemade' fruitcake was discovered to be a repackaged Waitrose consumable.

2: Mr Arthur Blewitt, 83. Retired factory foreman and war veteran, standing on a general anti-black, anti-gay, anti-Asian, anti-Pole, send 'em all back ticket.

3: Alistaire Simnall-Boothe, 24. Unemployed Volunteer Church Warden and Youth Club Worker. Retaking A levels at night school. Hoping to qualify for the clergy, having successfully defended charges of indecency in a Storton public lavatory.

The Petherton-Pugh charm, intelligence and trousers made light work of the selection process, but there was a greater challenge to win the seat. Braithwaite lived in, and secured as his, a largely suburban, lower-middle-class electoral ward, but there was always the growing threat of Liberal Democratic fervour amongst the younger, newly-wed faction and first-time buyers on the new estate. Labour ran a poor third in this ward, usually putting up a candidate who would have best suited a seat on the board of the Cats Protection League.

Despite his local notoriety, Simon surfed to victory on a wave of sympathy for the deceased Denzil. The Lib Dem candidate, a charity worker, demanded two recounts, but Simon's majority of seventeen stood firm. The total number of votes cast (173), did not live up to the expectation of such a pivotal moment in local politics. Simon though, saw it as the first steps in the long journey back…

CHAPTER 39

# FILLING THE GAP

Belinda Bellingham-Steele was beginning to have doubts about her gap year. Her original idea of voluntary service teaching in Nepal had diminished in scale and ambition, to tidying a terraced house in Storton, and preparing meals for Nigel Slot.

The undercover identity change had quickly worn off. Belinda had been seen around Storton during the summer and it was only a matter of time before her true whereabouts reached her parents, through the unlikely source of the *Daily Mail*. A fuzzy photograph of her taken at distance entering a supermarket was blown up under a page 6 headline:

**PUNK PRINCESS SPOTTED IN STORTON**

Belinda's father demanded she return home, but she declined, thus forfeiting the generous allowance she and Nigel had been living on. Belinda had no qualms in taking a job as a waitress to make ends meet, but she soon became a subject of curiosity. Stortfield pupils with nothing better to do after school would come into The Settle restaurant and ridicule the once distinguished Deputy Head Girl, now sporting a nineteenth-century milk maid's outfit.

Having burned his bridges with both of the town's senior schools and Lady Doulting, Nigel Slot was also in need of sustenance. He had never declared his financial commissions, and had long gloried in the anarchy of being a dole cheat. His years of sponging off the state came to an end that summer when the Department of Work and Employment served notice that he was to re-train in Horticultural Management'. Knowing this was a euphemism for gravedigging, Nigel took the only honourable option: He got a job.

Phoning up Raymond Chater in an attempt to ingratiate himself back into the patronage of Lady Doulting, he found the estimable Raymond unmoved by his condition, but he was good enough to suggest there was a vacancy at the quarry as a storeman, and he would give his personal recommendation for the job. Undoubtedly this did the trick, as Slot was the surprising choice from a shortlist of willing, if poorly qualified, applicants. Clearly Chater was having a little fun at Nigel's expense, knowing that the shift patterns, and heavy work, would give the sculptor a taste of what it really was like working with stone.

Nigel Slot became a slave to his alarm clock. The 4 am shift cruelly exposed the indolent artist, and he lost all appetite for sex with his nubile young concubine.

For Belinda, this was an education that extended well

beyond what she might have learned halfway up the Himalayas. She had become, to her sudden shock, a working-class housewife. With only part-time employment herself, she slipped into a routine of shopping, cooking, and cleaning, seeing little of the man she had chosen as her perfect sexual partner. Belinda's thoughts turned to better days and her adventures with Melissa Farnsworth-Rogers, who once again made the sensible decision and accepted a teaching secondment at a secondary school in Borneo. Having deferred, for a year, her place at Cambridge, Melissa's future looked predictably secure. Belinda had decided to apply for university during her gap year, but without the back-up of Stortfield's Careers department or her parents' support, she was struggling for advice. The excitement of her last school year had also given Belinda a taste for espionage, and despite not wishing to follow in her father's footsteps, a military career began to seem alluring.

For Jamie Timpson, a new school term was the opportunity to resettle into boarding school life. It had been suggested that, at the very least, Timpson might have been moved out of Churchill House, but Janine Jeffries, his Case Support Worker, had been ignored with contempt by Pelforth and Jenkins, his Housemaster. Both masters had decided Timpson could be a loose cannon, and retracted their offer to move him to a new house.

Janine Jeffries knew that with no access to Timpson's expatriate (and in-denial) parents, she had little influence over the boy's future. Through Jamie's reluctant testimonies, Janine was aware that Belinda Bellingham-Steele and her unnamed accomplice had unfairly taken the public flack for the Vigilantes.

A light, warm, late September day encouraged Janine to take a coffee break at The Settle restaurant. She took a seat in a quiet alcove. Sitting by the window was only likely to draw her to the attention of overdependent "clients" with little else to do other than parade along Storton High Street.

Having taken her seat, Janine noted two familiar faces appearing to be in earnest consultation at a distant table. Both were recognisable from their well-worn profiles in the *Storton Courier*. One was the waitress, Belinda Bellingham Steele, less elegant and more careworn than previously; incongruous in an antique serving wench costume and Mohican, which protruded into a bulge under the mob cap. The rest of her hair had grown out into a tight crop. Janine guessed that the girl had given up meticulous grooming, or had even decided that being a rebel was not as much fun it had seemed in her days as a daughter of privilege.

The customer, with whom the Belinda seemed uneasy, was Jed Crane, the *Courier*'s 'Ace Reporter'.

"All I want is a coffee," she heard Crane protest. "You can't ban me, you know. You're old news now, Belinda."

Belinda strutted off having reluctantly taken the order. Janine decided to make her move.

"Hi," she said, as Crane's attention returned to his copy of the *Sun*.

"Sorry to disturb you. You're the reporter on the *Courier*, aren't you?"

"Yeah. I hope I've not offended you too," he replied.

"Like young Belinda over there, you mean?

"Yeah. What does she expect? It was national news. I'm hardly going to turn a blind eye."

"Quite. But Belinda's something of a scapegoat. She was just the one they caught."

"Would you like a seat?" Jed looked slightly embarrassed by his belated invitation.

"Thank you. Er… I'm Janine. I'm a child psychologist. I work as case study support for children suffering from trauma.

"Oh, yeah." Crane kept one eye on the *Sun*'s gossip column in an attempt to seem only partially interested. "So, I take it there are other little terrorists running around Stortfield, are there?"

"Look–" Janine tapped the table in a subconscious attempt to gain his undivided attention. "What I'm about to tell you is a breach of confidence. You can't quote me, and I'm not giving you names. You're developing quite a reputation for controversy, so you can put the evidence together yourself."

"Fair enough," said Jed, slowly turning the page on his paper.

"I've been counselling a boy from Stortfield Academy. He's been deeply affected by bullying. He saw something he shouldn't have, and has been victimised ever since."

"So what?" said Jed, dismissively. "Bullying goes on in all schools. I was always being given a pasting in the toilets at my school. You just get on with it."

"It's not about the bullying, as such. It's what he saw."

"Go on."

"I feel rather bad about this. The boy was in hospital. A psychiatric ward. He was quite sedated when he told me this. He's frightened stiff I'll tell someone."

"Look – I'm not going to drive a child to suicide," said Jed, his voice descending to a whisper. Just give me the gist of the story and I'll dig the rest out."

"Well… it seems he got up in the night – at his boarding house – and ran into a bunch of older boys in black clothes and wearing balaclavas, with only their eyes visible. It didn't occur to him at first they were schoolboys. They were seniors, you see, well built, tall, and with deep voices. They grabbed him, roughed him up a bit, and told him to say nothing under fear of death. In the middle of the night it was, like a bad dream for the boy. Then they let themselves out of the house by the fire door next to the boy's room. They made him stay awake, sometimes three or four times a week to open the fire door to let them in on their return."

"The Vigilantes," said Crane, quietly.

"Sorry?"

"The Vigilantes," repeated the reporter. "I've heard the rumours. I tried to get names from Belinda over there, but she's grown a bit shy of publicity these days. I'm not surprised in that get-up. We've been following this story on and off for ages. My predecessor, Alice Turnbull, wasn't too keen on stalking the town streets at night to collect the evidence. There's also been a lot of deference to the Academy, and it was assumed Stortvale High School boys were to blame. Only when our friend in the dairymaid's outfit over there got busted, did anyone realise that it might have been Stortfield pupils."

"She's not much of a waitress…."

"No, you won't get served if you hang around with me. She knows I want her to dish more dirt on the school. The point is, no one can really collar the Vigilantes unless the police step up their patrols a bit – and they seem reluctant. I found out the Chief Constable and the Headmaster are members of the same Masonic Lodge."

"You're joking."

"We need to catch them red-handed. The trouble is, the Academy is a big campus and they're not just going to walk in and out through the school gates are they? I need to know the name of the boarding house this little night watchman of yours is living in."

"OK but that's all I'll tell you. Then, if you don't mind, I'm going to move to another table so that silly little girl will serve me."

"So…?"

"It's Churchill House. There's a hole in the fence two metres behind the house that leads on to the country lane at the rear of the campus." Janine's voice was shaking a little. She wasn't a willing conspirator.

"Churchill, eh?" Jed mused. "Then we shall fight them on the beaches."

From the corner of her eye, Janine saw Belinda trying to look away. She rose from her seat. "Remember," she warned, earnestly, "this is not just about an exclusive for you. A little boy's personal welfare depends on what you do with this story."

"Yeah, yeah – course," said Jed dismissively, trying not to overreact to her sanctimonious manner – "Not all newspaper reporters are completely unscrupulous."

"Right, well… hope to catch up with you sometime" Janine continued, whilst standing. "Now, where is she?"

Janine went to the counter where Belinda was pretending to tidy some teacups.

"Excuse me? Is it table service?"

"Yeah" replied Belinda, "Why?"

"Well, I'll save you the bother. Can I order a camomile tea, please? I'll be sitting by the alcove."

"Yes, of course" said Belinda – just a little more contrite

than before. Looking over Janine's shoulder, she spotted Jed Crane glancing at her. He was a confident, cool, and not unattractive bloke, she thought. Perhaps he might have his uses.

CHAPTER 40

# FIXTURE

Adrian Pelforth sat looking out of his study window towards the lake, and tried to imagine how his theatre might look on completion. The architectural plans featured a glass frontage, allowing natural light into the upper and lower foyers, and giving patrons an unprecedented view of the lake and lawns surrounding Stortfield.

His reverie was disturbed by the discomfort of knowing that vital changes to the planning brief were subject to unusually long and protracted discussions. He had no doubts that Simon Petherton-Pugh, now on Storton Council's Planning Committee, was busy behind the scenes causing chaos. The saving grace was that Petherton-Pugh, as a former Governor at the Academy, was not allowed to participate in any public debate on Stortfield's planning permissions without declaring an interest. The Bursar had pointed out that, in the past, it was possible to influence councillors with generous offers of entertainment at the school, but now, even the Tories seemed to be less biddable these days. Again, Petherton-Pugh's influence was cited.

Meanwhile, Pelforth had been informed that diggers had moved in on the corner of Stortvale High's playing fields earmarked for the new theatre. Whilst he tried to keep as distant from Stortvale as possible, he resolved that, this year, he would ensure his attendance at the Under 18 Storton Cup Challenge between the town's two schools. Frankly, the fixture had become an embarrassment in recent years with Stortfield Academy the inevitable victors by a country mile. This year it was Stortvale's turn to host the match on what remained of its playing field, and it would give him a chance to see, first hand, the theatre construction in its early stages.

Pelforth swivelled his executive chair to face his old oak desk, took out his fountain pen, and write a memo to himself: "See Head of Games, Monday. Stortvale match-must win fixture."

CHAPTER 41

# ALLIANCES

Gareth Chivers wasn't entirely sure what to make of Viola McIntyre. It was bliss having a Head of Drama who actually turned up to teach every day, but rarely had he encountered a teacher who complained so much, and so directly. Three times in her first few weeks at Stortvale, Mrs McIntyre had burst into his office, demanding, in no uncertain terms, he expel a pupil for offensive behaviour. On the third occasion it was Viola he detained, rather than the pupil, suggesting that she might have forgotten, thanks to her many years in private education, that expulsion, in the State sector, was near impossible.

Gareth also recognised that standards of discipline had fallen over the years. When he first began teaching, most pupils respected a teacher unless and until the teacher proved undeserving of it. Now it seemed that pupils were more inclined to hold a teacher in contempt until coerced into considering otherwise.

Viola though, seemed at home with her A level groups, who she noted, were naturally intelligent and talented. At Stortfield, some of her A level students would never have qualified without considerable nursemaid support. A private education is nothing if it cannot buy the kind of intense tuition needed to present all but the tardiest of dullards a university education.

It was the endless, turgid stream of lower school drama classes Viola hated. She never much liked teaching thirteen-year-olds at the best of times, but in classes of thirty-two, the noise and likelihood of chaos was intolerable. Very soon she learned that it was helpful to incorporate media studies into drama. Indeed, she was praised by the school's Director of Studies for an excellent approach to cross-curricular development. So, not only was it acceptable for her to allow her classes to watch *EastEnders* in lessons, it was actively encouraged. Watching soap operas, Viola found, was the best way to occupy class time, and the only way to keep some from climbing the walls.

Viola was however, proving a very useful political ally to Gareth Chivers. Her relationship with Simon Petherton-Pugh, if more distant than before, was still conducted at arms-length, thanks to a network of secret mobile phone and email accounts. By this means she had arranged for Simon to visit Chivers regarding "some interesting proposals" he had to make in the school's interest.

Simon couldn't help but feel sorry for Gareth. His Headmaster's 'study' looked out on a tiny, weed-strewn quadrangle in the 'Admin Block'. Despite attempts to adorn the room with personal mementos such as family photographs, winning football teams from years gone by, and a few geography books, the room had an uninspiring functionality about it. The cardboard substitute for one of the window panes was also telling. But Simon was a reformed man, a man of the people. He was determined to prove a caring and approachable councillor. He was also a man with a mission:

"Gareth, you know I've always supported what you do at Stortvale. Even when I was Chairman of the Governors at Stortfield, I always used to talk up what you're achieving here. I found some of the staff there terribly unaware of what life was like on the other side of the fence, so to speak…"

"Good of you," Gareth replied, trying not to sound too patronised.

"That's why I'm so glad your theatre project is well underway," continued Simon with a born-again zeal. "Yours will be a true community theatre-not something just for the toffs."

"Well, I'm delighted that Mrs McIntyre is with us now, and she tells me she'll bring with her the patronage of SODS." Gareth responded smirking just a little at Simon having the temerity to call others 'toffs'.

"Anyway," Simon continued, "I note in the calendar, that the annual Rugby Challenge is just around the corner. How's the first fifteen shaping up?"

"First fifteen? We'll be lucky to get eleven from our sixth form. We're mostly a soccer playing school you see. Unlike in Wales, where I grew up, rugby is seen as too much of a public school game in these parts. We're not so bad lower down the school, but in Year 12 we lose so many boys to the tech colleges in other towns."

"Yes, I thought as much. Seems a bit unfair when boarding schools like Stortfield can offer rugby scholarships to boys from all over the country."

"That's it. We just can't compete. Even if I had a specialist rugby coach on the staff, he wouldn't have much to work with."

"Yes, I see" Petherton-Pugh mused. "And the big match is just four or five weeks away?"

"Yes – about that." For Gareth this annual ritual had lost any real meaning.

"Well, it seems to me that if Stortfield can draw players from all over, you should be able too. Like the Ryder Cup. We wouldn't be much of a challenge to the Yanks without a few Europeans thrown into the mix."

"Nice thought Simon, but it doesn't work for the likes of us."

"Ah, but what if it did? What if I could draw on players internationally?"

"Sorry?" said Gareth. "You'll have to be a bit more explicit."

"The thing is," Simon continued in a hushed, conspiratorial manner, "the thing is… I was in France last week with the council's Twinning team at Chateau Valois Sur Seine. Do you have any twinning visits from their pupils?"

"We used to a few years ago. We had a very active exchange with the Modern Languages Department," Gareth explained, "but it died out when Criminal Records checks came in. Parents who hosted the foreign kids just lost interest when they had to go through Disclosure scans and all that palaver. All that legislation made them feel as if they were being scrutinised as potential paedophiles. What with that and the ridiculous health and safety legislation the teachers were expected to carry out on return visits, it's no surprise that the appetite for bon accord was lost."

"A bloody tragedy," said Simon. "Typical nanny state. Perhaps there's a way around all that. If the council could find the means to put up a few French lads on a rugby exchange, would you be prepared to accommodate them at the school? Just for lessons."

"Sounds interesting," said Gareth, raising a quizzical eyebrow.

"The secondary school at Chateau Valois has an academy scheme with the local rugby club. Top team. Attracts very good players who continue studying at the school, whilst training for a potential career in rugby. There's a twinning exchange heading to Storton the week of your fixture. What if I could persuade a few of the French school players to supplement your team?

"What? Ringers you mean?" remarked Gareth with slight indignation. "I don't know about that."

"Ringers?" Simon queried.

"Yes, that's what we'd do in the local clubs in South Wales, if we were short of a few players – bring in a ringer or two. Someone unsigned who would play under the name of an absent player. I don't think we'd get away with a group of Pierres and Marcels answering to the names of Darren or Wayne."

"No, no. This would be all above board. While they're there in Storton, the French boys would be officially on a school exchange. They'd be your responsibility – your pupils for a week. They'd be here officially to learn English."

"Yes, but what do you think the Academy might say? Would they pull out of the fixture?"

"Not likely! They're so confident, so bloody arrogant about rugby, they'd be really fired up. Besides, they needn't know until the day."

"Well, as I say, Simon, we are struggling to get a fifteen together, and of those, only half a dozen would be any good at all. I'll have a word with my Head of PE and let you know."

"Jolly good," ventured Simon, rising from his rather uncomfortable chair. "I'll get onto the French chaps as soon as poss."

Simon offered Chilvers his hand. With a twinkle in his eye, Gareth pulled Simon slightly towards him: "Oh, and if any of these French lads have got a bit of spare time at nights – you don't think they'd fancy doing a spot of terrorism on Stortfield's windows, do you?"

Simon knew exactly what Gareth meant:

"Well, I can't comment on those kind of rumours. Let's just hope the French are as good as they say they are. The council will take care of the accommodation. We'll put them in a hotel if we have to. Delighted to meet you again."

"And you, Simon – and you," replied Gareth. He was rather enjoying his new alliances.

CHAPTER 42

# THE HANGMAN

The Hangman was an old coaching inn in Storton High Street. With its knotty beams and leaded windows, The Hangman was one of the last standing remnants of Storton's historic past.

Waiting in the quiet corner of the saloon bar, Jed Crane seemed a little apprehensive. Jed was in his late twenties and couldn't imagine small town life would offer him anything worth hanging around for. Since joining the *Courier* he had met few eligible women in Storton and spent his free weekends back in London. Despite his affected 'cool', something about Belinda Bellingham-Steele made him a little nervous at their meeting. She was bright, intellectual, but also streetwise, edgy, and a little tough. He wasn't sure about her slightly androgynous look. It almost seemed an affectation to prove she could remain attractive, no matter how she dressed.

Jed himself wore jeans and a jacket with an open collar shirt. His hair was fashionably long but styled to look intentionally unkempt. His was an orthodox sense of fashion – he was more a bass player than a lead singer, in image. Cool, but not too self-regarding.

He looked up and saw Belinda enter. She looked left and right, her delicately honed profile turning like an elegant flamingo on a long, slender, neck. Jed quickly adjusted his hair into a more studiously crumpled mess, as he raised his palm to attract her attention. She saw him and her eyes widened. "Steel," he thought… the eyes had the blue coldness of steel. They were calculating eyes, intense and assured, but alluring too.

She wandered across. They shook hands delicately as she sat, and Jed sniggered ever so slightly.

"Sorry?" said Belinda, questioning his every move. "Something funny?"

He thought honesty was the best policy. "No – I was just looking at you as you walked in and thinking how self-assured you seem without your dairymaid's get-up."

"Oh, I know – gross, isn't it? That's the trouble when you're looking for a job to tie you over – there's not much about. The thing I hate is when kids I knew at school come in and start staring or giggling. Stortfield kids don't do part-time jobs. They haven't a clue about working – getting their well-manicured hands dirty. Most days I don't see them, but Saturday afternoons are shit. That's when they get time off to come into town and gawp. Mostly, it's the girls. The boys get more Games sessions on Saturday afternoons – thank God. If the girls take the piss I can usually find a way of ensuring they don't come back."

"So, are you local, then?" Jed enquired. "Is this your home town?"

"No – fortunately." Belinda had little but contempt for Storton. "I just ended up staying here this year. It's a long story. Can't really go back home. Don't really want to."

"You're with that artist guy, aren't you? The sculptor."

"Nigel. Yeah, I've been with him for a few months."

"He's quite – er… well… established in these parts."

"What are you saying? He's getting on a bit?" Belinda immediately read the inference of Jed's comment.

"No… I wasn't thinking that," he lied. "But now you come to mention it, he's quite a bit older than you, isn't he?"

"Why? What's wrong with that?"

"Nothing at all. Gives us all hope."

"What's that meant to mean?"

Jed looked a little uncomfortable. Her defensiveness indicated that Belinda wouldn't be an easy contact to make. He subconsciously decided to reveal his own, more vulnerable side:

"Well – I'm twenty eight now. I wonder if I'm too old for – you know – girls of your age. It seems that most women of my age around here are already married."

"Oh, you never need to worry about that." Belinda was sounding far more advanced than her nineteen years, Jed thought. She continued reassuringly: "If you've got your looks – look after yourself, keep fit you'll be ok. Many girls will go with older men. It's us women who get dumped the moment middle age starts to kick in. I don't see age as a big thing. Nigel's still a little boy anyway – mentally."

They both laughed. Jed felt the ice crack apart like a submarine surfacing in the Arctic.

"So Jed… I can tell you're not an ex-public school boy, otherwise I'd be calling you Jeremy. Anyway Jeremy, you've been pestering me for weeks now. When are you going to let it drop? You said yourself that story is dead."

"Well, the thing is, it's not. I mean, your side of it has been well used, and you've had your fifteen minutes of fame. There's some mileage in portraying you as the bright young thing, currently on her uppers and having to waitress for a living. The sort of story the *Daily Mail* likes. It proves to the readers that you should never take on the establishment. But, the fact is, you're on a gap year, right? Just biding your time before university, I guess."

"That's the general idea. I don't want to stay here longer than necessary."

"Me neither," chipped in Jed.

"I never did like Storton. Boring little shithole. So twee, yet lacking real class. Typical inoffensive little town. Ideal for a boarding school. No big distractions."

"Couldn't agree more, to be honest. I can't wait to get back to London. I'm just here as a stop-gap too."

There was a pause. Belinda began to empathise with the small town reporter, but reminded herself not to let her guard down too willingly:

"So – why'd do you want to talk to me – given that my star is so obviously on the wane?"

"Well, it's common knowledge that when you were identified as Stortvale's urban guerrilla, you were taking the rap for others. It's the whole thing about being a girl. The papers love a femme fatale. Look how much more interesting Myra Hindley was than Ian Brady."

"Fuck off, Jed!" Belinda interrupted with quiet assertion. "I hope you're not comparing me with her"

"No, no – of course not. What I'm saying is the daring, powerful woman is of great appeal to the press, especially an attractive one. The trouble is, they seem to have forgotten that you and the other girl, er…"

"Melissa"-

"Yeah, Melissa – were acting alone. You weren't really part of the bigger picture. It's the Vigilantes I'm after. I want names."

"Yeah, well, I could mention a few suspects – but really, it would mean nothing. The thing started up last year, and most of the group are still in school. One or two left at the end of the year, and from what I hear, it's an exclusive club plenty of others are queueing up to join."

"But as I understand it, they are from one boarding house?"

"Yes, Churchill House. Other boys from different houses have thought of copying them, but Churchill's unique."

"Why's that?"

"Well, to start with, of all the boys' houses, Churchill has the highest proportion of first team rugby players – maybe seven or eight. Secondly, the Housemaster, Jenkins is a pushover. He'd do anything for a quiet life and is a 'yes' man. The sixth formers run the house, not him. The bullying there is like something out of *Tom Brown's Schooldays*."

"What sort of bullying?"

"Oh, you know – dormitory raids on younger lads; humiliation tactics; fagging."

"Fagging?"

"You know – making younger boys servants to the older ones. It was banned fifty years ago but it goes on if the Housemaster doesn't stop it. Also, Churchill's placed close to a good escape route from the site."

"OK," said Jed, back in journalistic mode. "Why are they doing this? Why vandalise the local comp?"

"I don't know – you'll have to ask them. I suppose it's the obvious target. You know, town and gown and all that. Stortfield's pupils think themselves very superior to the locals, who they class as 'chavs'. And the chavs can't stand these outsiders coming in with their posh voices and uniforms. It's like being under an army of occupation. I see it from the other side now, working in the tearooms. Stortfield pupils are so bloody superior in their attitude to the waitresses, even the older ones. Worse still, is when they're just dismissive. I mean, if they're rude, you can be rude back, but if they just leave without saying thank you or leaving a one P tip, that's what really gets to you. That's what the other waitresses say."

So why don't the Stortvale pupils retaliate and just smash up the Academy?"

"Haven't you seen the place? It's like a bloody fortress – high fences, spotlights, warden patrols. The comprehensive's such a soft target by comparison. And I expect kids at Stortvale mostly grow up spending the evenings with their parents and watching telly. Everyone thinks most kids roam the streets in gangs every night, but it isn't true in a place like Storton."

Belinda saw Jed sipping his pint and looked down to realise that an untouched gin and tonic sat before her. "Is that for me?"

"You did say a G&T when I invited you. I think the ice has nearly melted by now."

"Cheers." Belinda was enjoying the evening out more than she expected.

"So, when did these Vigilantes raids start?"

"As far as I know it started after last year's senior rugby

match between the two schools. The game was ended in a brawl. The 'oiks' as we called them, were getting stuffed, so they started playing dirty and taking the piss. Then, one of our players, a pompous twat called Hetherington, told one of them, 'Go back to where you came from'. Hetherington said that he meant back to Stortvale, but the boy he said it to was black – and took it offensively. I don't blame him to be honest. So, a fight started and they all piled in. Stortvale were trying to get the game abandoned, so no result could be declared. There was talk of banning the fixture but both Heads agreed to continue it. Their Head is a bit of a rugby fan himself, it turns out."

"So, how do I find out when one of these raids on the comp will happen?"

"Well, as it started after the rugby match last year, the same might happen again. Otherwise, it's just sporadic. I don't think there's a pattern."

"When's the next rugby match?"

"Soon – three or four weeks, I think. It'll be on the school calendar."

"Can you get me inside information?"

"I still talk with one or two of the lads. They're allowed out into the local pubs on Saturday nights."

"I need to be there to catch them in the act. I'm prepared to pay for information. If you could show me the best way in and out of both those school sites, it would help. You're the expert."

"Listen," Belinda leaned discreetly towards Jed, "I'm happy to help – as long as I'm left out of the story. I don't want any more blame. The other thing is – I won't say no to the money. I've been cut off. The old man won't shell out for me anymore. Can I trust you?"

"Course. Like I said – you're old news now, Belinda."

"Oh, cheers Jed," Belinda responded sarcastically.

"No hard feelings. Bigger fish to fry and all that." Jed finished his pint. "Fancy another one?"

CHAPTER 43

# PLANNING

Adrian Pelforth was incandescent. A letter sitting before him from Storton Council planning committee indicated that they were unhappy with the original architectural plans for his new theatre. They would recommend the Planning Committee refuse permission to begin building unless changes were made. Amongst other objections, the height of the building was cited. The new theatre would "obstruct the view of the open countryside to nearby residents."

"That bastard Petherton-Pugh's behind this" he bellowed down the phone to Jack Wildblood. "We did a full fucking consultation with local residents. Hardly anyone objected."

"The point is," Wildblood interjected calmly, "adjusting the height of the building means losing the balcony and the fly tower. We'd end up looking like a community centre in Hackney."

"Might as well not bloody bother," snarled Pelforth. "In the meantime, the footings are already in at Stortvale. "They'll be up and running with some second-rate, left-wing diatribe directed by Petherton-Pugh's tart, and we'll still be struggling in the school hall."

There was a slight pause at the end of the line:

"I know what I'd do" calculated Wildblood.

"What?" snapped Pelforth.

"If this were industry, you'd bring in the spoilers."

"Spoilers?"

"Yes… saboteurs. Interfere with the supply of materials to the site. Make a few, how shall we say, minor adjustments to the structure when they're not looking. Slow things up. But most importantly, we need to get at Petherton-Pugh."

"And how do you propose doing that? said Pelforth. "The man's Teflon coated. He could hardly be more discredited, and he still gets on the fucking Council."

"I know a chap at Conservative Central Office," continued Wildblood, in a tone of conspiracy. "Simon P-P's had his name down for a safe seat in the Commons for some time. Perhaps if he could be persuaded to stop meddling in our affairs – a more favourable view might be taken as to his suitability."

"The very idea of helping that smooth-talking shit into Parliament goes against all my principles."

"Glad you still have some, old boy" Wildblood countered with a self-congratulatory wheezing laugh. "Persuading him to keep his nose clean is one thing. Getting him a safe seat quite another. I wouldn't worry about his prospects."

"Well, that's something" Pelforth responded with a sigh. "How you expect me to find the spoilers I don't know. I'm a headmaster, not Head of MI5."

"Oh, you'll think of something," reassured Wildblood, "You'll find a way." And before Pelforth could reply, the wheezing walrus had hung up, cutting him dead.

CHAPTER 44

# UP AND UNDER

It was Stortvale High School's turn to host the Storton Senior Cup Final. The game hardly qualified as a 'final' in that neither team had endured any kind of dramatic journey to reach this particular endgame. In that respect it was a local, schoolboy version of the Calcutta Cup (the annual bragging rights bean-feast slugged out by England and Scotland), but a little more one-sided.

It had been fifteen years since the Storton Cup last resided in the almost bare trophy cabinet of Stortvale High School. On that occasion, Stortfield Academy had fielded their second fifteen, saving their first team for a more important County Cup match the following day. The second fifteen were so complacent, that they began the celebrations the night before the game, and consequently, many were 'laid low' with what was described officially as a 'mystery stomach virus' on match day.

Stortvale's Physical Education Department had since looked on this annual confrontation with an ever-increasing sense of ritual humiliation. Derek Tate, the long-serving Head of PE, had even tried to persuade Gareth Chivers to abandon the fixture, but Gareth would have none of it. To Gareth, giving up the fixture would have been sacrilegious, "An insult to the great game of Rugby Union," he declared. "Rugby is greater than any individual fixture. If all weaker teams pulled out of competitions, there wouldn't be a game at all. Besides, we sometimes beat them at soccer. We wouldn't want that cancelled, would wc?"

Declining to avail themselves of Stortvale's menial changing facilities, the Stortfield team took the short coach journey to their comprehensive counterparts, fully changed into kit. Ever since a changing room break-in had disposed the entire first fifteen of their hefty wallets, Stortfield representatives were inclined to make the visit across Storton as brief as possible. Adrian Pelforth though, had decided to be a little more receptive to his counterpart, Gareth Chivers.

Following a particularly sour sherry in Chivers' shabby office, Adrian did his best to disguise ill-feeling, and allowed Gareth to show off the one impressive building Stortvale had to offer, albeit a building no further advanced than a line of bricks of less than two feet in height. With Chivers sporting green Wellingtons, and Pelforth looking less than dignified in a token pair of rugby boots, with suit trousers tucked into his rugby socks, the two wandered across the school playing field in bright orange vests and yellow hard hats. Derek Tate, a distant observer, allowed himself a wry grin as he watched Gareth pacing about the building site, waving the architectural plans under Pelforth's nose, prodding his fat finger at the paper and pointing excitedly, as Pelforth looked on, seeming more interested in brushing off the wet mud that had sploshed up around the calves of his smart suit.

It had been left to Derek Tate to tell his coaching counterpart, Carden Matthews, about his 'guest' French players. Matthews, a former England 'B' international, was, as ever, unfazed by the challenge. Carden Matthews had experienced the great highs and lows of life as a first class rugby full back, but it hadn't really prepared him for life beyond. A Cambridge Blue-Matthews found it easy to gravitate to the public school system, and didn't need a teaching qualification to do so. This was just as well, because he was only really suited to teaching rugby, and then only to the best boys Stortfield had to offer. This fixture proved of little significance in the greater scheme of things, and he was, in truth, quite heartened to hear of some exchange pupils being drafted in:

"Getting in a few ringers are we, Tatey?" he joked. He occasionally saw Derek Tate about town, and the two had a good sense of banter. Whilst Tate was a little in awe of his successful counterpart, Matthews simply couldn't understand how Tate could dedicate himself to teaching sport to the largely unwilling, in such difficult circumstances. He just assumed Tate was incapable of getting another job, and therefore regarded him with a mixture of sympathy and slight contempt.

For his part, Derek Tate, a sports fanatic, looked up to Carden as someone who had fulfilled a level of sporting achievement of which he, Derek, could only dream. Tate had been a decent Sunday league soccer right back, no more. Derek knew though, that the only way to earn grudging respect from the likes of Carden, was to beat his team.

Escaping quickly from Chivers' building site, Pelforth proudly stood guard as his fine young first fifteen descended from the team bus, demonstrably patting their backs and shaking hands.

Chivers decided to overlook the skivers who chose flagrantly to skip lessons and watch the rugby. He made a couple of token enquiries:

"What lesson are you supposed to be in young man?"

"Well, sir," came the hesitant response, "Mrs McIntyre said we could come out and watch sir."

"Oh did she?" he responded dubiously. "Well I'll be checking with Mrs McIntyre next time I see her."

In fact he had no intention of deterring much needed support for the first team. He fully expected to see Mrs McIntyre herself appearing on the touchline, to accompany Simon Petherton-Pugh, who arrived donning an elegant cream coloured raincoat, unbuttoned to reveal his beige flannel suit, as he picked his way through the divots and puddles of the school playing field in inappropriate Gucci loafers.

Studiously avoiding the hunched figure of Adrian Pelforth and his flunkeys, Simon made his way to the touchline to stand beside Gareth…

"How are the boys shaping up, Gareth?" drawled Simon, sweeping his blonde, foppish fringe back from his forehead.

"Our boys or the French lads?" replied Gareth, all too aware that Petherton-Pugh was probably even more apprehensive about the outcome of the game than himself.

"See Pelforth's here then?" Simon remarked. "Does he know about our little ruse yet?"

"I mentioned it, in passing. I don't think they'll mind two or three exchange students joining in, if it gives them a better test than usual."

"Two or three, is that all?"

"No – we might use a few more."

"How many, exactly?"

"Nine."

"Nine? Oh dear, perhaps that's overdoing it."

"Well, to be honest, we only had six Stortvale boys volunteer for the ritual sacrifice."

"And are the French boys any good?"

"Derek Tate was drooling when he saw them in training."

"Jolly good" said Petherton-Pugh with a slight grin.

The Stortfield squad, having declined the use of their opponent's 'grim looking' changing rooms, had been warming up in the drizzle for some time. They were becoming impatient. Some began shouting towards the changing rooms in a provocative way, slyly glancing across at Gareth Chivers for a reaction:

"Come on you chavs! Get a move on!" yelled a stocky young man in a scrum cap. Chivers thought there was something familiar about him.

"Get a move on! Come aaaaaahn!" bellowed a six foot five Stortfield forward through his gum shield. "What you frightened of?!"

Then, suddenly, gamesmanship stopped. Players confidently throwing and spinning balls between them, stood in silence and looked across the playing fields to the changing rooms.

Like the cavalry watching Sioux warriors appearing over the brow of the hill, the Stortfieldians stared with increasing surprise as a pride of scarlet-clad gladiators, swaggered towards them. This was not the sheepish, undernourished Storton boys of old, hunched and self-conscious, shirts askew, socks down, sniggering at the inevitability of their own fate. The blood-red shirts were firmly tucked into their flour-white shorts; socks taped tight below the knee, and headbands clamped to their heads, giving the impression of crop-eared bull terriers – fit to fight.

The reds strutted, as one, towards the field, looking imposing and muscular. The bulging biceps and thighs flashed in the wet, the white shorts stark against olive skin. Most were dark-haired and heavy-browed with purple shadow shading their necks and cheeks. One, who was lighter skinned, wore shoulder length hair and a full beard. For all the world, he was a Viking.

Approaching the touchline, the reds, as one, broke into a jog, and began freely passing elliptical balls amongst them with deft and skilful arrogance. Once or twice a speeding ball was directed at one of the fairer, slighter, members of their team, who dropped it.

Still astonished, the royal blues slowly resumed their warm up.

"The bastards are speaking French," blurted out the cocky Stortfield hooker in the scrum cap.

Quickly, Carden Matthews jogged onto the pitch to bring his players together for a final team talk.

"Lads, come on, gather round."

The team gathered around in a tight huddle around their coach, leaning in as he quietly addressed them, crouching close so each could hear him.

"Yes, we know about this. They're hosting some exchange students from France. These lads are regular players. They might actually give you a bit of a game this year. Should make it more interesting. Looks like they've got a bit of weight in the pack, but there'll be a few weak links amongst the local boys. We need to get in early – make our presence felt – show them a bit of team spirit." He then concluded his usual uplifting pre-match platitudes, and with a lot of clapping, growling, and fist shaking, both sides faced up to kick off.

The match began with bone-grinding collisions. Pelforth's confident, assured manner, turned to apprehension as some of his better players, suddenly looked a little shorter, slower, and less confident than usual... Edwin Slater, the oily bursar, slithered like a slug through the sludge to stand alongside him:

"Stortvale have upped their game this year Headmaster," he ventured.

"Huh!" responded Pelforth dismissively. "Stortvale have grown so desperate, they've been dipping into the transfer market."

"Sorry, Headmaster?" Slater had arrived late and remained uninformed.

"Most of this lot are French. From the twin town. The school there is an academy for the local rugby club."

"Oh, well that should liven things up!" said Slater, trying to put a gloss on things.

"Liven things up? Bloody cheats. Shameful, bloody cheats. There must be at least eight or nine ringers in this team. We were told there would only be one or two."

"Oh really? Tut tut. Shocking, Headmaster," Slater replied, rapidly changing his tune.

"And look who's over there gloating alongside Chivers. That smug bastard Petherton-Pugh. I bet he set this up. He's always freeloading on trips to Chateau Valois sur Seine. Oh damn!" Pelforth broke off just as a Stortfield pass was intercepted by a perceptive – and rapid –'guest' player. With astonishing acceleration, the tall, lean French student stretched his stride and sped away from the desperate lunges of pursuing blue. The try was placed neatly and undemonstratively beneath the posts, and converted with calm assurance by the French fly half.

By the second half of the match, the Stortvale 'Invitation Fifteen' (as Simon Petherton-Pugh had politely christened them) were demonstrating conclusive superiority and exhausting the will of their public school opponents.

With the score at 40-14, some of the Stortfield boys were beginning to grow agitated, humiliated and desperate. Also, exhaustion was setting in. They simply weren't used to 'chasing the game', and certainly were not prepared for this deluge at the hands of their local rivals. With five minutes remaining, a combination of frustration and pure cynicism overcame the team. The Stortvale half backs fed the ball slickly along the line to one of the local boys. Brian Smalls wasn't a bad winger, and though not skilful, was at his best when tucking the ball under one arm, his head down, and navigating his way to the try line. What a great finale this would be. The crowning glory of Stortvale's victory – one of their own – running in the final score of the match. It wasn't to be... As Smalls skipped past the last challenge; a Stortfield substitute, standing close to the touchline and overwhelmed by the humiliation of it all, discreetly stuck out his foot and tripped the streaking Smalls. Incensed by this, several Stortvale players ran over to the cynical sub and surrounded him – pushing and shoving. In the melee, a punch was thrown.

The Stortfield pack, never likely to turn their collective back on a fight, soon came to the errant sub's defence. Gareth

Chivers, close at hand, tried to intervene.

"Break it up! Break it up! Behave yourselves!" he bellowed. Little good it did him. It was clear that some of the Stortfield team could see more honour in the game being abandoned, than the shame of defeat.

Cries of: "French fucker!", "English pig!" and "Stortfield shits!" could be heard amongst the roving herd of fists and boots.

Whilst the mayhem continued, Adrian Pelforth tried to remain aloof and kept his place on the opposite touchline. Petherton-Pugh tried to help Chivers in separating the warring factions. His slender frame was soon swallowed up, however, in the human stampede. A swift push to the chest left him skating backwards on his Gucci loafers and, after a comical attempt to retain his balance, he fell flat on his back, his raincoat riding up and thick mud slushing up the back of his beige suit.

Pelforth bellowed with laughter from the safe distance of the far touchline. Parents and pupils from both schools alike looked on this outburst with astonishment. A Stortvale father, turned on him aggressively: "You shouldn't be laughing! You should be in there, sorting it out!"

"Nonsense!" retorted Adrian, realising his mask had slipped. "Boyish high spirits, that's all!" He looked at the Stortvale dad, and recognised him from the local golf club, a man of some standing in the community. "Oh! For heaven's sake! Alright then!" at which he ambled across the pitch, followed reluctantly by the shimmering bald head of the Bursar.

Neither the referee, nor masters, made an impression on the ruckus. As soon as they separated one fight, another broke out a few yards away. The Stortfield hooker in the scrum cap was particularly pugilistic. Turning to a teammate he instructed:

"Keep it going. They'll have to abandon the match!" Thereupon he threw a haymaker of a punch at the French prop forward.

Hearing this, Gareth Chivers temper finally broke. Grabbing the hooker by the shoulders, he spun him round and ripped the scrumcap from his head.

"I knew I recognised you, you little bugger! You're the one who broke my bloody collarbone!"

"Fuck off you Welsh wanker!" came the response, followed by a solid punch in the mouth. Chivers held his hand to his jaw.

"And now you've broken a tooth, you bastard!" He was riled beyond any thought for the professional consequences. As he raised his fist in response, they boy ducked, just as the intervening Adrian Pelforth had arrived in a token attempt to get his boys to back off. The momentum could not be stopped. Gareth's fist caught Pelforth flat in the middle of his square forehead. Pelforth was poleaxed. There was a sudden halt. The Stortfield boys could not believe what had happened. Lying flat on his back, mud squeezing up around the back of his head and in his ears, Pelforth opened his eyes, blinking in disbelief.

"Oh Headmaster!" exclaimed Edwin Slater like a love-sick leading lady, as he bent down to attend to the prostrate principal.

Pelforth quickly flicked away Slater's helping hand: "Leave me – I want no fuss Mr Slater. Right boys! Back on the bus! This disgraceful match is abandoned. And we're taking the cup back with us!"

Gareth looked at Pelforth, and then at Petherton-Pugh. "The cup!" he exclaimed looking to the table by the halfway line where the trophy was being displayed in anticipation of the final whistle. The cup though, had gone. Denied his moment of glory, and fearing the Stortfieldians would engineer an abandonment, Brian Smalls had slipped away from the squabbling ruck, and unbeknown to all but a few highly amused Stortvale parents and pupils, had started his own lap of honour to the home fans. Registering that all eyes were suddenly upon him, Smalls tucked the trophy under one arm and fled into the bowels of Stortvale High School.

"Shall we catch him sir?" said the Stortfield captain to his beleaguered Headmaster.

"Don't be ridiculous! Get on the bus – all of you!" Pelforth made a token attempt to brush the mud from his coat sleeves.

"And as for you Chivers" he said, pointing accusingly. "Don't think this will be forgotten!"

Gareth Chivers, his hand clamped to his aching mouth, spouted his reply through blood and spit.

"No, it bloody well won't! Now fuck off back to Stortfield Academy, the lot of you!"

As the mob dispersed amid cursing and threats, Jed Crane observing on behalf of the *Storton Courier*, couldn't quite believe his luck. With a barely perceptible grin, he shook his head and muttered under his breath:

"You couldn't make it up."

CHAPTER 45

# CIVIL WAR

The page 7 headline of the *Sun* had given Jed Trotter considerable pleasure:

**RUCK OFF! HEADS ROLL IN SCHOOLS GRUDGE MATCH**

But Jed Crane, despite selling the story to a national daily, noted that in provincial Storton, nothing counted quite so much as the front page of the *Courier*. Jed sat in The Settle restaurant with this week's edition spread before him, awaiting his cappuccino, wondering if his move to this quiet outpost wasn't a blessing in disguise.

Belinda, resplendent in dairymaid's attire, brought him the coffee:

"There you go," she delivered, with a smile. "I'm getting good at this."

"What?"

"Making coffee. Haven't had any complaints this week. Good front page, by the way."

"Cheers," Jed responded, raising his cup. "All about being in the right place at the right time. This civil war you've got here in Storton beats Hackney for a good story. You've heard the latest, I assume?"

"What?" replied Belinda in anticipation.

"I've been checking the police records – down at the station. They arrested Gareth Chivers for common assault. Pelforth must have reported it."

"The bastard!" responded Belinda, a little too loudly for her supervisor. "Better get on I suppose," she continued with a grimace.

"Sure – fancy another drink tonight? Need to pick your brains."

"Could do. Not too early. Need a bit of time to get out of this clobber and scrub up."

"Oh, I don't know. It does something for you" said Trotter, with a tinge of sincerity.

"Shut up…" Belinda drawled coolly. "Eight o'clock at The Hangman?"

"Yes, that'll do." Jed tried to hide his enthusiasm.

With that, Belinda turned and strutted off, casually glancing over her shoulder at him and giving him a little wink. He began to wonder if he was in with a chance after all.

CHAPTER 46

# GARDENING LEAVE

"We're behind you all the way, Gareth," said Raymond Chater, who had recently been elected unopposed as Chairman of Stortvale High School Governors.

"The Governors entirely accept this was a matter of severe provocation. We have witnesses, including Simon Petherton-Pugh, and several parents who knew you hadn't intended to punch Pelforth. However, your arrest makes your current position untenable, I'm afraid. We must act before it's forced upon us. You need to take time out."

"You're suggesting gardening leave then?" responded Gareth with a sense of the inevitable.

"'Fraid so, old boy. It's the last thing I want as incoming Chair of the Governors, I can assure you."

Gareth turned on his chair and looked through the window to the little quad outside. It was simply paved, and with a two-seat bench and a few faded pot plants to keep it functional. Nobody but him used it, and the weeds growing between the pavement cracks were only ever picked by Gareth himself, when he occasionally ventured out into the sun. The sun only shone in the quad for a couple of hours a day. Occasionally, he'd sit there when reading documents and reports, or eating the lunch Linda had dutifully packed. It was a brief sanctuary. Now he was to have more time than he could ever imagine to attend to weeds and compost.

"I dare say Philip Hart will relish the opportunity to take over," Gareth muttered, with a sigh.

"Well, we both know that Hart isn't half the man you are" Raymond reassured. "God knows, in industry, I've seen enough upwardly mobile pen pushers in my time. You expect school teachers to be a bit more inspiring, but the disease has taken hold of us all. The best we can hope is that he'll cope."

"Oh, he'll cope alright. He'll make sure the bells ring on time, if nothing else." Gareth was still gazing into the quad. A bird had flown in and was trying to make its escape between the high, narrow walls.

"Of course, you'll be on full pay, dear boy," said Chater with a slightly misplaced sense of bonhomie.

"Well, I suppose Linda won't mind too much. She's been saying it's time I had a rest."

"Look–" Raymond could see the despair in Gareth's eyes. "Lady Doulting's grown very fond of you Gareth. She's not the fool some believe. If you should need assistance at all with er –you know – legal costs – don't hesitate."

"That's very kind" replied Gareth swivelling his chair back to face Raymond. "But it won't be necessary. The union will cover all of that."

“Ah, yes, of course.” Raymond had never belonged to a union. It never occurred to him that a headmaster might be in one.

“Do you know what I regret most, Raymond?”

“No?” Raymond said, leaning forward to indicate he was offering counsel.

“That I didn’t hit that bastard Pelforth harder.”

CHAPTER 47

# GIN AND TONIC

The transformation in Belinda Bellingham-Steele was remarkable, thought Jed, as she entered The Hangman. The Mohican had grown into a loose, blonde, fringe which flopped forward masking the more fashionably cropped sides. Over the top of her denims she wore a white, cotton, blouse which almost reached her knees, and was tapered at the waist by a loose buckled leather belt. The Autumnal ensemble was completed by a leather jacket, cut high at the waist, and calf-length leather boots.

"Where'd you park the bike?" said Jed with a grin.

"Oooh, I'd love a motor bike," she replied. "Maybe I'll get one when I've saved up."

"What? On your wages from the caff?" Jed laughed

"It's not a 'caff'. It's a restaurant and coffee shop with a discerning clientele, for your information" Belinda countered with mock admonishment.

“Gin and tonic?” said Jed, rising from his seat.

“Go on then, mister” said Belinda in a mock cockney accent like Eliza Doolittle. “I’ll let you buy a poor gal a stiff gin.”

“I’ll make it a large one” Jed suggested. “Might be a long evening. A lot to discuss.”

“Won’t say no, darlin’,” said Belinda, and smiled ever so suggestively.

Later that evening, Marjorie Pelforth sat upright in bed, resplendent in her curlers.

“That poor man. Devotes himself to looking after the underprivileged and ne’er-do-wells of this world, and then bang! One moment of madness and it’s remorse for the rest of his life.”

Adrian was standing in socks and pants, shirt and tie, whilst studiously placing his trousers in the heated press. He was unaware that the trouser press was an ironic birthday present from his younger son, Jeremy. Jeremy had admitted exclusively to his mother that the item was, in fact stolen from the Premier Inn in Doncaster.

“For God’s sake, Woman! I still have a lump on my forehead the size of an egg!” Pelforth exclaimed, whilst glancing at himself in the mirror. “What more must a man suffer before taking the law into his own hands? If it hadn’t been my intervention, he would have punched a pupil at my school.”

“If you mean that repulsive little squat shit Percy Humphries, then a good thing too, I’d say,” Marjorie replied laconically.

“It hardly matters who it was. The man had become insensitive to reason. If that’s the sort of person they think suitable to run a state school – well, no wonder things are so dreadful."

"Well, perhaps he'll lose his job. But at least they might name the new theatre after him."

Without waiting for a reply, in one swift movement, Marjorie slipped down her eye mask, flicked of the bedside lamp, and nestled under the quilt.

The room was in darkness. Adrian was still in his underpants, shirt and tie.

"I haven't finished undressing yet!" he exclaimed.

"Good night darling," came the sardonic response. "Don't bump your head in the dark."

CHAPTER 48

# SHAG PILE

Belinda crept in quietly through the back door. Beelzebub the cat crouched on the fridge. Both were startled when suddenly the light came on. It was Nigel, standing before them in a T-shirt, and a faded pair of boxer shorts.

"Where you been?.." It was more an accusation than a question.

"I told you" said Belinda brazenly. "I've been meeting with Jed from the *Courier*."

"I thought we weren't – like – speaking to the press."

"Jed's different."

"Is he now?"

"Yes, he's on our side. Hates it here in Storton. Desperate to blow the full story on Stortfield. Wants to know all about the Vigilantes."

"Who gives a fuck?" Slot was clearly tired from shift work and suspicious that Belinda looked so well presented. "When will that lot learn to live in – like-the real world? And when will *you* – come to that?"

"What d'you mean?" Belinda replied pensively.

"Isn't it about time you just forgot about the old Alma Mater and – like – moved on with your life?"

"I intend to," she replied, turning away from him.

"First I've heard," he continued tetchily.

Belinda had been meaning to tell Nigel her intentions, but had backed off. This seemed like an appropriate time.

"I was going to mention it before," she began sheepishly. "I've applied for a commission. They'll support my university tuition. I won't have to be dependent on my parents."

"What commission?" The only commissions in Nigel's world were those procured from wealthy widows with a taste for bad art.

"Royal Navy." Belinda almost blushed. She knew as much as Slot that her brief days of Bohemian chic were but a passing phase.

"No shit. Royal Navy. What a dedicated little anarchist you turned out to be."

Belinda's response was angry, but measured: "Fuck off Nigel. I had always planned to go to university, you know that. This was supposed to be my gap year. I was meant to be teaching children in a primary school in the Himalayas. What did I end up doing? Working in a caff dressed like a farm hand, and washing your grimy pants."

Nigel, for once in his life, felt able to take the moral high ground: "I never made you. You chose this. I suppose slumming it with me hasn't turned out the great ideal you imagined, has it?" He grew increasingly sanctimonious: "Well, the fact is, working in quarries and caffs is what keeps a lot of families from being like – destitute. It's all very well you public school types learning about poverty in the third world. What about the way people live in this country? The likes of you think nothing of the privileges you gain on the backs of the taxpayer."

Belinda began to feel her face flush with rage, but endeavoured to remain calm. "The taxpayers? When did you last pay tax Nigel? Only since you finally took a proper job at the quarry. Before that you were only too pleased to sponge off the taxpayers and do a few 'side-projects' for cash. Fucking hypocrite!"

"Oh farking hypocrite am I?" Nigel barked back in exaggerated upper class fashion. "And how do we spell fark, darling? With a PH-AR-QUE?"

Belinda turned her back on him. His slightly careworn, chiselled look quickly became sharp and weasel-like when trying to be funny.

He spat and bit upon his words with spite: "Don't tell me your old man won't pull a few strings to get your little indiscretions overlooked? 'Cause that's how it works for you lot. The rest of us live with our mistakes for the all of our stinking, miserable, lives. Your type just conveniently forget the past and move on. Just sweep it under that nice, thick, shag-pile rug in the family mansion."

Belinda remained calm. "If you're so appalled by 'my type', why have you spent so much of your life mixing with us? If it's not those nouveau-riche prigs at Stortfield – it's Lady Doulting and her flunkeys. Now you're really working for Doultings – doing a proper job –getting your artist's hands dirty, it doesn't seem quite so attractive, does it?"

There was a pause. Slot narrowed his eyes and looked at her. She wondered what he was going to do next. If he turned violent, she was confident she could handle him. Momentarily she looked around the kitchen for a suitable weapon.

"What's he like?" Slot said quietly. There was more menace in his tone when he was quiet.

"What?" Belinda knew what he meant, but feigned ignorance.

"What's – he – like?" enunciated Nigel pointedly.

"Who?" Belinda tried to sound impatient.

"Jed. Jed the cub reporter. Jed 'Mr Exclusive' Crane. The man you've been out with tonight."

"I've not been out with him. It was a meeting. Anyway, what's it to you?"

"What's it to me? Well, strangely enough, I've assumed that since you've chosen to live under my roof, I might expect a little loyalty. A little bit of respect, for like – bailing you out when you blew it with everyone else."

"Look – there's nothing going on between me and Jed. I've just got some scores to settle before I leave this ghastly little town, and he's going to help me do it."

"Good for you, Belinda. You settle your scores and then you can like-clear off, and you'll never have to clap eyes on this place again. Storton and Nigel Slot will be just another unwanted piece of crap you can sweep under that swish Persian rug."

Before she had a chance to reply, Nigel had turned with as much dignity a man in a pair of boxer shorts could muster, and left the room.

She called after him: "I'll sleep in the spare room – with the cat – then."

The reply from halfway up the stairs concluded the conversation.

"Fine. But I don't see why Beelzebub should have to put up with you."

CHAPTER 49

# THE NAUGHTY STEP

Janine Jeffries was not cut out for espionage or subterfuge. She felt awkward, disingenuous, and distinctly uncomfortable about meeting with Jed Crane again. She had invited him to her house, but hoped none of her neighbours would recognise Storton's 'Mr Exclusive'. Nonetheless, she was also impelled by her own sense of decency and injustice to expose the appalling goings on at Stortfield. Her lifelong grudge against private schools was not helped by marrying Cameron Jeffries, himself a product of an exclusive fee-paying school, who she had met at university. Now, several years on, Cameron was living happily with his new wife Pippa, and their recent addition, Margaret Lily. Meanwhile, in a 1930's Storton semi, Janine did her best to entertain Tarquin and Grace, the abandoned older offspring of her ex-husband, whilst holding down a stressful and time-consuming job.

While Tarquin and Grace proceeded to squabble, fight, cry, and generally interrupt, Janine attempted to tell Jed as much as she dare. After the fourth or fifth interruption of "Mummy, Tarquin's put Plasticine in my hair" or; "Mummy, Grace just spat on my muesli bar," Jed politely suggested the children might want to "watch the telly."

"We don't have a television, actually," replied Janine. "I believe it's a bad influence. The role models they see on these TV programmes are so corrupting." Her flow was broken by a crashing sound and a loud scream. Tarquin entered a little sheepishly:

"Mummy, Grace was really horrible to me."

"So, why is she crying?"

"Well, after she punched me, I tried to stop her being horrible."

"She's screaming, Tarquin."

"Well, she deserved it!" Tarquin stamped his foot emphatically.

"What have you done?" Janine rose from the couch and went into the kitchen. Through the open door, Jed could see the wailing six-year-old, covered from head to toe in what was probably custard. Janine's tolerance had reached its peak:

"Right, Tarquin. It's the naughty step for you! Now!"

Whilst Tarquin sang happily to himself on the naughty step, Jed conducted the rest of the interview in the hallway, outside of the bathroom, listening to Janine supervising Grace in the shower. He felt distinctly uncomfortable, wondering if proximity to an infant in such circumstances might deem Janine to enquire whether he had been sufficiently monitored by the Criminal Records Bureau. In between screams to remove shampoo from the child's eyes, Janine was able to provide the information Jed had hoped for…"

"Strictly confidential of course. You mustn't say I told you. Jamie is a client. He has rights just as much as you and me. If anything happens to him, I'll never forgive myself…

"Yes, of course, Janine" replied Jed with as much patience as he could muster. "Now what did Jamie tell you?

"Well, he's upset. He was told he has to stay awake on Thursday night."

"Tomorrow?"

"Yes. The older boys are planning what he called 'a raid'.

"A raid?"

"Yes."

"On what?"

"He didn't know, but he's terrified at being implicated. I mean, with all this trouble at the rugby as well. Some nasty things are in the offing."

Janine continued shouting over the noise of the shower, and Grace's intermittent screams. "They plan to leave at midnight," she concluded.

"Any idea as to where this raid might occur?"

"Well, with all this bad feeling between the two schools, it's possible that it might be the High School."

"It usually is. Ends up with just mindless vandalism."

"Yes, but this time they're telling Jamie to wait until they get back, and say they might be gone for longer. He's terrified he could fall asleep."

"Right. OK – anything else?"

"Yes. They said the raid had a code name, and he was only to use the code name – and he wasn't to forget it."

"So what is it?"

"Well, it makes no sense to me – but you mustn't tell people you know. It might rebound on poor Jamie."

"No… no…" Jed could barely disguise his annoyance at Janine's procrastination. "I promise not to tell anyone. Really. I don't want our little mole compromised, now do I?"

"Mole? Oh yes." Janine permitted herself a little guilty laugh. "He is a bit like a little mole, now I think of it." It was the first time Jed had heard her laugh.

"So?" he pressed her.

"So? Oh the codename? Silly really. Like something out of a Dan Brown novel." She laughed again – "and what rubbish they are" she said self-consciously, with a hint of guilt.

"So?" Jed was trying, and failing, to sound patient.

"It's called…" she paused and lowered her voice as if the room was being bugged. "It's called Operation Holy Grail."

"Thank you Janine" said Jed, not wishing to be detained a moment longer. "I'll see myself out."

CHAPTER 50

# GIMP

Jed Crane rented a small, sparsely furnished, apartment above a newsagent in Storton town centre. He had never intended to stay for long in Storton and so the flat was devoid of personal effects such as photographs, books or records.

With Belinda due to call, he did, at least, tidy up. Tin foil containers of half-eaten takeaways, many days old, were duly disposed of; spent toothpaste tubes similarly thrown, the toilet cleaned, air freshener applied liberally in all rooms, and pornographic magazines stored safely under the two-seat sofa.

As instructed by Belinda, Jed was wearing black. He'd bought the polo-necked jumper especially. He studied himself in a full-length hall mirror, and affected a very poor Sean Connery impression: "The namesh Bond. Jamesh Bond."

His cool self-regard was abruptly shattered by three loud, firm knocks on the door. Jed adjusted his hair and pulled down the jumper, turned smartly, and went to the door. No sooner was the door off the catch, when it was thrust open, and a black-gloved hand shot through the gap and clasped him by the throat. He stumbled back in shock as a black balaclava-wearing figure pushed him down the hall. The figure tripped him at the ankles and he fell backwards onto the bare floor of the flat. The stranger fell on top of him, and forehead to forehead – growled.

"We've come to get you Crane! We know what you're up to!"

An expensive scent and the lightness of the figure lying upon him offered a split second of relief, before Belinda yanked off the balaclava and stared at him with open mouth and wide eyed.

"Ha-ha-gotcha!" she yelled, and flicked him on the end of the nose. Jed dropped his head back onto the floor with relief and laughed. "I knew it was you!"

"Scared you though," she replied, jumping to her feet nimbly. Jed remained prostrate.

"Took me a little by surprise, I grant you," he conceded, propping himself up on his elbows. He was conscious of the slight arousal he had felt as her body pressed to his.

"You'd better be on your guard tonight Jed. Can't afford to be taken by surprise."

"Yes, alright. I think you've made your point" he said, brushing the dust from his black attire. "Really must get a Hoover," he mumbled to himself, as he picked a large cluster of dust from the jumper.

"Got you a prezzie" said Belinda recovering a small black bag she had dropped by the door. Reaching into the bag, she pulled out another balaclava and threw it to him.

"There you go – belonged to a very good friend of mine

called Melinda. Now doing her bit for Voluntary Services Overseas. Managed to beat me to being Head Girl at Stortfield. I'm eternally grateful for that."

Jed put the balaclava on. "I look like a gimp."

"You are," replied Belinda. "Tonight, you're my bitch."

"Taking this a bit seriously though, aren't we?" Jed replied, quickly changing the subject.

"Oh I am. I know these bastards. Vicious. The worst of them are sadists. It's a public school thing. I expect two or three of them at least to end up as senior members of the Cabinet."

"I see," said Jed, raising his eyebrows.

"No, not really. Stortfield's not that kind of school. Most of our thugs end up with military commissions."

"So, run through the plan with me" Jed requested. "Er – tea – or coffee?"

"Coffee – please – cause that's all you've got" Belinda replied as she wandered into the living room.

"How did you know?"

"Looks a bit spartan – this place. Just moved in?"

"Sort of. I didn't want to settle in Stortford. I tend to go back to London at weekends. Take a seat."

"Where would you suggest?" responded Belinda looking at the meagre furnishings. "Oh – here we are!" she exclaimed, sarcastically, and leapt gymnastically onto the couch.

As he made the instant coffee, Jed listened to Belinda's plan and began to do doubt whether the story was worth it. Staking out a school; masquerading as a terrorist; aiding and abetting; breaking and entering.

"I must be mad going along with all of this" he said, passing the coffee mug and sitting tentatively beside Belinda. "I can't work out why I should need to go to these lengths."

"Because, Jed, you're being seduced," replied Belinda. Jed, for once, was lost for words.

CHAPTER 51

# ANONYMOUS

Philip Hart was nothing, if not diligent. Having completed a long evening meeting of the school governors at ten o'clock, he returned to his newly personalised headmaster's office to conclude important business.

On his desk sat an envelope marked: "To the Headmaster, Stortvale High School" in felt-tip capital letters. It had arrived late in the day and was obviously delivered by hand. He opened it assuming it to be yet another complaint from a parent with a grudge. The letter was neatly typed on plain paper. It was neither signed, nor were there indications of an address. It read:

"To the Headmaster, I cannot reveal my true identity…"

"Like a bloody Batman movie" said Hart under his breath."

"… but I think it only fair to warn you that I have it on good authority that your school may be under threat tonight from a group calling themselves 'The Vigilantes'. I cannot say more but I would advise you to notify the police. From a friend."

"For Christ's sake!" muttered Hart impatiently. He picked up the office phone. The Storton Police Station was on speed dial – such was the frequency of his calls there. There was a lengthy ring at the other end. Philip thought, for one dreadful moment that he was going to be put through to an automated response: "To report a burglary, press one. To report an assault on yourself or another person, press two. To report a murder, press…"

"Good evening, Storton Police Station, how can I help?" a gruff voice interrupted his train of thought.

"Yes, it's Philip Hart here, Acting Headmaster of Stortvale High School."

"Yes, Mr Hart, how can we be of service, this time?" said the voice with a tinge of weary familiarity.

I'm in my office. We've just had a governors meeting you see… and I just opened an anonymous letter, which must have been delivered by hand sometime later today. Of course, it might be from a crank, but it suggests we are going to be paid another visit tonight by some of our friends."

The Storton police had taken some criticism in the local press for failing to discover the source of these incursions in the past. It was all the desk sergeant at the other end could do to avoid a loud sigh.

"Right, well, we ought to take it seriously, I suppose. What exactly does the letter say?"

Philip read out the letter and patiently answered the follow-up questions about whether it was signed or addressed, and what kind of paper it was written on, before receiving an assurance that the police would keep a close watch on the school premises that night. The sergeant also urged Hart not to do anything silly, like take on an intruder. Hart agreed, with some remorse, that this would, indeed, be foolish. And yet his sense of diligence could not allow him to desert the school, especially in view of the fact that his elevation the Headmaster was temporary. He was determined to prove to the governors that he was the right man for the job, when Chivers was eventually to resign, as surely he must.

Hart picked up the phone again.

"Hello darling. Sorry, the meeting's just finished, and I've just received warning of another potential break-in. I'm going to have to stay here a while longer."

There was a sigh at the other end. Hart's wife, Caroline, was quite used to playing second fiddle to his career… He would have liked her to have shown at least some concern for his welfare – or perhaps have taken some interest in the crisis at hand. Instead – with a resigned yawn, she mumbled something about the shepherd's pie being burned, and he'd have to heat it up in the microwave we he got in. Philip Hart put the phone down with a sigh, and made his way to the senior students' common room, where, if he was lucky, the chocolate machine would still be in working order. More immediate sustenance was required. He was in for a long night.

CHAPTER 52

# WILFUL OBSTRUCTION

Belinda sat in the passenger seat of Jed's stylish but old BMW. Jed opened the door and climbed into the driver's seat.

"Better?" said Belinda maternally, her balaclava rolled up to form a black hat.

"Yeah, sorry about that. Too much coffee."

"Nerves can play a part too."

"Not nervous really," said Jed, placing his rolled up balaclava over his floppy fringe. "Be glad to see some action, though."

The car sat in a farm gate turning, facing out onto a country lane. To their left, above the hedgerow, they could clearly see the second floor of the three storey Churchill House. An exterior metal stairway connected the emergency exits at the end of each floor. Each floor comprised twin and triple occupancy rooms, thought to be amongst the best equipped and comfortable of any in the country. Since suspicions had been raised of boys escaping through the emergency exits, the doors had been fitted with sensors that triggered alarms, if opened. It didn't take long, however, for those amongst the Vigilantes with even the most basic knowledge of electronics, to work out how to disable this function.

It was eleven o'clock. Belinda and Jed watched intently for signs of a shaft of light from the second floor exit when suddenly, the silent lane was illuminated by the headlights of an approaching car. It slowed as it drew closer to Jed's BMW.

"Shit! It's a bloody police car!" Jed looked panic-stricken.

"Get your hat off!" said Belinda, grabbing both their balaclavas and throwing them under her seat. She also quickly zipped up her jacket to conceal the black jumper.

"It's stopping. He's seen us." Jed whispered unnecessarily.

"Don't panic. We've done nothing. Face them down."

The police car pulled in and both front doors opened.

"Follow my lead," said Belinda quickly, and then, without further warning, she turned, grabbed Crane firmly by the shoulders, pulled him towards her, and kissed him fulsomely on the lips. Between snogging manoeuvres, Belinda gasped further instructions:

"Hold me then! Don't make-it – look-like I'm seducing you. Come – on – get into it!"

The adrenaline pumping through Jed's body made him startle and jump in a convincing way, when his side window was rapped abruptly by a flat-capped officer. Belinda tried to look embarrassed as she sat back in her seat. Jed lowered the window.

"Er – yes, officer?"

"I was going to ask what you two thought you were up to – but now it seems fairly obvious."

"Erm, yes, I suppose it does. Nothing illegal though," Jed stuttered.

"No, perhaps not," replied the officer, while his colleague walked around the car, noting all identifying features.

"Can I see your driving licence, sir?"

"Yes, of course," said Jed, reaching across Belinda to his glove compartment.

"Not a very clever place to leave it sir," said the officer with ill-disguised sarcasm.

"I know, I don't usually – I –"

"Mmmm. Seems all in order. This your car?

"Yes"

"What's the registration?"

Jed told him, haltingly. The second officer, by now, had returned to the police car.

"You realise that you're causing an obstruction?"

Belinda couldn't resist chiming in with a little delicate sarcasm of her own:

"No, officer, I wouldn't let him cause an obstruction on a first date."

Jed turned towards her, his eyes widening, as if to say, "Don't make this worse."

"The obstruction I'm referring to, is this car being in a private farm entrance, madam. I have no interest whatsoever in your romantic assignations."

Jed could see the second policeman in his car conversing on the walkie-talkie. He responded quickly before Belinda provoked more irritation:

"Sorry, I thought it was a lay-by."

"No, I'm afraid not."

Belinda was not one to suffer aimless authority:

"So what are we obstructing then, at this time of night? Are you expecting a tractor rally along here or something?"

"Don't get clever madam. Your boyfriend here wouldn't like me to book him, now would he?"

"On what offence?" challenged Belinda.

"Wilful obstruction."

"You know as well as I do, that's not a traffic offence."

"Now listen, young lady–" the officer was interrupted by a tap on his shoulder. His colleague looked vaguely disappointed.

"All clear," he said, referring to the record check he'd just accomplished.

"Right" said the first officer, his moustache twitching in irritation. "I suggest you stop obstructing private property and move on."

"Ok," said Jed, trying to hide his relief. "Sorry and all that."

He started the engine and slowly moved away.

CHAPTER 53

# SHOTS IN THE DARK

Jed's mind wasn't really on the job in hand as they sat waiting in the car park of Stortvale High School. Belinda had literally thrown herself on him twice that evening, all in the name of role-playing. He couldn't really discern whether she was using the situation to get closer to him or whether she was a great actress and totally lacking inhibition. Either way, Belinda seemed totally unfazed by the impromptu snog.

Having been moved on by the police, Jed and Belinda had decided to wait at Stortvale, and, in a change of plan, hoped to follow the Vigilantes back to Churchill House. Philip Hart had been forced to raid a charity box for the National Society for the Prevention of Cruelty to Children in the school reception. He had completely run out of cash, but vowed he would replace the money taken, with interest. It was just enough to purchase a chocolate bar and a cup of coffee from the vending machines in the "Sixth Form Common Room" as it was archaically known. He vowed, when elevated to permanent Headmaster, he would immediately re-Christen it the Tertiary Education Resources Centre. Hart didn't like to appear behind the times, unlike Gareth Chivers, who positively embraced the past.

Whilst awaiting his freeze-dried coffee with powdered milk to splutter forth from the grubby machine, Hart stared out of the Common Room window across the car park. There he noticed an old BMW alone, apart from Mr Blenkinsop's Flat Panda, which had been awaiting collection by a scrap merchant for over two years now. Blenkinsop had maintained he was far too busy to deal with it, being, as he was, Head of Technology. By virtue of a distant street lamp, Hart could just make out the outline of two shadowy figures sitting in the front of the car. He snatched at his coffee, but thanks to the sticky surface of the dispenser, the plastic cup stuck to the tray, and as Philip freed it with a jerk, the hot coffee splashed out liberally onto his groin.

"Aaaaahhh! Aaahrgggh! Fuck! Fuckety fucking fuck!" squealed the Acting Headmaster, as he danced a little jig, tugging at his sodden trousers, so as to ease them away from the scolded flesh. He quickly ran to the boys' toilets, and splashed cold water around the red patch on his inner thigh. This gave him time to consider his next move. If he called the police, it might be a false alarm. If it was the Vigilantes, and he scared them off, then the mystery would continue. He decided he would creep up on the car and take a photograph of the number plate using his mobile phone. The only way to do this was to skirt around the edge of the school playing field and approach the car from the rear. He could take a short cut through the building site of the new school theatre.

Utilising his mobile phone – this time as a torch – Hart had realised there was limited battery available, and he need a good photo of the vehicle, but he could see well enough, he thought, to get through the building site. He could certainly read the sign: "DANGER – BUILDING SITE. KEEP OUT" well enough. Philip Hart pulled back the flimsy fencing that was designed to secure the site, and squeezed through the gap. The footings of the new theatre were already in place and the concrete floor enabled him to cut a diagonal through the building, knowing it would bring him out just behind the mysterious motor. It would also save his shoes collecting more mud. He hadn't accounted, however, for the deep trench, which had been left to accommodate electrical cables, and no sooner had he picked up speed across the concrete in the dark, than he felt his left heel slip away beneath him, sending him sliding, like a ski-jumper, down the three foot muddy trench, skidding to rest on the backside of his coffee stained, charcoal-grey trousers.

Sitting there in the dark, Hart felt the urge to scream, but composed himself admirably. Relieved to have damaged no more than his dignity, he clambered out of the trench and fumbled his way to the fencing on the far side of the building work. Silently pushing back the fence, Hart's skinny frame squeezed through the resulting gap. A protruding piece of fence-wire caught on his trouser back pocket and he heard a loud rip as the pocket tore into the shape of a smiling mouth, exposing the immaculately white underpants beneath… Philip closed his eyes in dismay, taking some consolation from the fact that dry cleaning the suit was now out of the question.

Reaching for his phone, Hart tip-toed to within ten metres of the rear of the BMW. He could see two heads, both wearing woolly hats. Hart's heart pounded. The flash light would surely alert them. He realised it might be better to wait until the car, or its occupants, made some kind of move. Just at that moment, the driver seemed distracted, as his head turned to the rear-view mirror. The two occupants suddenly adjusted their hats.

"Christ! They're wearing balaclavas!" muttered Hart almost audibly, whilst going dizzy with fear. Suddenly, the car doors opened – and just as Hart fumbled with his phone to catch the evidence, he too found himself in the glare of flashlights as two camera shutters fired off rounds like a tommy gun.

Just as suddenly, the shooting stopped.

"I know why you're here," screamed Hart in an embarrassingly high pitch. "I've got the evidence!"

"So have we," replied a muffled, feminine voice, behind the terrorist mask.

"What do you mean?" responded Hart.

"Oh fuck!" retorted the female voice. "It's him again!"

"Eh?" responded the other apparent raider.

"It's him," said Belinda vaguely. "Leave this to me."

"D-d-don't come near me… I'm armed, you know," bleated Philip unconvincingly.

Belinda tried to be reassuring, despite the disguise: "A mobile phone does not constitute an offensive weapon. Look, we're not here to hurt you. We're from the press. We heard you were going to be raided tonight and we want to get the evidence. We know who it is…"

"What? Who??" stuttered Hart, keeping his distance.

The girl continued: "It's a group of lads from Stortfield Academy calling themselves the Vigilantes."

"How do you know them?" said Hart suspiciously.

"We've met before. No photos now…and I'll take the hood

off. Ok?" And with that, Belinda Bellingham-Steele pulled off her balaclava to reveal a familiar blonde shock of cropped hair, now crowned with a floppy fringe.

"You!" The recollection sent a shudder of pain to his scalded groin. "Don't come any nearer!"

"Don't worry Mr Hart," said Jed reassuringly. "It's me too..!" Jed tugged at his balaclava. "Jed Crane from the *Courier*." The two had previously met.

Belinda quickly interjected. "Look, I'm sorry about what happened before, but the other girl and I had nothing to do with these raids. We were skipping out of school that night and took a short cut. We just got caught up with it."

"A likely story!" said Philip, his anger rising.

Belinda remained calm: "Then why would I be hanging out here with Jed, if that was the case? You wouldn't believe why I was really out that night. Needless to say, the story hugely incriminates Stortfield. And that's a story both you and Jed need. So I'm here to help Jed get the evidence."

"I'm still recovering from that kick in the groin, you know," Philip cut in, petulantly.

"So I see," said Belinda, noticing the wet stain on his trousers. "Still got the stains to prove it."

"No, no – it's just coffee. I spilt coffee.

"Yes, sure, bit nervy are you?" Belinda grinned.

"Of course not!"

"Look" interjected Jed. "You don't want to be handling this lot on your own. We think the police are turning a blind eye to all this. Let's get inside the building and we can wait there."

Hart was still a little unsure. "Alright, but no funny business. We'll go this way."

Hart walked past them, his trousers sticking to his thighs,

giving him something of a bow-legged gait. Belinda gently elbowed Jed, nodding towards Hart as he slithered past, a great streak of brown sludge smeared over the seat of his pants, and half way up the back of his jacket. The unstained underpants flashed vividly through the gaping split. The two roving reporters released the faintest hint of a snigger. Hart stopped in his tracks and looked over his shoulder.

"It's mud. I fell, alright?"

"We won't be taking photos" replied Belinda, as the three of them crept across the car park to the safe haven of the Headmaster's office.

CHAPTER 54

# A TIGHT FIT

Philip Hart suggested Jed and Belinda get themselves a coffee in the Sixth Form Centre under the pretence of hospitality. He then suggested they meet him back in his office in five minutes to give him time to change out of the soiled clothes.

Belinda and Jed kept an eye out for any signs of movement through the windows before making their way back to the Head's office. Passing through the school reception, they briefly stopped to ponder the trophy cabinet, empty but for the Storton Senior Rugby Challenge Cup, and were suddenly startled by two teenage figures in their midst. It took a second to realise that they were two eerie mannequins of a teenage boy and girl. Each was modelling a version of the rather dull Stortvale High School uniform. There was though, a glaring omission from the boy's uniform… a distinct lack of trousers, revealing a naked, androgynous, lower half, but for socks and shoes.

Jed politely knocked on the Headmaster's door and entered the study. Hart glanced at them as he stood looking earnestly out of the office window behind his desk. He then invited them to sit down, and emerged from behind the desk mustering as much dignity as a man wearing trousers six inches too short might.

Belinda let out an involuntary sudden screech of laughter:

"Sorry!" she blurted out. "I'm sorry but–" she pointed to Hart's bare, stick-like legs, protruding from the end of the skin-tight trousers, and tried to supress her giggling. She was reminded of the time she and Miranda giggled through their disciplinary in Pelforth's office. Looking again at the way Hart's brogues protruded like flippers, she lost all semblance of containment, and snorted and sniggered again.

Hart stood erect and unflustered like a well-trained butler. Even though Jed was amused, his own amusement was short-lived. He realised there was genuine hurt on Hart's face as he almost blinked away tears of humiliation. Jed looked across at Belinda who was straining to restrain tears of her own, and quietly, but assuredly said:

"Shut up Belinda."

Belinda bit her lip. "Sorry," she said. "I'm so sorry. Really."

Although the odd spasm overcame her, particularly when Hart was impelled to move, Belinda became as contrite as Jed had ever seen her, and he felt assured at being able to suppress the excesses of this wilful and confident young woman.

As midnight approached, the three discussed where the Vigilantes might strike. If they had left on time, it would take about fifteen minutes to jog from school to school. Philip pointed out that they usually accessed the school by going through the gardens adjoining the Stortvale grounds, but had encountered a dog attack on a recent reconnoitre. "Mostly they vandalise this end of the school as it's not visible from the road."

"OK," said Jed, "I think you should wait here. Let's exchange phone numbers. Belinda and I will have a discreet look around the grounds, to see if there's any movement. We'll need to text or call if we spot anything."

"We need a text code word in case we need support," concluded Hart. "Something short."

"Short?" replied Belinda. "How about 'trousers'?" on which she thrust the knuckle of her index finger into her mouth, but was unable to stifle the sniggering that followed.

"Make that 'S' – just the letter" Jed decided. "And – Belinda, do shut up. There's a snot bubble hanging out of your nostril."

Belinda wiped her nose on her sleeve, and for a moment looked a little contrite.

Belinda and Jed stalked the perimeter of the school grounds, hugging the fence like two prisoner of war escapees. It was twelve-thirty now, and nothing to report.

"We shouldn't get too far from Hart's office," said Belinda "They might just go straight through the front entrance this time. Might be getting cocky now. I heard about them being chased by dogs on the estate."

"I wonder if this isn't all a rumour," Jed surmised. "Just an attempt to wind us all up."

"Doubt it," replied Belinda. "The thing is, they secretly love people knowing what they are up to. It's all a big ego trip. I mean, this whole military approach – Operation Holy Grail," she half-whispered. "What a load of bollocks."

Jed stopped suddenly in his tracks. "What a pair of fucking

idiots."

"What do you mean?" Belinda looked slightly offended.

"We are. How I didn't see this, I don't know. 'Holy Grail' for fuck's sake! Did you notice the trophy cabinet? In reception?"

"Not really, I was too distracted by the smooth little pudenda of the teenage model."

"The only cup in the cabinet was the Storton Rugby Cup. The one that was carried off at the end of the game, when the fight broke out. It's the first time Stortfield haven't had that cup in years. The Holy Grail."

"I wasn't at the game – I knew nothing about it. You're the idiot!"

Jed's thoughts were abruptly curtailed. A short bleep signalled a text. Jed fumbled for his phone and then dropped it.

"Told you, you were an idiot, Jed" said Belinda, as she retrieved the phone in the dark.

"Here" Jed hissed, taking back the phone and accessing the text. "It's him. It's an 'S'."

"Shit!" replied Belinda, as the two of them took off at speed. Belinda was impressively fast. Fitness gleaned from years of public school hockey and netball, had not diminished in her gap year… The two pulled down their balaclavas as they ran almost the entire length of the school playing field. As they drew close to the front of the school, they could hear a commotion, a braying of male voices, chiding and laughing in uncouth and vulgar fashion, as if in a post-match rugby changing room, a strip club, or the House of Commons at Prime Minister's Question Time. Belinda and Jed reached the corner of the reception building and peered around the wall. Outside the reception, a group of fifteen black-clad 'terrorists' had gathered in a circle. In the middle of them stood Philip Hart in the excruciatingly tight, calf-length school trousers. Hart was the 'piggy in the middle' as the vigilantes taunted him with the Storton Senior Rugby Challenge Cup, throwing it over his head and around him like a rugby ball. The two mannequins had been brought into this little arena. One of the raiders had his arm around the female model's waist, his hand down the front of her skirt, and his lips pressed to hers. Another had acquired the trouser-less boy and was simulating anal sex with the model, much to the amusement of his Hooray Henry compatriots:

"Go on; give it to him up the bum – the Stortvale scum."

Some of the others began a chant: "Up, up, up the bum! Up, up, up the bum!"

Amidst the Bacchanalian furore, Hart was shouting: "That's school property! The cup is not yours! I order you to put it back! The police have been called! They know you're here!"

The young men just laughed uproariously at the pathetic figure in his ill-fitting trousers.

"Yeah," replied a large figure, who Hart took to be the ring-leader, "and they'll be coming for you. You're obviously up to something, wearing those trousers."

"Dirty fucker!" said another.

"Fucking paedophile," said one of the group, thrusting his face right into Hart's. Hart smelt alcohol on the boy's breath. He began to lose his fear.

"This is nothing more than common assault! Common assault and theft! They'll imprison you, you know!" Hart's voice was getting louder by the syllable.

"Fuck off you pervy streak of piss" yelled one of the raiders, and pushed Hart backwards. As he stumbled, the cup, which, by now was being hurled recklessly around the circle, with ever-increasing speed, caught him full in the face, bounced into the air and landed on the pavement, chiming like a bell. Hart went down holding his head. Blood ran through his fingers. He tried to get up, but seeing the blood, swooned, and unfolded in a faint.

"Fuckin' hell," said one of the Vigilantes. "We'd better scarper. Percy, get the cup."

Belinda and Jed had looked on in a moral dilemma. Jed had moved behind a bush and was taking photos on his pocket-sized camera. He knew the quality was compromised by being unable to use the flash. Belinda filmed the proceedings on her phone. She actually felt sorry for poor Philip and guilty about the way she had treated him previously, but she and Crane couldn't intervene without considerable risk to themselves. Hart had got in the way of their plan, which was simply to catch the Vigilantes in the act.

The raiders quickly scaled the school gates. The silver cup was thrown over and caught with care. Considering it had been badly dented after bouncing off Hart's head, the reverence with which they treated their prize showed a certain lack of irony.

Belinda and Jed waited until the Vigilantes had made their escape, and rushed to the assistance of the splayed figure of Philip Hart. Confused, Hart opened his eyes to see two hooded executioners leaning over him, and screamed. Belinda placed one hand over his mouth and with the other slipped off her balaclava.

"Don't worry, it's us. We couldn't stop them, but it's all on film. We'll get the bastards."

Jed looked squeamishly at Hart's bleeding temple: "I'm calling an ambulance" he announced.

CHAPTER 55

# ACCIDENT AND EMERGENCY

It wasn't easy persuading the police that his black attire was for journalistic purposes, but Jed was well known to the local desk sergeant. Jed also made sure that the evidence on Belinda's phone and his own camera was hidden in his car. He didn't want anything to be confiscated until he'd had a chance to run his exclusive in the *Storton Courier*. Belinda's footage might make great viewing on the paper's website.

Having been released from the police station after making their statements, Jed and Belinda got into his car in the sure knowledge that Philip Hart would be safely lodged for four hours on a paramedic's trolley, in Storton Hospital's Accident and Emergency Department, bleeding profusely, before having his wounds unceremoniously stitched by a student nurse, and his offending trousers removed with the aid of surgical scissors, in order to have his temperature taken anally.

"I'll drop you off then," said Jed to Belinda, a little reluctantly.

"Mmnn… tricky one Jed" Belinda responded pensively. "You see, I don't really want to go back to be honest. Nigel already suspects I'm up to something with you, and coming in at this hour won't help. I'd rather go back in the morning when he's at work. I can collect my stuff. I need to find somewhere to stay for a while."

Jed took the hint. "Look, you can stay at mine, if you like. I mean, I'm sorry Nigel thinks I'm to blame. I hope he's not the violent sort but – I kind of owe you. It doesn't mean I'm assuming…"

"Never assume anything Jed. But thanks. Maybe I'll sleep on your little couch tonight, then we'll see."

"Sure," said Jed. No problem. I have a spare quilt."

Ten minutes later Jed opened his front door and chivalrously indicated for Belinda to step inside.

"Cheers," she muttered, looking around with a little disdain.

"Tell you what Jed. I've changed my mind. I think I fancy your bed."

"Yeah, sorry. I should have offered you the bed. I don't mind the couch. Didn't make the bed though."

"That's alright" said Belinda, as Crane carefully locked the front door behind him. "Shame we didn't get close-ups of the bastards leaving the house, unmasked. That would have proved it."

"Yeah" sighed Jed, "but we have a story, and the police will have to investigate properly now."

"I don't trust them. Pelforth's too well in with the local Plod."

"You did great by the way. Brilliant," Jed quietly confided, looking at the elegant nose, the beautifully poised neck, and the blonde crop, protruding from the figure-hugging polo neck.

"Didn't do so bad yourself, Scoop," teased Belinda. "Sorry about the surprise snog in the car. All in the name of espionage."

"Oh, that's fine… I, er… I didn't mind. I've had worse." Jed maintained a cheeky grin.

"I bet you have," Belinda said, taking a step towards him. Jed stepped back instinctively, but Belinda moved again to press him against the wall.

"You liked it, didn't you?" She looked him in the eyes.

"What?"

"When I kissed you. You liked it."

What makes you think that?"

"You put your balaclava over your lap afterwards. Didn't fool me. Either that, or the car has got two gear sticks."

"Oh, you noticed."

"I don't miss much," Belinda replied with a smile, placing her cupped hand firmly to his groin. "Now then, I'll take the bed, and I suggest you do the same. Or shall we make up the couch for you?"

"Er… I'll put up with sharing, if necessary," Jed clarified, with just a little tremor in his voice.

"That's the answer I was looking for" Belinda whispered, and with that clasped Jed around the back of the neck and pulled him towards her. This time Jed kissed like he really meant it.

Neither actually made it to the bedroom. Copulation had taken place on the couch, in the kitchen, and in the shower, before they finally crashed out, exhausted on Jed's bed. There, they made love one more time, before falling asleep.

Jed had taken the initiative to text his editor to say he'd be in a few hours late, as he was following a lead. He was surprised, therefore, to be abruptly woken by a call at 8.45. Removing his arm from the sleepy, pretty head of Belinda, he reached for his phone.

"Hello?" He could barely croak out. "Jed Crane."

"Jed? Oh hi, it's me, Janine. Janine Jeffries. Are you alone?"

Jed glanced across to Belinda who had fallen back to sleep.

"Yeah – I can talk."

"I have some news. It's very important. It's Jamie Timpson. He has some information. There was a raid last night, as I said."

"I know Janine. I've already heard." Jed was reluctant to say too much.

"Ok. Well Jamie asked to see me this morning for a counselling session. I managed to get over to school before lessons. He said it was urgent. He said he can't go through it all again, so he took the law into his own hands."

"What d'you mean?"

"He's a clever boy is Jamie. Loves his *Harry Potter* books. He says it's his passport out of Storfield. He wants political asylum, I suppose."

"Asylum?" What the hell are you–?"

Janine quickly interrupted his train of thought:

"He rigged a secret camera. He recorded the Vigilantes leaving the House. He said quite a few could be seen without their hoods. He also caught them returning… with the Holy Grail."

Jed listened with mounting glee as the evidence unfolded. Belinda had slipped a naked leg from under the quilt restlessly. She slipped her arm out under the bedding exposing a firm, proud breast.

Jed Trotter, for the first time since leaving London, felt he was truly at home in Storton.

CHAPTER 56

# FURTHER EXPOSURES

Gareth Chivers sat slouched and unshaven, watching a daytime TV show which exposed the intimate and morally bankrupt social lives of society's dregs. It was way past midday and he was still in his vest and pants. Linda, his wife, taking a rarely observed lunch hour from her part-time job in a local primary school, came home in the hope that Gareth might, at least, have warmed some soup.

"What on earth are you doing Gareth? Look at you!" she stressed firmly but quietly.

"What's the problem?" Gareth replied, scratching his chest.

"It's nearly one o'clock! I've been at work for five hours, and I come home to find you undressed, unshaven, and the house looking like a bomb has hit it!" Her voice rose, despite attempts to remain calm.

"That's right Linda. Rub it in." Gareth was unusually inexpressive in his anger. "As if it wasn't bad enough being suspended from work… I now have to spend my day doing household chores."

"Well, you can't just sit there half-dressed, watching daytime television. You'll end up a zombie."

"God, Linda. What is there worth getting up for? Even the local paper is just a reminder of what I am."

"What do you mean?" Linda frowned as she turned over the newspaper lying face down on the coffee table. The cause of Gareth's disquiet then became apparent

**HAVE-A-GO HERO HEADS OFF RAID.**

A profile photograph of Philip Hart, his head swathed in a crepe bandage, looking suitably forlorn, appeared beneath the by-line, which read:

**School Rugby Rivalry Turns Violent.**

Linda glanced quickly through the text. The tenor of Jed Crane's expose had been toned down considerably. Malcolm Corby, the editor of the *Storton Courier*, feared reprisals from the town's famous public school, if the "Holy Grail caper" was seen as little more than a "prank that went wrong." "After all," he had told Jed Crane, "they spend a fortune on their annual advertising supplement." The matter was blamed on "high spirits" and Hart's "accident" as a result of "a fall whilst remonstrating with masked intruders." Corby had also handed in the video evidence to the police, rather than posting it on the paper's website. Jed Crane's reaction to this had been only slightly less despondent than the forlorn figure of Gareth Chivers.

Linda threw down the paper. "Oh, I see. That's your problem. Philip Hart's the hero now. Is that how you see it?"

"They're already calling me the ex-Headmaster" Gareth replied sullenly. And what about that bastard Pelforth? His pupils are running around like a bunch of gangsters, and no one suspends him. There's no justice."

Linda slipped off her coat and folded it neatly over the back of an armchair. She didn't know which she preferred-the Gareth Chivers who was rapidly working himself into an early grave, or the desperate, manic depressive for whom there was no life without work. She felt more than a little inadequate. She had hoped that Gareth would settle into a long and happy retirement with her, but now she had seen the future, and it was in creased underpants.

"I'll make a sandwich" said Linda with a sigh.

Jed's anger with his editor had subsided within a day of his story's publication. It may have had something to do with seeing the story in a full and frank report as sold on to his mate Barry at the *Sun*. More particularly, it was receiving an early morning copy of the *Sun* delivered on a tray, along with cereal and toast by a bright and grateful looking Belinda Bellingham-Steele, who was up and dressed for work, in her full rustic servant girl outfit. As he rubbed the sleep from his eyes, he realised the quaint image had become a little dishevelled.

"Wakey, wakey, you sleuth you. See what's on page 5." She leaned across him and engineered the sudden release of a delectable, pink breast from beneath the lacy blouse, which almost ended in his cornflakes.

"I'll skip page 3," he remarked with false nonchalance, and adjusted the breakfast tray.

CHAPTER 57

# GARDENING LEAVE

One by one, the cars arrived in the VIP car park beneath Pelforth's study window. Adrian was not expecting a full governors' meeting, but the writing was on the wall when the recognisable fleet comprising a Jaguar; a top of the range BMW; Mrs Worley-Darling's little red Mini; a modest but sleek, royal blue Rover, and a vintage MG sports, was trumped by Jack Wildblood's chauffer driven Rolls Royce which slid into its appointed dock marked "Chair of Gov's." In the back, Wildblood peered up at Pelforth from beneath Wolf Man eyebrows. His huge be-jowled face filled the side window. His stare met Pelforth's. It seemed unremitting, thought Pelforth. Three seconds of Wildblood's piggy eyes being enough to communicate intense foreboding to all but senior officers of a KGB Interrogation Squad.

Wildblood was clearly reading from a script agreed in advance. The other governors sat silently looking down at the boardroom table. The local vicar, the Reverend Merryweather, who had arrived in the vintage MG, clasped his hands in seemingly pious prayer, whilst others silently drummed, tapped, scribbled and picked with fidgety fingers. Even Wildblood, when it came to it, kept his caterpillar eyebrows creased down over his eyelids, only occasionally glancing over his pince-nez.

Wildblood's cold stare was, for once, matched by that of another. It was clear to Adrian that his fate was sealed, and sealed by the man who had once urged him to industrial sabotage. Wildblood knew that, as Chair of Governors, his own reputation would soon be tarnished by this latest scandal, and a column had already appeared about his involvement with Stortfield in the satirical magazine *Private Eye*, which made regular derogatory references to his affairs.

Jack Wildblood tried to sound conciliatory and reluctant to pass judgement on Pelforth, but failed completely:

"Adrian, Adrian, Adrian," he repeated, shaking his head in feigned sorrow. "We are as one in our views of you as a dynamic, authoritative, highly respected Headmaster. You have driven this school onwards with dogged determination and skill. Stortfield has flourished under your leadership. The building works you have envisaged here has made this school one of the most desirable boarding schools in the country. In fact, one of the reasons I have called this meeting, is also to report that I have had reassurances, in the last twenty-four hours, that the local authority will drop all their objections to planning permission for the new theatre."

There was a ripple of staged applause from around the table. Pelforth smiled wryly at Wildblood, sensing the preamble was only an attempt to soften the passing of sentence. "But of course," continued the porcine industrialist, "we cannot ignore the expose in yesterday's *Sun* newspaper Adrian. This story has run for too long." Wildblood's Churchillian pretentions gradually emerged as he became more combative. "It is clear the good name of Stortfield can endure no more of this scandal, and that Mr Jenkins has lost control of Churchill House, and you have failed to advise him accordingly. Only this morning I received a call from the parents of the boy Timpson who, it appears, is seeking refuge in the home of a social worker after exposing these 'Vigilantes' as they're called. Now we both know that the boy should never have returned to Churchill, following his spell in hospital."

Adrian wasn't going to allow Wildblood an easy passage: "I don't recall you objecting to his reinstatement at the time," he interjected, staring down the length of the table.

"Well, as ever," countered Wildblood spitting out his words, quite literally projecting saliva over the carefully arranged fruit bowl before him: "I have always deferred to your greater experience in these matters. It has never been my inclination to undermine your integrity in educational issues."

"Until now–" responded the surly Pelforth, almost adopting the cynicism of some of his least favoured students.

"Well, you see Adrian… you've always been brave enough to stand or fall by your own decisions."

Adrian said nothing. He knew what was coming.

"We feel Adrian, around this table…" (Wildblood opened his fat arms as if to embrace his fellow governors) "… we feel that Stortfield needs a fresh start. A new image. We need to put this scandal behind us. Nobody wants to see these boys in the gang expelled. God forbid we should destroy such young lives." He emphasised 'young' all too explicitly for Pelforth.

"My friend, the Chief Constable suggests that the evidence of the video is inconclusive, and that the photographs only incriminate one or two boys, who I'm sure, can be dealt with. But first we must remove Mr Jenkins from his role as House Parent."

"And then?" prompted Pelforth, wishing to cut to the chase.

"Well, Adrian…" Wildblood took a deep sigh. "You're fifty-nine next birthday aren't you? You have the luxury of a good pension at sixty. I'm sure we'd make it worth your while to take an early retirement on, say, 'health grounds' at the end of the term."

"And we'd honour you, of course, Adrian," interrupted the Reverend Merryweather, trying to soften the blow.

"Yes, indeed," continued Wildblood. "We have a special honour in mind. We've been mulling it over, and we think it entirely appropriate to create a new award at prize-giving day, in your name."

Mrs Worley-Darling saw her moment: "Yes, we've been planning a new cup. The Adrian Pelforth Cup for the school's finest annual sporting achievement." She clapped her hands in misplaced delight, and looked to the room for approval. There was silence.

"That's it, is it?" Pelforth slightly chuckled as he spoke. "Years of service, of sacrifice, of dedication to the cause, and all you can give in return is a bloody tin-pot."

"Well a cup got you into this situation, Adrian," sneered Wildblood. "It seems entirely apt."

"And you, Jack?" re-countered Pelforth. "What will Stortfield dedicate to you, I wonder?"

"I have never done this for recognition, Adrian. Surely you know that?"

"Then–" said Pelforth, hitting the table with his fists, and standing– "I shall assume you will decline any suggestion that the new theatre be dedicated in your name."

"That is not for me to decide, Adrian."

There was a lengthy and uncomfortable pause as Pelforth stared down the table. The rest of the governors cast their eyes downwards. Pelforth suddenly realised how Caesar had felt in his last moments in the senate. Their discomfort was palpable.

Adrian walked slowly to the door. "I shall be out of the Headmaster's House by the end of term. I shall vacate the office to my First Deputy by the end of the week. You will, at least do me the service of granting me leave of absence with immediate effect. My resignation… and terms… will be with you tomorrow morning."

And with that, Adrian Pelforth departed the room – and his career as Headmaster of Stortfield School.

An hour later Wildblood's chauffer pulled into a quiet layby. The industrialist wanted to make sure his call would receive a good signal. The mobile phone was almost swallowed up into his sweaty, hairy hand:

"Hello Simon, Jack here. The deed is done. He's going. End of the week effectively. I'm expecting you to keep your half of the bargain."

Simon Petherton-Pugh put his feet up on the polished oak-panelled desk and smiled wryly.

"Of course, Jack. We're in this together. A safe seat for me, and I would think a 'K' is the least I can recommend."

Wildblood allowed himself a hint of a smile. He had long felt cheated of a 'K' as Simon had put it. He knew full well his combative, uncompromising personality and low beginnings had not helped him to win friends. His dubious business practices had brought him before parliamentary subcommittees on more than one occasion, and his party donations had not resulted in the elusive knighthood. Charm was not his speciality, so he had bought the one man he knew had it in spades – Petherton-Pugh.

"And you won't forget the other little part of the agreement, I hope?" Wildblood purred.

Petherton-Pugh looked less smug. He knew full well that this part of the deal could cost him dearly, particularly in his rekindled relationship with Viola McIntyre.

"I'm sure I have enough influence, if not with the school governors, then certainly with the council, to delay the building. You'll get your theatre first, Jack."

"I hope so Simon. I hope so" said Wildblood. And without so much as a polite farewell, his fat thumb fumbled for the 'off' button.

"Drive on" he barked to the chauffer, rapping on the glass divide between them… and then, almost to himself… "Drive on…"

CHAPTER 58

# DANCING WITH THE DEVIL

Belinda Bellingham-Steele was made of stern stuff, but her courage deserted her when it came to further confrontations with Nigel Slot.

Having moved her belongings to Jed's flat, she returned for one final, flaming row with the disgraced artist. The argument concluded with her hurling a door key directly at Slot, with force enough to cause him a sore eye for the best part of a week. Literally blinded with rage at the act, Nigel attempted to chase Belinda through the side passage of his terraced house and out into the street. As Belinda threw open the waist-high front garden gate, Slot's temporary blindness caused him to run with full force into the wrought iron construction as it was opening, bringing the sharp-pointed corner into contact with his groin.

Nigel was winded and wounded to such a degree that he

could barely stagger back into his kitchen. There, on the stained linoleum, he lay and moaned for some time. The moans soon became a cry, and the cry developed into abject weeping. Nigel had genuinely loved Belinda, and was of an age where finding such a young, intelligent, anarchic and sexually charged woman again was increasingly unlikely. He had danced with the devil, and he knew it.

Subsequently, Belinda had memorised Nigel's shift pattern with depressing familiarity, and so waited for him to leave the house early one evening, from the vantage point of Dorothy's house across the road. Dorothy was an elderly woman who Belinda had befriended, and who was only too pleased to receive Belinda's company.

Hidden by well-laundered net curtains, Belinda watched Slot close the slightly buckled garden gate, having wheeled his bike into the street. Finishing her tea and making her farewells to Dorothy, Belinda walked casually across the road to her old address, and slipped down the side passage into the back yard. Night was falling and Belinda had come prepared with a torch. So used to subterfuge was she, that this little act of breaking and entering was attempted with almost carefree abandon.

Belinda had returned to claim some important documents relating to her university application. These documents had been hidden from Nigel under an old dressing table in the spare room, the room she had taken to sleeping in during the latter days of their relationship.

Looking up from the backyard, she noticed the upstairs bathroom window was open. The bathroom was directly above the old, now defunct, outside toilet, and an adjoining outhouse of the century-old dwelling. Shinning up the drainpipe, Belinda climbed on the tiled roof of the outhouse. The roof was slanted and the tiles, old and worn. The outhouse had been used for storing garden implements and household junk. She carefully stepped across the roof. A tile slipped and smashed on the concrete yard below. "Shit!" she exclaimed under her breath. The next-door neighbours would have clearly heard the commotion as their kitchen window looked out on Slot's yard. She rapidly moved towards the upper bathroom window. Suddenly, she felt the tiles beneath her start to give, and the sound of rotten timber creaking. Belinda grabbed the drainpipe and took a high step onto the bathroom window ledge, but couldn't keep her balance. Another tile slipped, she stumbled backwards, planting her right foot down firmly to break her fall. This time, the roof gave way under her weight, and a hole opened up beneath her. Belinda held her breath, expecting a heavy landing, but was spared possible injury by a short stack of wooden boxes, forming a convenient platform onto which she broke her fall. Her knees gave way and she slipped down onto the firm crates beneath her. For a moment she lay back, staring at the hole in the roof. A flashing neon light suddenly reflected on the wall now visible above her. Clearly the kitchen light had come on next door. She thought it better to wait in the musty outhouse, and took out her pocket torch. The crates beneath her were clearly marked "Property of Doulting Stone."

"Typical" she thought, "Nigel's pension plan. He'll be flogging this on the net." Belinda decided it wouldn't be a bad idea to find out more about Nigel's felonies, thus accumulating useful evidence against him, if ever the need arose. The boxes on top were marked, "Paint-Green." She levered open the top of the crate with a small garden spade. Nigel wasn't the type to decorate, she thought. As she shone her torch into the case, she realised that this was not paint, but something far more intriguing. A slight shiver ran through her as looked more closely at the packed items. Under the tiny torchlight she saw something only a fool, madman, or hardened criminal would wish to conceal in their shed. The labels read:

"PROPERTY OF DOULTING STONE LTD. DANGER-HIGH EXPLOSIVE. STORE IN COOL PLACE. KEEP AWAY FROM NAKED FLAMES."

Belinda had been sitting on enough dynamite to start a small war.

CHAPTER 59

# BUCKLED

Nigel Slot shivered as he paced in the layby. He looked down and realised he was still wearing his cycle clips. He rapidly bent down and removed them, hanging them over the crossbar of his bike.

It was a long ride to the layby on the road out of Storton, leading to its eastern lying villages, but at least the journey was mainly flat.

Ten minutes after the allotted time, he saw headlights approaching from a distance. The pace of the car was cautious and controlled. Slowly it pulled into the layby. Slot was confused when a second car pulled in behind the first. From the second car, two heavy-set men emerged and approached him menacingly.

"Can I help you?" said Slot squeamishly.

"Yes, sir, you can" replied one of the men politely. He had the bearing of a soldier, and before Slot could continue, the man had quickly stepped behind him and held him firmly by the shoulders.

"Oi! Fuck off! What is this?" Slot shouted.

The second 'heavy' took the initiative. "Nothing to be frightened about Mr Slot. It's just that before you go for a little drive with Mr Wildblood, we need to search you. Mr Wildblood is a very influential man. He has had to step up his security of late."

Rapidly, the man behind Slot lifted the artist's arms, while his comrade conducted a body search.

"What? Wildblood thinks I'm tooled up, does he? For fuck's sake!"

The henchmen said nothing. "What's this?" said the one facing him, pulling out a cell phone from Slot's inside jacket pocket.

"It's my phone. What does it look like?"

"This could be problematical," replied the dark clad military-style man. "Mr Wildblood appreciates his privacy. He wouldn't want you using the phone in his company, would he? I mean you could be relaying this private meeting, or recording it. Now we can't have that." With that, the smaller man who searched him, snatched Slot's phone away.

"What are you doing with that? That's –like – private property." Slot realised he was beginning to sound like a bullied schoolboy.

"You'll get it back," said the small man, "just as soon as this little interview ends." He slipped the phone into his jacket pocket and tapped twice on the passenger window of the first car, a Range Rover, which had remained stationary, with its engine running throughout. The electric passenger window descended slowly. Slot looked up to glimpse Jack Wildblood's wide head silhouetted against the driver's side window. "Get in," the gruff voice called out from within. Dutifully, Nigel clambered aboard.

Wildblood was unfamiliar in casual dress, wearing a beige Fair Isle sweater over a cotton checked shirt, like a gentleman farmer. He engaged the gears with the crunch of a driver more used to being chauffer driven.

"Where are we going?" demanded Slot. "I've got a bike in the layby."

"My boys will look after it. We'll just drive for a while and then I'll drop you back."

"What's this all about then?" Nigel enquired impetuously.

"There's been a change of plan."

"Yeah?"

"We don't need you to do the work."

Slot paused for a second, keeping calm.

"Why?"

"Well, I'm not necessarily obliged to tell you – but the matter has been resolved –diplomatically, you might say."

"What d'you mean?"

"We've laid off Pelforth. The Vigilantes have been rumbled anyway. We couldn't blame the job on them now. The police have been called in. Criminal proceedings against some of the boys. They were caught on film. So much of this small town espionage seems to be going on now. That's why I had you searched. Apparently your ex-girlfriend was involved – and her new man – the ace reporter."

"I know – I heard," replied Nigel, sulkily. "I still want paying."

"Even though you've done nothing. I don't see why I should pay you." Wildblood's voice dropped.

"Done nothing?" Despite them being in a car, Slot felt obliged to drop his voice – suppressing his anger behind a course whisper:

"Done nothing? Have you the faintest idea what it took to smuggle that stuff out of Doulting's yard?"

"You said you worked in the warehouse. Can't have been that hard."

"Yes, but they don't let you take fucking Semtex home to play with. It's not Plasticine."

"Did anyone suspect?"

"No – not that I know of."

"I'm astonished," replied Wildblood shaking his head in mock disgust. "What with all these terrorists about, and you can just walk out of a quarry loaded up to your arsehole in dynamite." He laughed wheezily, and broke into a cough.

"They're not really looking for a man on a bike."

"How much did you get?"

"Not a lot. Just enough to make the kind of mess you asked for. Anyway, it's no use to me now. What the fuck am I going to do with it?"

"Where is it?"

"In my outhouse at home – next to the outside toilet."

"Christ on a bike!" wheezed Wildblood. "You don't want to be smoking on the lav!"

"You might think it funny" Nigel whined under Wildblood's continued rasping laughter. "I haven't a fucking clue what to do with it. You said you'd pay me enough to set me up in a pad in Goa. Now what?"

"Look, I didn't expect things to turn out as they have," Jack Wildblood abruptly responded. "Take a look in the glove box."

Slot did as he was told. The glove box light came on to

reveal a roll of banknotes sitting on a neatly folded pair of Wildblood's driving gloves.

"It's yours. Take it."

"How much?"

"Three grand. Not bad for doing nothing."

"It's not nearly enough" said Nigel, snatching the money and stashing it rapidly in his breast pocket, before Wildblood could change his mind.

"Not enough?" snorted Wildblood, with contempt.

"I've put myself on the line for you. If I was caught nicking that stuff, I'd go down. And I'd have to tell them everything, as well. You owe me."

"Everything?" Wildblood replied calmly. "Who's going to believe you?"

"What would I have to gain by demolishing a school theatre?"

"Revenge, Nigel. You were planning on doing the job and blaming it on your little girlfriend. Ex-girlfriend I should say. And you'd want to stitch me up, wouldn't you? And Pelforth too, I shouldn't wonder. You have motives enough. And form. You have a past."

"What do you mean?" Nigel was unsure as to how much Wildblood knew about him.

Well, that little escapade at the Parents' Day for a start."

"That was nothing."

"Then there was a little matter of the art fraud."

There was a pause. Nigel shifted uneasily in his seat.

"What do you know about that?"

"I make it my business to know."

"I did my time for that."

"Oh yes. You did your time for the two they discovered. But

what about the others, Nigel? The police knew you were the forger, but the paintings were on their way to Dubai by then. I know one or two well-connected businessmen over there who would love to know your address."

There was an uncomfortable silence. It began to rain. Wildblood switched on the windscreen wipers.

"Dirty night," he said with irony.

Nigel knew had had no response. Wildblood had him bang to rights. Perhaps if he could get more information…

"What I don't get is why you wanted me to go to all that trouble. What's it to you? Stortvale's a run-down, bog standard comprehensive. Why do you need to interfere with their one chance to make an impression?"

"You're getting into the kind of detail you don't need to know about."

"So–?"

"Well, let's put it this way. I've put up a lot of time and effort into developing Stortfield. A theatre was all the school needed to make it one of the best equipped public schools in the country – the world, even. And that's important to me, personally and politically. It reflects on me. A modern day philanthropist. It wins one friends. So when this 'bog standard comprehensive' comes along and attempts to steal my thunder, I simply can't allow it to happen."

"Yeah but your deal will always be – like – bigger and better. Pretentious theatre types would always prefer the prestige of the snooty surroundings of Stortfield to Stortvale at – like – the arse-end of town.

"I'd agree. But when our friends Petherton-Pugh and Viola McIntyre climbed into bed with Stortvale, the local Operatic mob-bloody SODS, went with them."

"Big deal."

"Big deal indeed. The Stortvale lot are supported by Lady Doulting, a woman with more political clout than you'd ever believe. And a woman who doesn't like me much. She's already got far too much recognition for patronising the great unwashed. Not only that, the cow has bad-mouthed me in all the most influential places. A man in my position would have expected greater recognition long before now. There was something rather satisfying about destroying her little dream with her own… well, never mind." Wildblood stopped short.

"So – that's it? You just want a fucking knighthood or something, and she's put the oar in?"

"Not entirely. This project had financial implications," said Wildblood.

"What do you mean? Nigel looked at him from the corner of his eye.

"Prestige. Deals were done. Favours called in."

"Bribes?" interrupted Nigel.

"That's a little harsh Nigel. It's a competitive field. Harrow is planning an art gallery you know. We're all playing the same game. Public schools are non-taxable – and want to stay that way. But they can't exactly make political donations, can they? To claim non-profit status they need to re-invest their surpluses into building projects. So the right builder comes along, charges a substantial price for the work, but agrees to make a healthy donation to the appropriate party in return. Wheels within wheels."

"Fuck me. It's even more bent than I imagined. So, you're already up against Harrow and you need to keep the construction businesses sweet."

"Well done, Nigel. You're very good at subterfuge."

"Yes, but Stortvale High School isn't in your league, is it?"

"Not knowingly, but Lady Doulting would certainly be looking for favours from friends in construction as well as me."

Nigel shook his head and sighed. "So what's changed? Why don't you need me anymore?"

"Ah well, you see, none of us much liked old Pelforth. A little man by nature. He was looking to take all the credit. In the end he allowed his little gang of thugs too much leeway. He would have let them do a bit of a wrecking job on Stortvale's shitty little theatre, but nothing that couldn't be rectified in five minutes. He hated Petherton-Pugh and his bitch, and was desperate to see his name in lights on the theatre billboard. Now I've got Petherton-Pugh back on my team and he's using his influence to hold up the Stortvale project, so we don't need to go to extremes."

"And, of course, 'The Wildblood Theatre' does have-like-a dramatic ring to it."

"Do you think so, Nigel? I'm so glad. This is where you get out." Wildblood turned quite suddenly into layby. They had circumnavigated the Storton ring road but something wasn't right.

"Hang on. This isn't where you picked me up."

"No, I shot past it, about a mile ago, sorry."

"Fuck off. Drive me back you double-crossing cunt!" yelled Nigel. At which point the car door opened and a large fist bunched around Slot's collar.

"You – out!" came the voice in the dark.

Nigel was dragged from the car. "Alright, alright. I don't need any help!" he spat, recognising Wildblood's bodyguards.

"I think you do," replied a second voice.

Suddenly Slot found himself wrestled to the ground. He

looked up with his left eye as his right cheek was pinned to the tarmac. Wildblood was lying flat across the car seats, his fat head protruding through the open door. It was a fearsome sight, and Slot pitied any woman forced to look at it from such an angle.

"Now then Slot, you lying little bastard," Wildblood enunciated. "Let this be an end to your devious little game of espionage and sabotage. You've got your money and if you breathe a word of what's happened here tonight – you may never sit on that outside toilet of yours in confidence again. You'll be flinching every time you fart. Ha ha! Remember, there's many a rich Arab would like to cut your fucking hands off!"

With that, Wildblood's head disappeared from view, and the car door was slammed. The two henchmen lifted Slot to his feet.

"Now then," said one, staring at Nigel from no more than six inches away. Each staccato syllable of what he said next was emphasised with a prodding two fingered jab to Nigel's solar plexus: "You–do–as–Mr-Wildblood–says. Get it?"

Slot bent forward. There was just enough air in his lungs to exhale "Fuck off" into the cold night air.

The second thug pulled Slot up to his full height by a handful of hair.

"I don't think you understand." This time a forcible punch to the gut, made Nigel fold in two, like a drunk spewing in the gutter.

"Yessss," he hissed, hardly able to catch his breath. He fell to his knees, gasping. "Just leave it. Leave me. I'll do whatever."

"Of course you will" came the reply, followed by a boot to

the ribs.

Nigel whined in agony, clutching his side. “No more… please… no… more.”

“Now fuck off back to your fucking push bike” said the ‘goon’. As Nigel tried to rise, he felt the force of another boot into his coccyx. “That’s the way!” laughed the thug as if about to kick him in the right direction. Hearing an approaching car, they quickly moved to their own vehicle, its engine running and ready for a quick exit.

“Oh, and here’s your phone,” said the smaller man, before stamping on it with the heel of his boot, picking it up and throwing it over the hedge into the dark of the field beyond. Before Nigel could raise himself up fully, he was blinded by the car’s headlights as it took off, swerving close enough to cause him to fall back into the hedge, which clung to his clothes and scratched his face and hands. The wet tyres flashed up a shower of rainwater, which mingled with the blood around his face. He spat and wiped his hand with his sleeve.

Staggering breathlessly through the rain, Slot seriously doubted whether he had the strength to pedal his bike home. He needn’t have worried. When he returned to the original layby Nigel’s bicycle lay on the ground, the wheels buckled, and the frame flattened to the road.

CHAPTER 60

# FANCY DRESS

To the innocent bystander, it might have appeared that they had ventured into a time-warp in which King Richard the Third was making love to Tess of the d'Urbervilles. This was, however, a fairly normal scenario in the costume barn of Storton Operatic and Dramatic Society.

Despite their best intentions, and the threat of unpleasant outcomes for them both, Simon Petherton-Pugh and Viola McIntyre had resumed what was (for them) normal practice.

Neither were truly happy in the more mundane environment of Stortvale High. Whilst Simon saw his role on the Board of Governors as a public duty, Viola had become steadily depressed by the daily grind of classes of over thirty. She had also underestimated how difficult it would be to cast a school play from teenagers whose essential extracurricular activities were stacking shelves, babysitting and serving burgers.

Her first attempt at a school play had been heavily

dependent on willing girls playing grown men. *The Accrington Pals* a First World War epic, did have its virtues, and was a great deal more polished than any previous production in the old school hall. It had been a good start, and some of the performances highly commendable, but Viola knew she was in for a long slog.

Simon had decided to break the news to Viola at a more strategic time – that is to say postcoital. As they reclined on the moth-eaten pile of old costumes on the mezzanine floor of the barn, Simon conveyed a suitable, if Machiavellian, charm in his Richard the Third costume – complete with padded hump:

"So – er, what's your next show with the school then? Any ideas?"

"Well," replied 'Tess' coyly from beneath her Victorian Sunday bonnet, "I was actually thinking of having a go at *Tess of the d'Urbervilles*," she said in a mock Dorset accent whilst opening the palm of her hand and moving it down her body, in simple demonstration. "I've read a good adaptation. Lots of girls' parts – and the males in it are all a bit stereotyped, so I expect we'd find a couple of lads who might cope."

Viola was sounding more optimistic than usual. "I think the theatre will be an incentive, don't you?"

"Oh absolutely, absolutely" Simon responded, a trifle too enthusiastically. "It's just that it might be a good idea to keep your powder dry for now."

"What do you mean?" Viola was immediately suspicious. She was familiar with Simon's diplomatic manoeuvrings.

"I mean that before you decide on your opening show for the new theatre, you might be advised to make sure it's all on schedule."

"What's the problem?"

"The builders have hit a snag."

"Oh God… no…" Viola exclaimed in anticipation, as she sat up.

Simon continued: "There's been a complaint to the Planning Department."

"What sort of complaint?" said Viola, impatiently tearing off the ridiculous bonnet.

"Worthy type in the Equal Opportunities Department, says we need a lift up to the balcony. Disabled access, you see."

"But you said as long as we had wheelchair access downstairs, it wouldn't matter."

"Well it turns out that there's a case for disabled people wanting to use the lighting control room. They won't be able to. It's a fair point."

"Yes – but what other theatre has disabled access in the control room?"

These new regulations are very tough. Only apply to new buildings."

"So, what are we going to do?"

"Looks like we'll just have to put in a lift."

"Well, do it then."

"It's not as easy as that. To start with, the architects will have to redesign the foyer and the balcony to accommodate the lift shaft. Then there's the cost."

"How much?"

"Anyone's guess really. Could be twenty, thirty thousand – of that order. There's grants of course, but applying for them can take time.

"How long?"

"Well… I'm loath to be pessimistic but…" At this Viola braced herself, Simon's hesitation was self-evident: "Indefinite,

I'm afraid. Six months at best, perhaps a year." Simon tried to look sympathetic. "I know how much this means to you."

Viola almost jumped to her feet, simmering. "What it means to me?! Look at me! Look at all this! This stupid bloody get-up!" She started tearing at the costume, struggling temperamentally with the eye hooks in the back of the Victorian dress. "You meet me here. I get into these ridiculous costumes. I risk being humiliatingly exposed and pried upon, my entire marriage at stake; and when you've casually had your fun, you completely dash my hopes of any kind of relief from this appalling, drab, mundane, unremitting bloody torture." With each adverb she tore at the eyehooks, loosening some from the shabby costume.

Simon stood up, raising his hands defensively: "Calm down… really… this isn't my fault. I'm doing what I can to make it all work."

"Are you Simon?" yelled Viola as the dress dropped to her feet. "Are you?" she repeated, kicking the costume across the floor.

Simon, similarly peeling off his Mediaeval tights, was slightly turned on by her insane striptease, but realised this was not the time to make further advances. "Of course, darling. You know I'd do anything to help things work out for you."

Viola was given to a diva's temperament. She had endured years of frustration. The failed marriages; the classroom conflicts; the local amateur scene which provided a poor refuge for her considerable gifts as an actress; and the debacle that left her humiliated at Stortfield. At least there she had a semblance of self-esteem.

"Would you do anything Simon? Would you walk away from that indulged little wife for me? Would you give up your political ambitions for me?"

"Oh don't be ridiculous Viola. We're not about all this."

"All this what? Commitment?"

"Look, it's a setback, that's all. I want to build this theatre as much as you do."

"Do you Simon?" Viola snapped back as she slid into her slacks.

"Will you stop doing that?" Simon replied sharply, as he fumbled amongst faux clothing, for his own.

"What?" replied Viola, hurriedly buttoning her blouse.

"All that questioning: 'Do you Simon? Will you Simon?'"

"Then tell me, Simon; if we're 'not about all this', what are we about?"

"I don't bloody know. Why have you suddenly turned on me? It's as if you're blaming me."

"Why? I'll tell you why! Because you persuaded me to lie to my husband to come out here for a quick shag in a silly fucking outfit, and then, when you've spilled your semen all over a tatty costume, you calmly tell me that I'm going to spend another year in that stinking, sweaty excuse for a school drama studio, before I get the one thing that's kept me in hope since I started there. And you know what's worse? It's knowing that those bastards over at Stortfield will now get there before us, and the Society will be clamouring to move there instead."

"It's just a bloody building, Viola, bricks and mortar."

"It may be bricks and mortar to you Simon, but to me – it's a lifeline." At this point, she slid her antique neckerchief from her throat and threw it, with a backhanded flick, at him. She picked up her handbag and began to pick her way through the dusty costumes to the door.

"Viola, darling, I understand. It must be terribly frustrating."

"You know it's fucking well frustrating! Anyone with an ounce of feeling would know that. Anyone with the slightest sensitivity would know what I've been going through. And that person might think it appropriate to discuss the matter with a bit of urgency and tact. Not, Simon, after a carefully arranged fuck in fancy dress."

And with that, Viola McIntyre, stomped to the door, dragging and kicking at the ill-kept loose garments around her. "I'll leave you to lock the door behind you" she hissed, and made her final, dramatic, exit.

Simon was of a mind to follow her, but there was only so much guilt he could take. Someone in the Council Planning Department had told him that the best way to obstruct building development was to: "Play the disabled card. Always gets the sympathy vote."

"He obviously wasn't accounting for the greater self-interest of Viola McIntyre" thought Simon.

CHAPTER 61

# PRETTY VACANT

Belinda Bellingham-Steele was also feeling a little guilty. She wasn't really interested in her old neighbour Dorothy, but arranged to pay her another friendly visit for a cup of tea as soon as word got out that Nigel Slot had left town.

Since discovering the explosives, Belinda hadn't slept well. She knew Nigel was a trifle unhinged, but dealing with dynamite was more than she imagined of him. Ever since telling Jed, the two of them had grown quite paranoid. Jed had taken to checking underneath his car for suspicious packages.

Belinda had considered going to the police, but she wanted no more to do with Slot and feared provoking unnecessary reprisals from him. She had also been breaking and entering when she discovered the cache. Then there was Jed's nose for a scoop. "Why let the local plod bugger up the investigation anyway?" he had flippantly remarked.

Belinda had hoped, naively, there was a simple, innocent explanation, but couldn't put her mind at rest.

As she sat drinking tea with Dorothy, Belinda kept her eye on the house across the street with its To Let sign propped up by the front gate. Nothing stirred.

Having promised disingenuously to Dorothy that she would call again, Belinda slipped out of the spinster's house and discreetly down the side passage of Slot's former abode, opposite. She grabbed the drainpipe by the outhouse and, with accustomed agility, anchored her feet sufficiently to take a few steps up the wall and step out onto the outhouse roof. The broken tiles had been repaired. It was an amateur job, no doubt the handiwork of Nigel. The old tiles had simply been placed over the hole and stuck down with an instant adhesive. She kneeled down and prized up the broken tiles with the merest resistance from the white paste holding them in place. Removing a small torch from her jacket pocket, Belinda shone the light down into the hole. The old coal store was empty. Nigel had gone, and his arsenal had gone with him. On the bare floor below her, she saw a piece of cardboard, torn from a box, fixed in place under a couple of small stones. There was an enigmatic message, written in thick black felt pen:

"BELINDA – GONE-BUT NOT FORGOTTEN – KEEP SAFE"

Belinda didn't know whether to feel relieved or not.

CHAPTER 62

# SENTENCES

Gareth Chivers stood in the dock. Linda had made sure he looked his best, but a shaving cut had opened by his throat, and a speck of blood had infiltrated his collar. Gareth's tie knot had slipped under his collar too and his shirt was hanging out to one side. He was sweating profusely. Linda wept when she saw him in the dock. An otherwise clean shirt couldn't hide a broken man.

Adrian Pelforth hadn't waited for the verdict. He had given his evidence and wanted to return as swiftly as possible to his new home in Dorset. Edwin Slater, his old Bursar, had served as an eyewitness and stayed on, vowing to phone the former Headmaster as soon as he knew.

There was a point when Pelforth nearly withdrew his evidence, but when his wife Marjorie told him he was being "an utter fool, vindictive, and an idiot" for allowing a fellow headmaster to be prosecuted, he obstinately proceeded. He wanted to leave Storton with "right on his side."

Pelforth had been surprised however, by the level of support for Chivers in the local paper, and expressed by a gathering of thirty or more very verbose friends, parents and pupils outside the court rooms. Adrian's own appearance that morning had been met by howling, derisory chants and hostile catcalling. He left the court by the side door in fear of further physical recrimination.

The Crown Prosecution service had brought a charge against Gareth Chivers of Common Assault. Gareth had denied the charge on the grounds of Diminished Responsibility. Indeed, his subsequent behaviour was sufficiently unorthodox to have persuaded Linda that he really was going quite mad and needed to retire before it was too late.

Gareth resisted the idea at first, but reality eventually struck him, as surely as he had struck Pelforth on that fateful day. No matter what the outcome of the trial, his reputation had been tarnished. The adrenaline rush he experienced on waking every morning was no longer there. He began to feel tired and listless, as he used to during the summer holidays, but this was without end. Recharging batteries was all very well, but trying to let go was more difficult than he imagined. He knew another school inspection was due and he couldn't face the intrusion, the scrutiny and the inevitable anger it would cause. He also knew the type of person who became a school inspector in these times, and even if the court found him innocent, the inspectors would be sharpening their knives.

"It wouldn't be so bad if you played golf, I suppose," Linda had said.

"Never had the time love," he had replied mournfully. Besides, he couldn't face the local golf club. Full of old

Stortfieldians, and their parents alike.

Gareth stood staring into space as the judge, a tired looking man of sixty, pronounced the verdict:

"Gareth Owain Chivers, this court finds you guilty of the serious offence of Common Assault. While it is apparent this incident has had a profound effect on you, it has not been possible to prove that you were in any way suffering from the symptoms of diminished responsibility at the time. Indeed, witnesses for both Prosecution and Defence have noted you were apparently robust both physically and mentally, when the assault took place. I find it extraordinary that, in your defence, you admit that you hadn't intended to strike Mr Pelforth, a highly respected member of your own profession, but that you had intended instead, to physically admonish one of his pupils. We do not live in Dickensian times, Mr Chivers. I shouldn't have to remind a man in your position that this shows a level of irresponsible yobbishness, unacceptable even amongst your own pupils. Furthermore, you are lucky, Mr Chivers. Had you made contact with a pupil of school age, whether in your own school or another, the charge would have been very much more serious, with the possibility of you leaving an otherwise respectable career in abject shame, and perhaps even with your pension rights withdrawn."

Gareth's solicitor had warned him that claiming self-defence against a school pupil would do him no good, but drowsy and confused by the effects of antidepressants; Gareth had fallen into the prosecution's trap.

The judge, his face grimacing in distaste continued: "This whole, ridiculous rivalry between two local schools has become wildly out of control. You did nothing to subdue this conflict. Indeed, by allowing your own school to import professionally trained rugby players from France, you showed a distinct and cynical disregard for the spirit of fair play and integrity. For you, winning and revenge were more important than the game itself, and when there was an inevitable explosion of aggression, you were only too ready to become involved. It would appear that you have suffered enough for your loss of judgement. I am, therefore, passing a sentence of some lenience. You are fined £1000, and bound over to keep the peace for a term of eighteen months."

Linda Chivers wept audibly. Gareth just stood and stared, as if in a trance, his face immobile.

Within a month, the same judge presided over the case of the Crown versus three pupils from Stortfield Academy including Chivers assailant, Percy Humphries. In summing up, he took pity on the pupils, believing that the charges of Trespass Causing Wilful Damage and Common Assault on one Philip Hart, were no more than "high spirits." The students had been "led astray" and suffering expulsion from "such a well-respected public school" was surely punishment enough. It was the judge's view that Community Service would only bring these "impressionable young men into the company of those who would be an inappropriate and pernicious influence."

The judge concluded that their parents had suffered enough, having spent so much on their education, and to endow the boys with a criminal record would destroy their intentions to seek commissions in Her Majesty's Armed Services.

Pelforth, having slipped away from court unnoticed by the mob, took a short walk to the station. The train journey back to Dorset gave him adequate time for reflection, and he felt satisfied and exonerated. He had, at least, brought that smug bastard Chivers down with him.

As the taxi pulled into his drive, he noted the reflection of the harbour lights in the bay, and the tranquil sound of a settled sea. Perhaps, he thought, he could now move on with his life. Perhaps, following this experience, he would volunteer his services as a magistrate.

The house was dark. The in-set lights flickered on, illuminating the state-of-the-art kitchen, upon which Marjorie had insisted, but rarely used. He saw a note set on a glass-topped kitchen table secured in place by an empty prosecco bottle.

Adrian sighed, expecting another "dinner in the oven" missive. He had grown used to this since his retirement, Marjorie having found it easier to socialise than him, in their new life. He could see though, the note was a little more detailed than usual.

"Congratulations!" it began. "That vile man Slater phoned me with the good news. You must be very pleased with yourself. No one I ever met in Storton had a bad word to say about Gareth Chivers – except you. His poor wife used to volunteer at the local hospice you know. She must be devastated. Anyway – you've had your revenge – and now I shall have mine. Jeremy is unwell. Minor surgery involved-gall bladder. Nothing serious, but he will need time to recover. He didn't see the point in bothering you with it. I said I'd go up to Aberdeen to help in the shop. It may not be as tranquil and twee as down here, but at least, up there, his life seems to have taken on some kind of meaning. Perhaps mine will too… I intend to stay for as long as he will let me. I've taken the car. I don't see why I shouldn't. Perhaps if you'd let me drive more often, I would have managed to stay sober. I'm sober now – in case you're thinking otherwise. I emptied the bottle down the sink.

"I think what I'm trying to say, Adrian, is for the foreseeable future at least… I'm leaving you. Dinner is not in the oven. Nor is it likely to be again… Marjorie"

CHAPTER 63

# TEA

"So he's gone?" said Lady Doulting, raising her bone china cup. "Oh dear."

"Afraid so m'Lady," Raymond Chater confirmed.

Raymond's weekly briefing with Lady Doulting was very much in the mould of the prime minister's audience with the Queen. The difference was that most prime ministers only had to put up with it for a few years. Raymond was now twenty-eight years into his tenure as PR Executive of Doulting Stone.

"Yes, I rather liked Nigel," Lady Doulting said, with a sigh. "A maverick of course, but very talented."

"Indeed," responded Raymond, imperceptibly raising his eyes to the ornate drawing room ceiling.

"Any idea of his whereabouts?"

"Don't know, I'm afraid. He just didn't turn up for work one Monday morning. E mailed Human Resources to say he's been called away on family matters and wouldn't be returning. That was the last we heard of him. Apparently hadn't paid his rent for two months."

"He never spoke to me of his family. I do feel a little let down. He was desperate for work. We couldn't have been more accommodating."

Raymond was eager to move the conversation on:

"Well, if we hear anything, you'll be the first to know. More importantly, we've had some bad news on the Stortvale Theatre plan."

"Oh dear, builders I expect," came Lady Doulting's clipped reply.

"No, planning problems. There's been a hold-up. The planners apparently overlooked the need for a disabled lift to the balcony. It's quite a set-back. It'll add another thirty thousand on the bill.

"Thirty thousand? Oh dear. Doulting Stone has already put enough in. The Board wouldn't stand for more. We're laying off men at the moment, you know."

Chater tried not to sound patronising. "Yes, I'm aware of that m'lady. I wouldn't suggest another donation," he added disingenuously. "There are grants available, I understand, but it takes a long time to make all the applications. Even then, we may only receive a contribution."

Lady Doulting, having been looking through the window to Slot's horrific sculptures, returned her gaze to Raymond. "Does this mean Stortfield will steal a march on us?"

"Undoubtedly, Lady Doulting. The theatre there is now progressing rapidly," replied the remorseful sounding Raymond.

"Hmmm, Jack Wildblood will be smug. Perhaps we should

have stuck to Nigel's sculpture park after all. Pity someone couldn't put a spoke in their wheels."

"Yes, indeed, a great pity" Chater responded, hoping she'd take the hint.

There was a pause as they simultaneously sipped their Earl Grey, and gazed across the gracious lawns.

Lady Doulting broke the silence. "So how did we find out about this planning problem?"

"Simon Petherton Pugh was told directly by the Head of Planning."

"And nothing mentioned before?"

"No, apparently not. New legislation he says."

"Strange you know" Lady Doulting began, with a dry sense of mischief in her tone: "When I was at a charity function at the Savoy last week, Wildblood was also there with Petherton-Pugh. The two of them were like peas in a pod. It seems Mr Pelforth's fall from grace has proved the bloodletting Stortfield needed.

"Really, m'lady?" said Raymond, raising a quizzical eyebrow. Well, isn't that interesting?"

CHAPTER 64

# HAND GRENADES

Raymond Chater was nothing if not well connected. A swift meeting over lunch with the Chief Executive of Storton District Council had confirmed his suspicions: There was absolutely no requirement for a disabled access lift in the theatre, but even the Chief Executive himself couldn't override the council's decision to insist on the provision.

On discovering the news, he felt it essential to impart the information to Viola McIntyre who, he suspected, had renewed 'operations' with Simon Petherton-Pugh. If anyone could stop Simon's double-dealing, he thought, it would be Viola. If not, then at least it might have the effect of getting rid of the traitor in their midst.

Viola was cleaning up the drama studio after another frantic day of endless noise and confrontation. The door was open, so Raymond knocked politely before entering. Viola was picking up screwed up balls of paper from the floor. A group of fifteen year old boys had decided that 'hand grenades' were needed in their improvisation around life in the First World War trenches. The impro had escalated into a full scale riot, over which Viola had virtually no control.

Delicately bending over to pick up the paper, she didn't hear Raymond knocking:

"Er… hello. You got a minute, my dear?"

Viola was not one to be patronised, but somehow when Raymond Chater called her 'my dear' it was done with a genuine sense of avuncular affection and old-fashioned courtesy. He had always been one of the more amiable and less egotistical of her leading men in the Storton Operatic and Dramatic Society.

"Oh hello Raymond," she said, trying unconvincingly to sound cheerful. As she stood and brushed back her hair from her eyes, Chater could see that she'd been crying.

"Oh dear. Have I called at a bad time?" he asked.

"No. Shut the door, please… if you don't mind." Her voice was about to break.

"Of course." Raymond closed the door and turned to see Viola sitting on a sad looking plastic chair, its legs bent and wobbling a little. Her knees were clamped together, her feet turned in, her head bowed and her hands clasped before her.

"I'm sorry," she sobbed. "You've caught me at the end of a very bad day."

Raymond realised his timing might be disastrous.

"Oh. Difficult classes?"

"They're always difficult" said Viola between sniffs. "But it isn't that."

"What then?" said Raymond, pulling up a chair and sitting beside her…

"I should never have taken this job. I'm sorry Raymond; I feel I'm letting you down."

"You're not letting me down in the least. You're the best Head of Drama this school's ever had."

"No, I'm not. I'm useless. I'm alright with the brighter ones. I can put on a show in the hall. But that's all I do. Put on a show. The rest of the time, it's a bloody battle. I've been spoiled, I know, at Stortfield, but I was arrogant enough to think I could just walk in here and make a difference."

"Well, you have. You have no idea how bad it was before."

"Oh thanks," Viola sniggered through her sobs. "Damning with faint praise."

"I didn't mean it like that, of course, my dear," Raymond rapidly responded with a gentle pat on her wrist. "This isn't an easy school. It takes time to adjust. You'll be better prepared next year."

"No – I don't think I will, Raymond. I'd like to believe you, but really I took this job for all the wrong reasons."

"What do you mean?"

"Well, I needed to work. I wasn't going to be a kept woman. My marriage was on its last legs. I needed security. This was just offered on a plate. It was just too convenient."

"Too convenient for Stortvale too. It's not every day a teacher of your standing comes along," replied Raymond.

Viola was not easily consoled. "I could see that, by coming here, I would inherit the new theatre. I dreamed of having that theatre at Stortfield, and it was taken away from me. I wanted to get my own back on that bastard Pelforth, and I knew I could steal Stortfield's thunder, but I can't go through this every day, just so I have a toy theatre to play in. I never was that struck with teaching, even at Stortfield. I muddled through and lived for school plays and the long holidays."

"Oh, you're being hard on yourself Viola. Everybody has times when they just get by… when the job gets the better of them."

"But this is every day. And it gets worse. When Gareth Chivers was here, at least I knew I could get support. He could deal with the difficult kids in his own way. Philip Hart is – well I shouldn't say this to you, but I have to – he's useless. I hope to God he doesn't get the job permanently. He does everything by the book. He's more interested in scrutinising the staff, than supporting them. He walks in, watches my lessons for ten minutes, and then sends me notes about 'reinforcing learning outcomes' and 'plenary sessions'. And yet, when I send him some errant young hooligan who has just told me to 'fuck off' – it is recorded in some register and nothing else is done. I just didn't know it could be this bad."

"Oh dear." Chater was mentally abandoning his plans to reveal to Viola his news. "Well, I'm glad you've mentioned it. The governors need to know these things, if we're to consider Philip as the permanent Headmaster…"

"It's not just that–" Viola said abruptly – but then paused.

"Yes?"

"It's Simon."

"Ah." Raymond sensed he knew what was coming.

"We started seeing one another again," said Viola with a hint of shame.

"I had a feeling that was the case."

"I really wanted to let go when I left Stortfield, but having him on the governors here made it too easy to fall back into old ways. I needed some support. My husband has never been a good listener. Simon has always been kind."

"Indeed," Raymond acknowledged, with as much sincerity as he could.

"But–" there was more from Viola.

"Yes?" Chater countered.

"But I've seen the other side of him."

"Right…"

"This business over the delay in the building. I don't know why he didn't warn me earlier. He's become so distant. Even more engrossed in his own importance. We had quite a row."

"Well…." Raymond took a deep breath, seizing the opportunity that was beginning to emerge. "I suppose I'd better tell you why I came here."

"Is it to do with Simon?"

"Yes. I'm afraid he seems to have fallen back in with Stortfield. Did you know?"

"I suspected as much."

"Yes. He's made his peace with Wildblood. It seems Pelforth's sacking has helped heal the rift."

"He didn't actually say, but I could tell he'd mellowed towards them. I think, like me, part of the reason he wanted to get involved here was just to get his own back. I don't think he really cares or understands how things work in this world. It just looks good on his CV. He's desperate to get a safe seat at the next General Election."

"Yes, I know. But there's more to it."

"What?"

"This hold-up on the theatre. I don't know that I should tell you really, but I have to. Simon's trying to throw a spanner in the works. It seems like he wants it stalled. I've found out there isn't any need to fit a lift. The disabled access is more than adequate. Simon cooked the whole thing up."

Viola looked at him without expression. "I knew it." Her answer was studied and a matter of fact. "I knew he was hiding something. Do you think he's made all this up to help Stortfield beat us to it?"

"I can't think of any other reason."

Viola stared into space, her eyes glazed over in thought. There was a sudden change in the way she looked. She brushed away the tears with the back of her hand, and flipped back her hair. She took a deep breath.

"Right," she announced with calm determination. "Right. We'll see about that."

Raymond wasn't entirely sure what he'd done.

CHAPTER 65

# VITRIOL

Wildblood's determination and Petherton-Pugh's stalling, ensured that Stortfield had stolen a march in the race to complete the first purpose-built theatre in Storton. Neither Raymond Chater nor Lady Doulting could influence the Council's (in his words) "red-tape brigade" to reverse the disabled access ruling before several subcommittee sessions, site visits, and Planning Committee meetings had elapsed.

Viola McIntyre observed daily as the new theatre lie dormant in its muddy womb, and knew that another winter of discontent would be endured before she might take ownership of the building.

In the meantime, Petherton-Pugh had recently resigned from the governors of the comprehensive and, with indecent haste, was quietly restored to the parallel body of Stortfield. One or two parents objected to his return on the grounds of

Simon's sullied reputation, but a reply from the school chaplain, using terms like "complete transparency" and "utter contrition" seemed to quell any further uprisings. Simon and Viola no longer met. She had ended their relationship in a long and bitter email, ranting about her regrets and the "wasted years." Simon, for his part, was not unmoved. Viola was an exciting, spirited woman who he had once loved intensely. He knew though, they could never be together. His political career and his sense of duty to his family simply couldn't be compromised any further. He knew he had betrayed her, but Viola's response would always be tempered by her similar conflict of loyalty to her own husband and children. He simply endured her words of spite and vitriol, and let the matter lie. Simon had hoped they would always remain friends. It was not to be.

Gareth Chivers, following the court case, suffered a decline in self-esteem and morale which had greatly disturbed his wife Linda. She had never liked beards, but at least Gareth's decision to grow one meant she wouldn't need to nag him about not shaving. He had always had a thick head of hair which, when allowed to grow, became mane-like and unfashionable. Gareth was unconcerned by this, or by the way he dressed.

"You are beginning to look like a tramp!" Linda told him at one point.

"Yes, I've always fancied a life on the open road," he replied, drawling like an ageing Jim Morrison. "You know, hitchhiking down Route 66. Chicago to LA… fabulous!"

For Gareth, the M4 became a poor substitute for Route 66, when he mysteriously vanished early one morning after saying he was "just going down the shop to get a paper." He was brought back by two policemen, having been picked up wandering along the hard shoulder en route to Merthyr Tydfil singing 'Land of My Fathers'.

Gareth was arrested again for being drunk and disorderly, and causing an affray in a ladies fashion shop, where he said he was "trying something on for his wife's birthday." Sadly, having been previously bound over to keep the peace, Gareth found himself sentenced to Community Service, along with some of his more notorious ex-pupils.

Antidepressants seemed to have a calming effect, but Gareth's mood was diminished further when he saw in the *Stortford Courier* that Philip Hart, the 'Have-a-Go Head', had been rewarded for his "loyalty and determination" by being appointed Gareth's full-time successor as Headmaster of Stortvale High School.

Hart's appointment was, by no means, unanimous. Raymond Chater opposed the decision, but Simon Petherton-Pugh, in one of his final acts as a school governor, had led the campaign for Hart. Chater's favoured candidate, a smart, intelligent, and plain-talking woman of considerable experience, was considered "too dour" by Simon. Chater didn't trust Simon to judge the candidate by much other than her looks, but, moreover, he almost sensed Petherton-Pugh knew Philip Hart was a pushover, and no threat to his old alma mater, Stortfield.

A few days after reading of Hart's elevation, Linda Chivers, who had never told a lie in her life, found herself falsely verifying an alibi regarding her husband's whereabouts. When the police had called in connection to an incident in which a bearded man was seen throwing a brick through the art room window of Stortvale High School, Linda claimed that Gareth was at home with her, despite recalling that he left the house claiming to be "going down the pub" on the night in question. She just couldn't face another court case or even the possibility of prison for her disturbed spouse.

Linda began to see that Gareth shared more in common with their errant son Dominic, than she had previously recognised. All it ever needed, she thought, was the wrong set of circumstances. She vowed that, as soon as she could find another job, they would move away from Storton.

Having already escaped Storton, Adrian Pelforth found himself surviving on beans on toast. The beans were opened on a state of the art can opener, cooked on an elegant ceramic hob, and the toast prepared to the exact shade by the digital toaster. Other than that, Adrian mostly ate and drank out every night.

Moving to a coastal retreat afforded little comfort to Adrian. He was, to the core, an institutional man, a club man, and proud of it. He had joined the local golf club but spent too much time at the nineteenth hole. There, in the club bar, he found his new friends quick to drink up and move on. Besides, too many were married couples.

Marjorie had failed to return from Aberdeen. She had flown back just once in several months and then only to pack another suitcase, and arrange for her belongings to be sent on. His pleas to "pull yourself together" and the "start acting your age" brought an icy lack of compassion. Marjorie had pulled herself together. She was more together now than she'd ever been. "I don't drink anymore, Adrian" she told him. "I only ever drank to help me tolerate you. Now I don't need to. I think you'll find I have grown up. Rather successfully."

Adrian wished he'd not left Storton, but living close to the school would only have been a constant reminder of how dispensable he was in the end. Also, his reputation had been so tarnished he didn't really know who, amongst his old colleagues, would continue to welcome him into their company.

Adrian was often the last to leave the golf club bar. Sometimes he would drive down to a sea front hotel to linger longer over a whisky and water. One night he stumbled across a small, seedy hotel, but thought he might give it a try… There he was accosted by a brightly dressed middle-aged woman who asked him for the time. She invited him back to her place. He was sober enough to know he was too drunk to drive, but escorted her to the car. As he pulled out in the new Jaguar (a present to himself on retirement), the sudden flashing of blue lights in his rear view mirror sent a shuddering nausea through his body. "I think you'd better pull in sir," said the woman in the passenger seat, with a telling sense of authority. She then revealed her police ID. Adrian Pelforth was arrested on charges of driving under the influence of alcohol and attempting to procure a prostitute. The story made page 5 of the *Sun*.

CHAPTER 66

# DEPOSIT

Nigel Slot did not find disposing of a quantity of high explosive particularly difficult. Through contacts, he was able to cut a deal with a Mr Shah of Southall, London, who owned a "highly reputable" demolition firm.

The money received, when added to his pay-off from Wildblood, was enough to secure him an apartment on the coast close to Goa in India. There, it was his intention to 'hang out' with some of the more Bohemian migrants to paint, and then sell his landscapes in the local tourist shops and bars.

Nigel kept his whereabouts as secret as was possible, and decide to cut all ties with Storton, a town he had never really liked. Before departing British shores, Nigel had decided to hold back a little of his explosive material for other uses. On the evening prior to his departure for India, he entered the grounds of Stortfield Academy and found his way inside the empty shell of the rapidly emerging Wildblood Theatre. There, he discovered a suitable spot, and made his deposit. He fully expected his investment to earn him higher interest than might be gleaned from a Savers Account in the Storton and District Building Society. All he needed was a willing accomplice with a little disposable income, and an enormous grudge.

CHAPTER 67

# SOUND AND FURY

The final day of the summer term had been eagerly awaited by the staff and governors of Stortfield Academy.

Instead of four assemblies being repeated across the morning for various year groups in the school hall, the new Wildblood Theatre held half the school at a time, much to the relief of Jeremy Rowbotham, the school's Acting Headmaster.

Rowbotham's glory was fleeting. A perennial Deputy, largely responsible for timetabling and other, more mundane, duties, Rowbotham was to stand down at the end of the summer term, returning to his supporting role. His place was to be taken by Marcus Alexander Valentine MA Oxon, a greying Greek god of a man. Formerly an Oxford Blue and British Olympian in rowing, Valentine was already Headmaster of one of Stortfield's bitterest of rivals on the sports field, Rathbone College, situated in a neighbouring county. Despite being smaller and less well funded, Rathbone had often ‘punched above its weight’ in all departments, and the lower school fees were modest enough to enable Rathbone to poach some of the more talented but less well-to-do pupils from local comprehensives. Adrian Pelforth always hated losing to Rathbone College, and so loathed its charismatic principal. Worse still, Marjorie always seemed to show up when Valentine was in town.

Marcus Valentine was a guest of honour on Parents’ Day, having bid a fond farewell to Rathbone the day before. Being carried out of the Parents and Visitors marquee on the shoulders of the first fifteen rugby team, proved a moving finale to a ten year tenure which commenced when he was only thirty eight – one of the youngest headmasters in the competitive world of the British public school. Now, at just under fifty, Valentine had time enough to turn around Stortfield’s ailing reputation before a well-earned and lucrative retirement.

The Headmaster-elect, was not the only special guest on the final day of term. To open the new theatre, the school had invited Emile (formerly Eric) Gardner, an ex-pupil who had risen through the ranks of the Royal Shakespeare Company in recent years and had impressed some with his Richard the Second. Emile had accepted the honour of opening the Wildblood Theatre on discovering Viola McIntyre was now part of history, and banished from the kingdom of Stortfield as would befit an obsessive Shakespearean. It was Viola, bewildered by ‘Eric’s’ success who, it was recalled, initiated a very ugly, drunken scene in the Dirty Duck at Stratford upon Avon.

Simon Petherton-Pugh, when replying to Emile, very much assured his ‘star turn’ that Mrs McIntyre would not appear unannounced at the party, like Banquo's ghost. Emile's mother, also a stalwart of SODS, could not keep such information under her pink, wide brimmed hat, and it was not long before this rebuttal leaked all around the Society, finally reaching the ear of Viola herself.

Also, in an act of truce brokered by Petherton-Pugh, Philip Hart was invited to the grand opening in a very public "gesture of reconciliation" between the two Storton schools, and a desire to "begin afresh." At least those were the words quoted in the Academy's press release to the *Storton Courier*.

Back from her very productive gap year in Nepal, former Head Girl Melissa Farnsworth-Rogers was also high up on the guest list. She had spent much of the preceding week giving talks on her experience to current Sixth Formers, urging them to get the first plane out to the Himalayas. Melissa had returned looking lithe and tanned, with a maturity that belied her years. She had decided to avoid contact with her old compatriot Belinda Bellingham-Steele, despite hearing that her dysfunctional deputy was still in Storton. Belinda, for her part, having heard through the grapevine that Melissa was in town, was quietly relieved not to have to face Melissa in her gingham teashop best, preferring to defer a reunion until she had finally begun to make something of her life. Yet something still appealed to her about her alma mater, and she was particularly remorseful to be working a shift in the café knowing Jed was invited to the theatre opening on behalf of the *Storton Courier*.

The Wildblood Theatre was, by standards of modern architecture, an impressive building. The auditorium was in two tiers with conventional stalls and a gallery. The stage was a thrust-style construction with seats surrounding it on three sides, adding to the Jacobean intimacy. Wildblood, recalling his distaste for crowded theatre foyers "where one can barely raise a glass, never mind get served," had insisted on the inclusion of spacious foyers on both levels, and two well-stocked bars. Both upper and lower foyers were encased in glass, offering wonderful views of the school lake, and the meadows beyond. Jed Crane could not have been more impressed, despite going with a spoiling agenda.

Jack Wildblood looked on and smiled as his old friend Lord Haverstock, the main Guest of Honour, mumbled a few slurred and indecipherable words, cut the ribbon, and declared the theatre open. Wildblood was a man who rarely smiled, and when his lips spread back, it was easy to see why. The wide grin and slanted eyes gave him the look of a particularly pugnacious Staffordshire bull terrier, but one with incongruously fleshy gums, and short stumpy teeth. The formalities done, parents, guests, senior staff and select pupils filed into the new auditorium in expectation of the dedication and speeches.

Belinda was not particularly busy in the café that day. The weather was hot and so most potential customers, it seemed, were sensibly taking their refreshments in pub gardens and in Storton's more al fresco Italian-style pavement cafes. The phone by the till of the humid tea room rang abruptly. Miriam, Belinda's superior, took the call. Miriam was living proof that a dairymaid's uniform could only look increasingly ridiculous with age.

"Who wants her?" Miriam shrilly responded to the mystery caller. "Well, she's supposed to be working, so it better be urgent. "Oh alright then, I can spare her for a minute. Don't keep her long please. Belinda! It's for you! Wouldn't give a name. Long distance."

Handing over the phone to Belinda, Miriam put her hand over the receiver and mouthed at her "Keep it quick" with an exaggerated mime, her lips alive with elasticity. This was accompanied by a "cut throat" gesture across her fat larynx.

"Yeah, yeah," said Belinda, with as much contempt as she dare, collecting the phone from Miriam's fat greasy, palm:

"Hello? Who's this?"

"Belinda, best not ask."

Nigel's attempts at impersonation could not easily be disguised, even with the obligatory handkerchief over the phone.

"Nigel?"

"Just don't ask – and don't attempt to – like – trace the call – the phone isn't mine, and will be – like –destroyed… yeah?"

"What do you want?" Belinda replied dismissively

"I'm having a crisis of conscience. I know something will happen, and friends of yours may be in danger."

"What do you mean?"

"Perhaps you know that Stortfield's new theatre opens today?"

"Yes, of course."

"The place isn't safe – that's all I'm saying. Someone… and it isn't me… depending on-like-who you think I am… is going to cause something – like – very nasty to happen."

"Who?"

"Never mind who. Just to say, if you value your friends you might want to do something about it. It all kicks off at midday. There will be carnage."

There was silence. Nigel had hung up. Belinda tried to call back, but after a long delay in connecting, all she got was a call-minding service.

Belinda immediately thought of Nigel's dynamite stash.

"Miriam, sorry." said Belinda, tearing off her mob cap and apron. "An emergency. I have to go."

"What emergency?" enquired Miriam, more out of intrigue than concern.

"Can't say. Must go – sorry. Explain later." And with that Belinda Bellingham-Steele ran from the room disappearing into the street to the faint sound of Miriam shouting after her: "There'll be no explanations. You'll be sacked! Do you hear?"

There were no taxis. Belinda tried to call Jed on his mobile but it was switched off. A text message received no reply. It was ten to twelve. He was probably already in the theatre. Belinda knew she could make it to Stortfield, if she ran, in about ten minutes.

Wildblood, having been pleased with events so far, realised that he had ten minutes in which to relieve himself before the assembly began. Few knew this, other than a succession of ex-wives, but Wildblood was "a martyr to irritable bowel syndrome." Not wishing to be indisposed in the theatre's gleaming but very public lavatories, Jack took himself to an hitherto un-Christened, disabled-access lavatory in the backstage area, as other guests mingled in the auditorium.

Wildblood lifted the lid and peered into the sparkling lavatory pan. His ruddy face reflected, in distortion, back at him in the clear water. He loosened his belt and his tie, and suitably divested, sat on the cool lavatory seat, checking his watch.

Meanwhile, in India, Nigel Slot, having made his final call from a mobile phone he had stolen on a visit to an upmarket hotel in Goa, took out the sim card, and threw it, case and all, into the sea.

The special guests began to assemble backstage. Jeremy Rowbotham had rounded up the participants and was going through the motions in the dressing room. He guessed that the Chair of Governors was also going through the motions when he noted the red flash on the disabled toilet door, indicating that it was engaged. He delicately steered Lord and Lady Haverstock into the wings to avoid a less pleasant engagement with the evacuating Wildblood.

Stortfield sat on a gently sloping hill on the outskirts of town. Belinda had ascended this gradual but persistent slope many times, and knew of its energy sapping qualities from many a cross-country run. As she ran, Belinda turned her mind to her moral and practical dilemma. To call the police would involve unnecessary timewasting. Besides, they would never believe her, given her previous record of disrupting Parents' Day. But what if it was assumed she is party to this conspiracy? Jed would certainly vouch for her, but both of them could be held to account for not reporting the explosives in Nigel's house. Yet, none of it mattered now. Jed, Melissa, and countless others may be about to suffer an unexpected fate. Maybe, Belinda thought, this was her redemption.

Jeremy Rowbotham took it upon himself to knock delicately at the toilet door.

"Er – is that you Jack–?"

There was a grunt – followed by a fart – then a cough. "Yes… yes… out in a second. You go ahead," he snapped impatiently. "Please," he added as a polite, but barely sincere afterthought.

"Right… right. See you there," replied Rowbotham with slight embarrassment.

Belinda Bellingham-Steele could see the school gates ahead as she passed a banner fluttering from the length of the school iron railings which proclaimed 'Welcome to Stortfield Academy Parents' Day'. She had expected to be confronted by two rather timid girl prefects but her spirits sank on noticing two security guards on the gates. Security 'bouncers' had become an increasing presence in recent years, and Belinda took momentary satisfaction in having contributed to the sense of paranoia apparent around the school. Thinking quickly, Belinda took hold of the railings and hoisted herself up to perch astride of the school fence, delicately avoiding the upward thrust of barbed spears.

Glancing towards the gate, she realised that a guard some way off was pacing curiously towards her. She jumped – and the voluminous uniform skirt caught on the spike. As her feet landed, she heard a tremendous rip, and felt the flapping of torn material against her calves. She had no idea to what extent the skirt was torn, but there was no time to investigate, as she took off at speed across the school grounds with both security guards deserting their post and giving full chase.

Fortunately, Belinda's knowledge of the school campus was greater than these hired hands, and she was able to shortcut down familiar alleys that were empty due to the revels taking place in the theatre.

Cutting across the Maths quad, Belinda sprinted onto the rugby field and headed towards the theatre, its new glass front reflecting the lake's summer tranquillity. As she reached the lake, Belinda could see one of the security guards gaining on her, the other having stopped to crouch forward and catch his breath. By shape and size, she ascertained that the more persistent of the black-uniformed 'bouncers' was a rugby player. This was no nightclub doorman, weighed down by endless late evening suppers of kebab and chips.

Through the bright reflection on the theatre windows, she viewed shadowy images of a few suited men and women in summer dresses floating into the theatre, as the last arrivals. It was one minute to twelve. She feared she may be running into the breath of hell.

Jack Wildblood, finally relieved, struggled to release the first tissue on the toilet roll, and swore belligerently as the virgin roll span uncooperatively, in its holder.

Bursting through the front doors and past the ineffectual programme-bearing prefects, Belinda looked in desperation for fire alarm buttons. Spotting one by the inner door to the theatre, instinctively she picked up the fire extinguisher beneath the button, in order to break the Perspex shield and activate the alarm. Afterwards she realised this was a pointless exercise as the shield would have broken with the pressure of a thumb. Perhaps it was a moment of fate – but as Belinda swung back the fire extinguisher, she caught the approaching security guard full in the testicles. As he stumbled and exhaled with the pressure of a steam train, Belinda brought the fire extinguisher into contact on the up-swing. Immediately bells and alarms began ringing and whirring. Belinda turned to the stunned prefects and yelled: "Get out! Get out now!" She then span on her heels to run. Barely recovered, the security officer caught her ankle with a determined grip and brought her down like a lightweight fly-half.

"Christ!!" snarled Wildblood. "What the fuck?" He was still struggling with remnants of toilet paper as the alarm whooped. "That's all I bloody well need!" Eventually, the tight toilet roll submitted to his tugging, Wildblood released a handful of torn tissue, and began preparing himself with dignity for a further, unwanted evacuation.

Rowbotham announced to the assembled audience that the fire alarm was "undoubtedly a teething problem, so let's quietly leave the building by the marked exits and congregate on the rugger field. All good practice. Ha ha. We'll soon be back inside, no doubt."

The guard was now pinning Belinda to the floor, sitting on her with little respect for her more fragile frame. The spectacle had been witnessed by the emerging parents and pupils. As she screamed at the guard to "let me go, you fat fuck, and get out!" he seemed even more determined to restrain her, heavily influenced by passing pupils, who recognised Belinda and assured him she was up to another act of sabotage. "Don't let her go," one of them said. "She's a trouble maker." Jed, emerging from the auditorium, recognising the torn checked gingham outfit splayed out from beneath the guard ran to her.

"What the hell are you doing?" he shouted.

"She set the alarm off!" yelled the guard.

"Not you – her!"

"Jed – please don't ask. Get out now! This place is going to explode. This idiot won't listen. Get out!"

Jed quickly realised what had happened and crouched beside the guard: "OK, OK listen man, she could be right. We both know something. Take her if you must, but please just leave the building."

"I'm not letting her go. My colleague has called through to the police. Who are you anyway?"

Jed noticed the guard's walkie-talkie was live with static and realised he wasn't joking. "I'm from the *Storton Courier*, alright? The police will know me. I know this isn't a hoax. It could be a bomb. Now both of you get outside – now!"

The guard rose to his feet, carefully guarding his aching balls, whilst holding Belinda in an arm lock. Suddenly Belinda was confronted with the red, angry faces of Petherton-Pugh and Rowbotham.

"Belinda Bellingham-Steele! Haven't you caused enough problems around here?" shouted Rowbotham with as much anger as his reedy voice could muster.

"For Christ's sake Belinda!" Simon Petherton-Pugh breathed his fumes of fury over her. "When is this going to stop?"

Belinda was unrepentant as the guard pulled her towards the theatre door.

"This has nothing to do with me. Don't shoot the fucking messenger. You may be grateful for this."

"Oh, for God's sake. Keep hold of her. Someone call the police!" shouted the Acting Headmaster, not knowing that his instructions had been pre-empted.

"It's not the police you need, it's the bloody fire brigade!" shouted Belinda. "Seriously!"

Wildblood had finally finished his inconvenience in the convenience. He stood up, tugged up his trousers, breathing heavily, as he bent forward, then fastened his braces and his belt, and reached for the button marked "Heavy Flush." Simultaneously, Belinda was being led through the theatre doors into the daylight beyond, followed by Jed, imploring the guard to "go easy" and shielding her from the insults as she was led through the well-groomed, milling crowd. Then, from the rear of the building, there came the sound of a cannon, followed swiftly by a low, menacing rumble, rapidly expanding into a propulsion of air, dust and other fragments that threw

Belinda, Jed, and her guard forward, stumbling to the earth. There were screams, confusion, chaos. Some threw themselves to the ground; men threw themselves on their wives and daughters. Women clasped their children. Boys ran, girls hugged.

The dust began to clear. "Keep moving," shouted the security guard. "Move away from the building." The shock had blown Belinda from his arresting arms, but he made no attempt to recover her, too preoccupied by attending to the injured. He realised there was little point in bothering about Belinda, as he turned to see her tearing at the hanging cloth from her ridiculous dress, and using it to bind the bleeding hand of an elderly woman.

At the back of the theatre, the dressing room roof had caved in. Doors hung by one hinge, or had fallen completely. Windows had shattered entirely. The lighting gantry above the stage was hanging like a broken bridge to nowhere. Lighting bars had fallen, creating dents and holes in the polished floor of the splintered stage. Somewhere amongst the backstage debris lay the prostrate corpse of Jack Wildblood, his thick eyebrows singed, his dense hairline burned back, revealing a scorched, pink scalp. His ruddy complexion was now earth brown and his bull terrier grin frozen. A lavatory pan was embedded in his torso.

CHAPTER 68

# SUSPECTS

For Jed Crane, the 'Scandal School Bomb Blast!' story presented mixed fortunes. On one hand, his girlfriend was a prime suspect, on the other, his 'on-the-spot' reporting and photos had been syndicated worldwide, whilst his eyewitness accounts were broadcast on all national radio and TV news networks.

At first, a terrorist attack was suspected. Stortfield Academy had, in the past, taken in a number of oil rich sons of the desert who may have graduated through the University of Al Qaeda. Motives would suggest a more local culprit however. Detective Inspector Moss and his team from the County Constabulary rather relished their moment in the headlines, and had meticulously drawn up a web-like diagram of interconnecting chief suspects on a white board in the Crime Room:

Nigel Slot: … Reputed to have stolen explosive materials from his former employers Doulting Stone. May have been 'mystery' caller to Belinda Bellingham-Steele, warning her of the impending event. Call traced to Goa, India. Since disappeared… Evidence suggests he was working with an accomplice who primed the explosion…

Belinda Bellingham-Steele: … Grudge against Stortfield Academy. History of disruption at school. So-called 'Vigilante' attacker on Stortvale High. Seen as fantasist. Raised alarm, but failed to notify police of call received possibly from Slot…

Viola McIntyre: … Personal grudge against Stortfield Academy. Wanted theatre project to fail. Former lover of Petherton-Pugh. Alibi: In London 'shopping'. Till receipts from Harvey Nichols suggest absent at time of explosion…

And so the list went on. Gareth Chivers, whose wife Linda had claimed he was with her on the day in question, remained a suspect, given, not only the motives, but his recent lapse into criminality and insanity.

The Vigilantes – or some opposition group from the comprehensive – was considered. Perhaps this was a tragic 'prank', intended only to scare. Petherton-Pugh's double-dealing brought him into focus. Even Lady Doulting herself was not beyond suspicion. The newspapers had never been so intrigued by this country town 'whodunnit' since the famous Mr Whicher of the Yard headed west to pronounce his famed 'Suspicions'.

Given the explosion had taken only one serious casualty – Jack Wildblood – the possibility of a deliberately targeted murder could not be ruled out. Trouble was, Wildblood had no limit of potential enemies.

And then there was Adrian Pelforth. The recently disgraced, corrupt, and abandoned former Headmaster had every reason to wreak revenge. Indeed, he was the only suspect with the appropriate training in the use of explosives from his time in the military. There was just one problem: On the day before the murder, Adrian Alexander Pelforth was reported missing after his clothes were discovered on a remote stretch of Dorset coast. A body had yet to be recovered.

CHAPTER 69

# EPILOGUE: A FEW YEARS LATER

A stinging sheet of freezing rain swept across Red Square. As tourists and locals scattered into elegant coffee bars, a lone female figure strutted along elegantly, despite the cold wind that threw her upright. She wore a raincoat and headscarf, like a remnant extra in a sixties movie.

The figure cut across the square and stayed close to the wall along the side-streets that eventually led to her apartment. Fumbling in an expensive, classic handbag, the woman found the key to the front door, and ascended the stairs to the fourth floor flat. She discreetly drew a handgun before entering. Opening the door almost silently, she glanced around in nervous apprehension. First of all, she checked the living room and the kitchen. Finding no one, she moved to the bathroom, kicking open the door and pointing the gun towards the shower. Finally she checked the bedroom. As the door eased back – she emitted the slightest gasp – a combination of faint shock and frustration. In the wardrobe mirror, she saw a familiar reflection. It was a middle-aged man, well built, and quite handsome. He lay on the bed in his boxer shorts, dead. A stain of dry blood had dribbled from a small wound in the side of his neck, no more than a puncture mark. Exploring the room thoroughly, the woman left, closing the door behind her. As she paced back to the living room, she put down the gun on the functional coffee table and took off the drenched headscarf, to reveal shoulder length, chestnut-brown hair. She removed her wet Mac and hung it over the corner of the door where it dripped onto the linoleum. The woman delicately stepped out of her shoes and took a phone from her hand bag. Her fingers worked agitatedly at the keyboard.

The answer came: "Yes?"

"The garbage has yet to be collected," the woman replied tersely.

"They were held up."

"I don't give a fuck." Despite the underlying tension in her voice, she tried to maintain a matter-of-fact manner. "I shall be checking into a hotel. Sleeping in an infested room is not in the contract."

"The garbage men are on their way," came the reply.

"Too late, I'm afraid. I've kept my half of the deal. You can explain the hotel bill to head office."

She took the phone from her ear and pressed the 'end' button. As she did so, she heard a belated attempt to placate her:

"Just give us–" and the line went dead.

The woman closed the curtains to cover her balcony window, scanning the windows of the apartments opposite. She collected clean clothes from the bedroom and began to change out of her wet attire. Even she could not stand naked in front of the incessant stare of the man she had recently made love to – and killed. A spider scuttled from under the headboard and across the man's immobile face. She swallowed hard, and suppressed a scream. She hated spiders, despite the cruel nickname applied to her by colleagues – the Black Widow.

Standing before the mirror in the living room, she hooked her thumb below her soft, brown fringe, and gathering some hair in her fist, lifted away the chestnut wig. Underneath lay a blonde, close crop that accentuated her fine features whilst remaining feminine. Belinda Bellingham-Steele ruffling the hair upright, suddenly looked only a little older than her schooldays, but there was a slightly careworn look replacing that of eager innocence.

Belinda stared into the mirror above a faux fireplace. Her eyes, once cool and blue, now seemed cold, and grey. Her reflection revealed an uneasy mixture of admiration and self-loathing. She knew that despite her natural tendency towards rebellion, Belinda Bellingham-Steele was indeed the archetypal product of that renowned institution – the British public school.